This book is dedicated to my daughters, Elayna and Darline
Who have yet to get a character named for them.

In memory of
John Nikolas Kelly

With heartfelt thanks to the people of Tipton, Oklahoma
Who asked: When is the next book is coming?

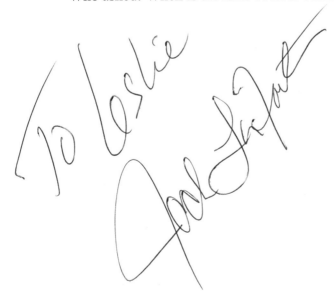

Hatchlings

An Anchored Book

First Printing April 2011

Published by Anchored Publishing
Tipton, Oklahoma

IBSN
978-0-615-45867-0

Printed in the United States

www.jacklafountain.com

Hatchlings

Table of Contents

The Wolfbat of Missouri Flat

"You can't go in there," Ernie said. "That thing will eat you alive."

Eddie looked at Rich. "If it does; kill Lefty for me."

"Done," his brother promised.

"You want Bro. Ray to do the funeral?" Jack asked.

"Sure, why not?"

"You three are crazier than a pack of outhouse rats," Ernie said.

Eddie stepped from the shelter of a tall pine. His companions leveled their rifles at the entrance. Eddie slipped into the cave. The fading light at his back didn't penetrate more than ten feet. Maybe that would be enough. Wounded grizzlies didn't need much provocation. Eddie decided to let her know company had arrived.

"Hey," Eddie shouted.

The she bear's roar ripped through the dark confines of the cave. Eddie backpedaled as the wounded bear waddled out of the shadows. There was dried blood behind its right ear. The putrid scent of infection rolled off the bear in waves. Eddie's stomach lurched. If he puked now; he was a dead man. He clinched his teeth and drew his gun.

Three shots thundered from the cave. In their wake sprinted a wide-eyed Eddie Powell hightailing it for anywhere but here.

"Run, boys!" Eddie yelled.

That was all the invitation Ernie Carson needed.

Five hundred pounds of enraged muscle, teeth and claws exploded from the cave. From the cover of a pair of Ponderosa pines, Rich and Jack opened fire. The bear absorbed a half dozen slugs before it rolled to a stop twenty yards from the cave.

"Reckon Ernie's still running?" Jack pointed in the direction of the sheriff's retreat.

"I'll bet a round of drinks he don't stop short of the Flat." Rich said.

"You're on," Jack accepted. "Speaking of skedaddling, have you ever seen Eddie move that fast before?"

Rich slowly shook his head. "Never in all my days."

"I think he deserves a drink."

"Dang right I do," a voice from above answered.

Jack and Rich looked up to find their partner perched on the limb of an old oak. Eddie wiped the sweat from his brow and began working his way down the tree. The two men on the ground did their best to bite back the laughter. They succeeded until Eddie missed the last toe hold and fell squarely on the seat of his pants. The dam broke. A river of laughter flowed all the way down Forni Hill.

In Missouri Flat, Ernie Carson wasn't laughing. He sat on the steps of his office huffing and puffing like an engine on the Great Northern. He was too old to race grizzlies; too old and too soft. He liked it that way. I t was time he took it easy. If he had known being sheriff meant accompanying Jack and the Powell brothers on their hair-brained schemes, he'd have never taken the job.

"Speak of the devil," Ernie said.

"C'mon Sheriff, drinks are on Jack." Rich slapped Ernie on the back and gave Jack a wink.

"Don't worry Uncle Ernie," Eddie said. "We're tight lipped sorts."

"Says the fella we found twenty feet up an old oak." Jack shot Eddie his best cheese-eating grin.

Sure, why not? And quit calling me that. I ain't your uncle." Ernie pulled a plug from his pocket and bit off a fresh chew. He couldn't figure out why Eddie Powell decided to start calling him uncle, but it irritated him to no end.

"You boys just going to leave that carcass up there?" the sheriff asked.

"Yep. The stink coming off that wound would gag a maggot," Eddie told him.

"But I saw plenty of stout hearted ones working away on the critter's brain," Jack volunteered.

The thought turned the sheriff's stomach. It was enough to put a man off his drink---almost. Ernie spit tobacco.

"The Red Dog?" he asked.

"The Red Dog," Jack said.

The Red Dog Saloon was one of three watering holes on The Flat in 1852. The Flat, meaning Missouri Flat, one of the rowdy camping popping up all over California's gold country at the foot of the Sierra Nevada. Missouri Flat sat in a wide bend of Shinbone Creek a half day's ride southwest of Hangtown. There wasn't another piece of level ground for miles in any direction. The Flat was three inches of red clay atop solid rock. It wasn't worth a lick for crops. There was enough grass growing in the breaks between the oaks, ponderosa pines and manzanita to support cattle, but

no one showed much interest in ranching in those days. Gold fever was sweeping the country.

Missouri Flat got swept into the mix in April when an ornery cuss by the name of Lefty Nickels made a strike on Shinbone Creek three-quarters of a mile from The Flat. Overnight, Shinbone Creek was lined with tents. The news brought miners running. Shopkeepers, whiskey peddlers, and gamblers were not far behind. The flat ground was just right for building and the color from the creek showed no sign of fading anytime soon. In a month there shot up three saloons, two general stores, an assay office, and a blacksmith's shop. Missouri Flat was born.   Like most youngsters, The Flat was a trifle on the wild side. It was a rare Saturday night when someone didn't get shot or stabbed. There was no doctor, unless you wanted to count Seb Collins. He worked a hospital tent in the Mexican War and knew a thing or two about sewing up the big wounds and making bandages the actually worked. The fortunate ones who didn't bleed to death before Seb arrived to help rarely died of their wounds. The blood alcohol of the typical miner was too high to allow infection to set in. Which was a good thing given the astronomical number of bacteria on their unwashed exterior.

The miners spent their days scratching in the dirt and looking for a flash of color in the pan. Some days they came up empty, but over the course of a week, most of them managed to collect enough dust to buy a few staples and get rip roaring drunk. Then, the process began all over again. On a few rare occasions big strikes turned crusty miners into San Francisco millionaires. But those were few and far between indeed. No matter, stories of instant wealth were all that was needed to keep gold fever burning from Orville to Plymouth. There was no shortage of tales around gold country campfires. The strangest story ever to come out of El Dorado County is the one about the Wolfbat of Missouri Flat.

The story and the blame for what happened centers around the aforementioned Lefty Nickels; three brash ne'er-do-wells and a wounded grizzly bear.

One Sunday Lefty, half awake and only half sober, stumbled on a she-bear rummaging through the garbage behind the Gold Nugget Saloon. Lefty loosed several shots managing only to disturb the bear's breakfast and the morning quiet. But as luck would have it, the bear stopped at the tree line for one glance back at Lefty. His last shot caught her in the neck just behind the right ear. The bear roared in pain, but kept running. Lefty staggered back to his camp. Case closed--or so everyone thought.

Three days later Sandbar Jack and the Powell brothers, Rich and Eddie, rode into town with Red Campbell's body. They found Red chewed up and spit out near a cave on Forni Hill. The culprit was obvious. The solution was too. Somebody had to finish off that bear. Everyone in camp agreed that someone was Lefty. When Sheriff Carson delivered the news to The Flat's richest miner, Lefty promptly offered a hundred dollars to clean up his mess.

The boys took him up on the deal for $100 apiece and invited the sheriff along as a witness that the job was done. It was easy money--much easier than mining or chopping wood. The Boys always liked easy.

"The Boys" that's what folks around Missouri Flat call them.

Sandbar Jack, who seemed to have no last name, was a stubby little man rumor said out ran a lynch mob on his way to The Flat. He didn't look like much on the outside; just an oily haired kid with a hint of a moustache. Inside, beat a heart of stone with a vein of pure mean. Jack was a fair hand with the Colt tucked in his waistband. However his real talent for settling disputes was the hidden stiletto in his left boot.

The Powells were the first white folks near The Flat. The titular head of the clan, Asa Powell was a first rate blacksmith. Asa gave up a thriving business in Benicia to join his sons, Harold and Jonas, neither of whom had any talent with an anvil, in a sawmill scheme in the mountains. The Powells had a mill on Diamond Creek a year before Sutter got into the game. Rich and Eddie, along with cousin Ray, worked the mill with their fathers and listened to their steadfast assertion that timber was the real treasure of the Sierras. Belief in their father's dream lasted until Lefty Nickels yanked a finger sized nugget out of Shinbone Creek, Rich and Eddie traded their saws for shovels. Grandma Powell had other plans for Ray, but that's another story altogether.

Rich was a tall, rough cut bean pole who shared his father's business instincts and streak of independence. He was the most sociable of the trio. He kept his partners from jail and abject poverty one more than one occasion. Unfortunately, Rich had a hair trigger temper that flushed bright red beneath his sandy whiskers and required frequent rescuing himself.

Eddie was built more on the order of a small horse with the strength to match. His left eye had a disturbing habit of wandering off on its own. This made it dang near impossible to figure out what Eddie was thinking, or where he was looking, at any given moment. All the more disconcerting because Eddie Powell was the fastest gun anyone on The Flat had ever seen. Just how these two got hooked up with the likes of Sandbar Jack is still a mystery. They were spotted panning gold together one day and seldom apart thereafter.

The Boys made a fair show of panning gold, but never to put together more than a pair of double eagles at a time. They were as apt to spend the day hunting as working their claim. What gold they found was quickly invested at the Red Dog Saloon. The Boys' claim bordered on that of Lefty Nickels whose good fortune and constant crowing was an endless vexation to the aspiring idlers. After relieving Lefty of $300 for dispatching the bear, The Boys retired to the Red Dog and regaled the customers with exaggerated tales of the hunt. True to their word, Ernie Carson's quick departure was omitted though Rich, at one point, offered to buy the sheriff a new pair of drawers claiming his present pair would never come clean. Erin went along with the good-natured ribbing; reached his one drink while on duty limit and left the Boys to celebrate alone.

"Nothing like turning a disagreeable varmint into easy money," Eddie said.

"To easy money." Rich held a bottle high.

Two sets of eyes turned to Sandbar Jack. Jack didn't seem to notice. Eddie waved a hand in front of his partner's eyes.

"Nobody's home," he said.

"I don't like the looks of this." Rich snapped his fingers in Jack's face.

Jack was unmoved. Real concern began to creep into the others. Jack's face began to change, subtly at first, a smile began working its way up from his innards. The smile stalled a moment on his lips, then broke into radiant beams from his eyes.

Eddie leaned forward for a better look. His couldn't help but imitate Jack's smile.

"Still ain't nobody home, but the lights are on," Eddie said.

"You're going to love this," Jack said at last. "Listen, here's what we're going to do..."

The three men crowded close together. Voices low, they took turns nodding and mumbling until all three were smiling; their eyes alight with avarice. They promptly disappeared from the Red Dog and The Flat for almost a week.

***

Backlit by the first rosy hint of dawn, Sandbar Jack hammered on the front door of the Red Dog. The noise continued until Zeke Tucker, the owner, poked his head from an upstairs window.

"Who's making that racket?" Zeke hollered.

"Get down here and let us in," Jack called up.

"Like hell I will. You boys go sleep it off." Tucker pulled his head inside.

"Zeke, you get down here or Rich is going to set your place on fire," Jack warned.

Zeke's head reappeared. "Okay, okay, don't do nothing crazy. I'm coming."

Cursing under his breath, Zeke stumbled downstairs to let them in. The sight of these three at dawn was blight on Zeke's foggy brain.

"We need a bottle," Eddie said.

"Make it three," Jack corrected.

"Ain't you Boys had enough?" Zeke plopped the bottles down. It was just easier to go along.

11

"We ain't had any; that's the trouble," Rich answered.

"You go to seein' crazy things cold sober; it's time to get drunk." Jack took a long pull on his bottle.

"Shut up, Jack," Rich said.

"Ah, Zeke don't care, do you Zeke?"

"I ain't got the slightest idea what you're talkin' about," Zeke said.

"Good. Let's leave it at that," Rich said.

"Leave what, where?" Zeke wanted to know. He was awake now and his guard was up.

"You leave us...and put some clothes on." Eddie shielded his eyes and downed a second shot. "Seeing you in your drawers ain't exactly conducive to proper drinking."

Zeke glanced over his attire. "Dad-blast it, you three come in here before the sun's up and you want *me* to leave? Oh, all right. I'm goin' back to bed. But you keep it quiet in here or I'll be back with double barrels of shut up."

Zeke retreated up the stairs. Once out of sight, but not out of earshot, he took a seat on the stairs. He'd find out what was really going on. Something was up and there just might be a profit in it for the man who found out first.

"Here's to getting' out alive," Jack raised his bottle.

Bottles clinked.

"What are we gonna do? Eddie wiped his mouth on his sleeve.

"I don't care as long as I never see another one of them things," Jack said.

"I'm for that," Rich agreed. "What was that thing anyway?"

"You seen it," Eddie said. "It was a danged wolf."

"With wings?"

"What else could it be?" Eddie asked.

"A bat?" Jack offered.

"There ain't no bats that big," Rich said.

"I'll bet it was something the danged Chinese brought over," Jack said.

"You're crazy." Rich gave Jack a nudge. "Everything's the Chinese with you."

"Well, it ain't nothing American."

"That's for dang sure." A light came on in Eddie's eyes. "It's a wolfbat."

"A wolfbat? There ain't no such thing as a wolfbat," Rich protested.

"There is now," Jack said. "It was a danged old wolfbat. I say let's catch it and charge a dollar a head to see the thing. Hot dang we'll be rich."

"Just one catch." Eddie scratched his head. "How we supposed to catch it? I know I put half dozen slugs in that thing."

"I don't know," Rich said. "But, Jack's right. We'd make a fortune showin' it around. We've got to take a crack at it."

"Let's start by getting drunk," Jack said.

Bottles clinked again. The conversation quickly degenerated into jokes about bodily functions in slurred syllables. Zeke Tucker slipped from his listening post and returned to bed. The situation bore watching, but he had time to sleep on it.
***

Zeke tumbled out of bed at the crack of noon. He went downstairs hoping the damage was minimal and clean up quick. Eddie Powell was passed out on his pool table. Rich and Jack were lying on the floor nearby, but nothing was broken. The Red Dog would see another day. Zeke decided it was best to let sleeping dogs lie. He tiptoed out; saddled his mule and took a ride out to Shinbone Creek.

Along the creek, miners were washing gravel. Everything looked normal--until Zeke reached the camp of his uninvited guests. Boxes were overturned; supplies scattered everywhere and there were a dozen bullet holes in the tent.

"Dang," he whispered.

Zeke talked to a few miners on his way back to town. They heard the shots. Most figured The Boys were tying one on and none was willing to poke his nose into something involving The Boys and shooting. Zeke couldn't fault them there. He headed back to town, but decided on one last stop--Binkerman's Store. Zeke despised the know-it-all shopkeeper, but wanted another opinion. Binkerman had never heard of wolfbats either, although he conceded that strange creatures must surely live in China.

"You sure they didn't know you were listening?" Binkerman asked.

"Sure, I'm sure."

"You think it's a trick?"

"Didn't sound like it. It sounded like they were scared. It don't make sense, but that's the way it sounded."

Chapter 2

Secrets were hard to keep along Shinbone Creek. Miners kept an ear open as they jostled one another to wash gravel in the clear water. Voices carried at night and gossip traveled faster in gold camps than at a quilting bee. Word spread along Shinbone Creek that The Boys had spotted some strange creature near their camp. The miners claimed to put no credence in the tale of wolves with wings, but stole an occasional glance at the sky just the same.

A week after The Boys early morning drunk at the Red Dog, things settled back to normal; the mythical creature forgotten. Twilight sent long shadows across Shinbone Creek where miners washed the last pan of the day. Without warning the peace was shattered by revolvers being emptied in a hurry followed by Rich Powell splashing down the middle of Shinbone Creek like his hair was on fire. He was followed, at a somewhat slower pace, by Jack and Eddie; guns drawn; eyes on the sky.

"What's got into Rich?" a miner asked.

"What you boys shootin' at?" A crowd was gathering.

"Wolfbats," Jack said. "You see any come this way?"

Rusty Neal dared ask. "What the heck's a wolfbat?"

"A wolf--with wings...big wings," Eddie said.

"From China," Jack added.

Eddie shot him a menacing glance.

"You don't know they *ain't* from China," Jack persisted.

"No," Eddie agreed. "But I know better'n open my big yap."

"What are you tryin' to pull?" Lefty asked.

"Yea, you're joshing us...ain't you?" Scotty Benbow looked worried.

"Sure," Eddie answered. "We run up the creek, shootin' for the fun of it."

"Now, get outta our way," Jack ordered.

The crowd of miners parted with a shrug and went back to their pans.

"Them three are crazy than outhouse rats," Rusty said.

"Wolfbats; who they kiddin'?" Scotty added.

"I tell you they're up to no good," Lefty promised.

Joke or no joke, vigilance reigned along Shinbone Creek. After sunset, miners gathered around fires to plates of beans and whispered speculation about the possible existence of wolfbats. No campfire burned at the twist in Shinbone Creek that The Boys called home.

The next morning, Rich and Eddie staggered back to camp dragging a snoring Sandbar Jack atop a large bundle. The smell of whiskey emanating from the three of them gave several bystanders an early morning buzz.

15

The Boys had a genuine talent for "finding" rare commodities. Where they found a huge fishing net no one knew. But they had one and began stringing it from the branches above their camp. The sight was too much to ignore. Miners dropped their pans and gathered to watch. Nate and Billy Johnson even pitched in to help. Once the net roof was in place, Jack set on coffee while Rich and Eddie stacked boxes of cartridges.

"Okay, enough. What are you up to?" Lefty asked.

"We told you," Jack answered.

"There ain't no such a thing as wolfbats and you dang well know it," Lefty insisted.

"Fine," Eddie said. "You boys go back to your unprotected camps. We'll see who's loco come dark."

"Yeah, you're blockin' the field of fire," Jack said.

There being nothing more to see, the slowly crowd melted away. Jack and the brothers sat by their fire and waited.

"I think that went well." Jack pulled a bottle from his pack.

"None of that," Rich said. "I don't want to git shot cause you're too drunk to see straight."

"We all gotta go sometime." Eddie smiled at his brother.

"But not today. Put that away both of you."

The day passed with no wolfbat sightings or gunfire. Nonetheless, tension built as the darkness grew. Dinners were eaten undisturbed and one by one campfires went out along Shinbone Creek. The cool night air lifted the waters of Shinbone Creek. Wrapped in a foggy embrace the camp was still.

The Sierra foothills are never completely quiet at night. Sound carries and varmints are out and about. Fog adds a spectral quality to the night song as it bends distance and direction. The miners couldn't agree exactly where the sound came from, but everyone agreed as to the varmint responsible.

"Wooo--wooo--wooo--woof--woofbat!" The sound warbled through the shrouded pines.

Miners scrambled from their tents. Scotty caught his boot in the rigging of his tent pulling the whole thing down on his head. As Scotty struggled to free himself from the canvass, his pistol went off and took out Nate Johnson's lantern. A second shot sounded from God knows where touching off a spree of wild gunfire. Miraculously, nobody was killed.

"Wooo--wooo--wooo--woof--woofbat!"

The second cry set off a general stampede. A hundred wide-eyed miners crowded under The Boys' net shivering with the cold--or so they claimed.

"Well, well, looks like we got company," Eddie crowed.

"Nice of you boys to drop by," Jack said.

"Dang near got one." Rich trotted into camp from the far side of Shinbone Creek. "I know I hit it, but the thing just kept going."

"*What* does it take to kill those things?" Eddie said.

"Anybody hurt?" Rich asked the crowd.

The only injuries were assorted bumps and bruises. Although a large number egos were deflated by pieces of half swallowed crow.

"So, now what?" Lefty asked. "We stand around like jackasses?"

"You'd be good at that," Jack said.

"Lefty, you're welcome to leave whenever the notion strikes." Eddie pointed the way. "As for the rest of you, anybody want a drink?"

The tension broke as bottles went around. Lefty helped himself to a shot for the road. No one else seemed in a hurry to leave. The need for sleep and the relaxing comfort of distilled spirits took their toll on the others; they followed Lefty-- eventually.

News of the wolfbat attack spread the length of Shinbone Creek and circulated around The Flat. The following evening, floor space in the saloons soared to two dollars a night. Bro. Ray offered church pews for the same price and threw in a nightly prayer for each man's safety. Jim Binkerman sent to San Francisco for fishing nets; advertising them for $100 while supplies lasted. Two hours after posting the sign, Binkerman pulled it down, cancelled all orders, and announced an auction for noon Saturday.

Folks were scared, but gold has a way of overcoming fear; nobody was giving up their claim just yet. Besides, no attacks occurred in daylight. The miners pronounced the wolfbat nocturnal and kept panning. There were no more stampedes, but no one was getting much sleep either. Each night exhausted miners closed their eyes only to be awakened by the haunting cry of the wolfbat. Inevitably, a few shots were fired before quiet returned. Nerves grew raw; tempers flared; and the number of wolfbats grew.

On Saturday the miners made Jim Binkerman a rich man. A dozen brawls, four stabbings and a shooting interrupted the bidding, but it was a mild affair given the explosiveness of the populace. That night, the fortunate few slept under their new rooftops. The wolfbat was silent. It was the first real sleep anybody had in a week.

Chapter 3

As September became October, miners split time between panning, building cabins, and cutting firewood for winter. The Boys found hauling firewood more lucrative than panning. They all but abandoned the search for gold and began bringing wood in from Forni Hill by the wagonload. The Boys felled trees, cut, split and stacked firewood with the exuberance of a small colony of beavers. They could also be persuaded, for double what their father charged, to haul an occasional load of lumber in from the mill.

The wolfbats left the camps undisturbed the first week of October. Although The Boys reported seeing one or two out near

Forni Hill, none ventured close enough to Missouri Flat to be bothersome.

The calm unraveled one evening when The Boys didn't return to camp. The eerie sense that misfortune had befallen them turned to certainty when shots rang out in the darkness. Lefty, Scotty and the Johnson brothers gathered near the trees that backed up onto Lefty's claim. The silent men shifted from one foot to the other; cocked their heads towards Forni Hill, ears straining to hear; and worked their tobacco harder than need be.

"How far off do you make it?" Scotty broke the quiet.

"Couple of miles." Lefty spit.

"Out near Forni Hill."

"Uh huh."

"Reckon we ought to go see about them?"

"Be my guest." Lefty looked at Nate and Billy who had found something interesting on their boots.

"We just gonna leave 'em out there?" Scotty asked.

"Yep."

"Uh huh."

"Guess so."

Scotty stomped back to his camp.

"What's with him?" Nate wondered.

His companions shrugged.

The next morning, Rich and Eddie returned with a blood soaked blanket atop their wagon. They carried the bundle into their cabin without a word. An hour later, a crowd gather when the Powells came outside to sit. No one asked, but the question hung in the air like putrid flatulence.

"We got a late start," Rich explained. "When we reached the clearing near the foot of Forni Hill, we spotted a wolfbat. The varmint had its head buried in a deer's guts, so we figured to sneak up on it. Jack got up on it. The danged thing never looked up, it just shot into the air. Jack was down before he got off a second round."

"Rich whopped it with a stick of wood trying to get it off Jack." Eddie took up the story. "We heard bones crack. It finally turned on Rich. That's when Jack…"

"Stuck it with that stiletto of his," Rich finished. "Sliced its wing plum off. After that the fight went out of it."

"What'd you do with its wing?" Lefty asked.

Rich nodded in the direction of their wagon.

"You got it with you?"

"Dern right," Eddie said. "Step up and take a look."

In the bed of the wagon lay a black wing nearly four feet long. Broken bone protruded through its leathery skin.

"Does that look like a bat or what?" Eddie asked.

"Dang sure does," said Scotty.

Pressed by the crowd behind him, Cletus Brown held the wing aloft for all to see.

"And you say this came from a wolf?" Nate asked.

"Looked like a wolf." Rich corrected "I didn't for sure see a tail."

"That ain't the worst of it," Eddie added.

Heads turned in Eddie's direction.

"It was foamin' at the mouth."

Nods and muttered curses issued from the men beside the wagon. Finally, someone worked up enough courage to say the word.

"You're talking about hydrophobie."

"Yeah," Eddie admitted.

"You got to get him out of here," Lefty said with a jerk of his head towards the cabin.

"Later," Rich said.

"Not this time Rich," Lefty said. "Jack's got hydrophobie."

"We got to burn the body," Nate added.

"You ain't gonna do nothing." Eddie drew his pistol. "I'll kill the first one that tries."

"You'll get the one Eddie, but that's all," Lefty said.

"It'll be all the same to you." Eddie pulled back the hammer.

"Hold it," Rich said. "Ain't no need for this. Jack it...ain't gonna...after...we'll do what needs doing."

There was no panning that day. The miners wandered back to their tents to think things over. Sandbar Jack was dying; prey of a rabid wolfbat. As it turned out, he wasn't at the top of the Reaper's list.

Cletus Brown and Scotty Benbow sat across from one another in their newly constructed cabin. The silence between them took on a presence all its own. The world, as they knew it, was slipping away.

"Scotty?" Cletus said.

"Yeah."

"Is hydrophobie, you know, catching?"

"Dang right it is." Scotty noticed his partner rub his palms on his jeans.

"I mean, a man couldn't get it just by touching something could he?" Cletus asked. He was scrubbing harder.

"Nah, nothing like that." Scotty glanced at Cletus' hands.

Scotty sounded calm, but Cletus saw the truth in his partner's eyes.

"Oh God. I got it. I got hydrophobie. Help me Scotty," Cletus pleaded. He reached for his partner.

Scotty jumped from the table. There was no hiding his fear. "I'll get you a doctor. I will, honest. Settle down now. It'll be alright. We're partners ain't we?"

"You and me, Scotty."

"You and me, Cletus."

Scotty returned to the table. Cletus relaxed, but continued to try and wipe the disease from his hands. Scotty eased the Colt from his holster. Cletus never saw the gun. It hardly registered at all when Scotty put three slugs in his chest. Cletus fell to the floor with a dull thud.

"Oh God," he moaned and was still.

Scotty shied away from the pool of blood growing on the floor. He had to have help. He had to get rid of the body before he was infected too. Scotty Benbow stepped over his partner's body.

The camp was quiet--too quiet. It had taken on the appearance of a ghost town. Tent flaps fell and doors closed wherever Scotty chanced to glance. There was only one place he was going to find help.

"Rich open up it's me, Scotty."

The elder Powell poked his head through the door. "Guess I don't need to ask what all the shootin' was about."

"Rich, I need help," Scotty moaned. "You got to help...with the body."

"Tarnation, couldn't you have waited for a sign he had it for sure?" Rich stepped from the doorway and took Scotty by the arm.

"I..." was all Scotty could say.

"It don't matter now. Let's get it over with."

Rich dragged Scotty along. The sun shining through the cabin door fell over Cletus Brown's face. Rich looked around; he and Cletus were alone.

"Get in here," Rich ordered. "I said I'd help. This is your mess and you're going to clean it up."

"Don't touch him," Scotty warned.

Rich spread a blanket alongside Cletus' body. With the toe of his boot, he worked the blanket under the dead man's shoulder and hip.

"Get a shovelful of dirt to throw on that blood," Rich directed.

When Scotty returned, he did his best to avoid looking at his ex-partner. He piled dirt on as much of the blood as he could before looking to Rich.

"Now, shovel him over on the blanket." Rich heard Scotty choke back his supper as he pried the body up.

Cletus cooperated and rolled face down on the blanket. Rich nudged Cletus closer to the center and bent to grab the blanket.

"Grab the other end," Rich said. "Oh, go on, you'll be okay as long as you don't get his blood on you."

Wrapped in his bedroll Cletus swayed between Rich and Scotty as they carried him to The Boys' wagon.

"On three," Rich said.

The blanket swung in widening arcs as Rich counted. On his third trip towards the wagon, Cletus sailed through the air and landed with a thud that sent air rushing out both ends of his body. Scotty gasped and lost his dinner. Cletus' limp right hand flopped out onto the wagon bed. Mercifully, the rest of him stayed wrapped in the blanket. Rich agreed to take care of Cletus and sent Scotty packing.

A few hours later, Rich and Eddie carried out a blanket of their own. The threat was over--for now. Nobody in Missouri Flat was breathing any easier. There was still a rabid, wounded wolfbat lurking out there in the dark and folks weren't too sure the Powells hadn't been infected.

"Geez Louise," Eddie whispered as they drove out of camp. "This is getting out of hand."

"People do stupid things when they're scared. we can't do nothing about that."

"Shut up back there," Rich snapped.

Eddie turned the wagon west; skirted The Flat proper and started up the Green Valley road. They followed the road's many twists and turns wanting to be far enough from town to escape prying eyes, but close enough that the fire would be seen on the Flat.

"This ought to be far enough. Pull over there." Rich pointed to a small open patch of ground.

Eddie steered the team off the road and circled the open ground so that they could make a fast getaway if the situation called for it.

"Okay, let's do it," Rich said. "It don't need to be too deep."

"Thank God for that." Eddie's spade hit rock six inches down.

An hour later Rich was satisfied with the hole. They dragged Cletus off the wagon. He hit the ground; bounced once like a load of planks and toppled into the hole. That's when things began to go wrong.

"You've got to be kidding," Rich moaned.

The grave was six inches too short. Furthermore, Cletus had become stiff-necked about the whole thing. In fact, Cletus was stiff all over. No amount of force could compel him to bend his knees.

"Break his legs with the shovel."

"You get out of here," Rich said. "We'll handle this. Eddie, get the kerosene."

Eddie piled brush on top of Cletus and soaked everything with the kerosene. Orange flames climbed from the hole throwing long, distorted shadows across the clearing. The smell of burning hair and flesh was not far behind. The Boys pulled bandanas over their faces to escape the stink. It didn't help.

"How long we going to stand here and smell that?" Eddie asked.

"Until we're sure nobody's gonna recognize who's in that hole. Then, we cover the whole mess up and get back.

"Are you sure we shouldn't just cut and run?"

"No, are you?"

"It's tempting."

Scotty Benbow pulled up stakes the next day. He said he'd been thinking about going to Jackson for some time. This seemed as good a time as any. Scotty stopped long enough to pay a call on Rich and Eddie. The Boys were trying to wash away the taste of the previous evening's cremation and burial.

"Hoped I'd find you here." Scotty handed Rich a neatly folded piece of paper.

"Your claim?" Rich passed the paper to his brother.

"It's yours, legal and proper," Scotty explained. "You boys are the only ones I trust not to sell it to Lefty the minute I'm gone."

"It'll be here if Jackson don't pan out." Rich tucked the deed into his coat.

"Obliged to you," Scotty said and was gone.

The Boys left the Red Dog planning to make it back to camp before dark. They were no sooner out the door than Frog Henry called them aside. Frog swapped errands for drinks at, Avery Hawkins place, the Lucky Strike. Seemed Avery wanted a word with the Boys.

"He's upstairs." Frog pointed the way and licking his parched lips; retired to the bar.

Rich and Eddie exchanged puzzled looks; shrugged and headed up the stairs. Rich knocked on the door marked Private.

"Come in Boys," Avery called. "Have a seat."

"What're you up to Hawkins?" Eddie asked.

Avery Hawkins leaned back in his chair and crossed his arms behind his head. "Now, that's the very question I was going to ask you."

"We ain't got time for this." Rich stood to go.

Avery leaned forward slapping the desk with both hands. His face was flushed; his eyes narrowed to slits.

"Sit," he hissed.

Rich's hand was on his gun. Eddie's were already trained on Avery's head. Avery didn't appear scared, but neither did he dare flinch.

"I wouldn't do that," Avery said. "I was over at Lotus Hill yesterday. You'll never guess who I passed on my way home. Why, it was none other than the recently deceased Sandbar Jack. Don't you boys find that interesting? I'm sure the sheriff would."

Rich returned to his seat. Eddie holstered his weapons.

"Ah, that's better," Avery told them.

That night, the wolfbat was back.

"Woo-woo-woo-woof-wolfbat!" The cry echoed up and down Shinbone Creek. Campfires were built up. Guns of every shape and size bristled from tent flaps and cabin windows. A few stray shots were fired into the dark, but no wolfbats were killed. Jonas Everwhite claimed the sight of a wolf with one wing running through the trees expedited his visit to the latrine. Floyd Looney and James Mayo swore the coarse black hair stuck to a tree behind their tent came from the same creature.

Saturday night the crowd at the Red Dog was in a somber mood.

"We got to do something about the wolfbat," Jonas told the room.

"I ain't slept more than an hour at a time for a week," Jud Voorhees complained.

"Ain't nobody sleepin'. I'm thinking of pulling out," Jonas said.

"I'll buy the claim of any man foolish enough to sell," Lefty offered. "Wolfbats, you're all crazy."

"Don't see you taking many strolls in the moonlight," Eddie said.

"Maybe, Jack was right," Rich said.

"Right about what?" Jonas asked.

"Wolfbats, blast it all," Rich spat. "Maybe they do come from China. It could be we're going about this all wrong. What we ought to do is ride over to Lotus Hill and talk to that Chinaman."

"Yea," Eddie agreed. "He's supposed to be some kind of witch doctor or something. It might work."

"What are you waiting for?" Jonas asked. The question was followed by a general murmur of approval.

"Daylight," Rich said.

Three cheers went up. The atmosphere at the Red Dog returned to its usual rowdy festiveness. No one noticed the harbingers of all the good cheer weren't joining in the celebration.

Rich and Eddie got under way early the next morning. The few folks on Missouri Flat still standing offered up another three cheers. It was a day's ride to Lotus Hill; another back again. Rich and Eddie took another whole day persuading the Chinaman to come along. By the time they returned, the entire community was as sober as it ever got. Young and old gathered in the street to hear the news.

The noise in the street was too much for the Chinaman's frail voice. The decision was made to repair to the Red Dog. The miners and townsfolk packed themselves into the saloon; perched in the rafters and spilled into the street. Once refreshments were served, wet whistles and eager ears turned towards the bar. Eddie put a chair atop the bar and hoisted Wei-ho into the seat.

The little Chinaman's funnel shaped hat hid most of his face, but not his age. A braided white lock fell down his back and a wisp of snowy beard hung from his chin. He wore baggy black pajamas that pooled atop his woven grass sandals.

"This is Wei-Ho." Rich announced. "I don't want everyone shoutin' at him. Ho is gonna tell you what he told us. You can ask questions when he's done. Until then keep your yaps shut and go easy on the whiskey."

"This is ridiculous, Lefty shouted from the back. "Everybody knows you can't trust a Chinaman."

A flying beer bottle caught Lefty between the eyes.

"Any other questions?" Eddie asked. There were none.

"Good," Rich said. "Ho, tell these men what you told us."

The Chinaman bowed and nearly fell from his perch. He recovered with a giggle. Ho's mangled English mixed "l" and "r" but his message was clear.

"Mista Rich; nice man. Thank you, listen. When Ho little boy, grandfatta tell story of Yamhoachung--whatta you call wolfbat. Big wolf, very big wings--so." Wei-Ho stretched out both arms.

"Wolfbat always come into village atta night. Take away animal; chicken, goat, sometimes pig. One time take away baby. After that children no safe."

Ho's claim brought a gasp from the room.

"Yes, very much so. Wolfbat take baby…never see again. Men of village hunt wolfbat. Ancient ones say: 'Don't go.' Men of village no listen. Gun, arrow, sword no kill wolfbat. Many die. Wolfbat come back every night."

"Ho, tell these people how they finally killed the wolfbat," Rich said.

Ho looked at Rich. His head dropped and his braid swayed slowly side to side.

"You mean we can't kill it?" Ernie Carson said.

Rich held up a hand. "Go ahead Ho, tell them."

"Ancient ones say can only kill Yamhoachung with sirva or gord." Seeing puzzlement on the sea of white faces, Ho looked to Rich.

"Silver or gold," Rich explained.

"Ah yes, silver, gold, they poison to Wolfbat. Ho's grandfatta, very brave, make golden arrow. Kill wolfbat."

"What the hell is he talking about?" a brave soul asked.

28

"His grandfather made a gold arrowhead," Rich explained. He used the gold to kill the wolfbat. It's a kind of poison to wolfbats."

"Hold it right there." Lefty had recovered. "Just how stupid do you think we are?"

"Lefty, you know the answer to that," Rich said. "You're dumb as dirt."

Laughter rippled through the saloon, but Lefty was not to be denied.

"This whole thing is nothing but a load of bull. It's a trick, I tell you. There ain't no such thing as wolfbats."

"I know it's crowded," Sheriff Ernie told the crowd. "But somebody throw that jackass out of here."

A cheer went up. Lefty was propelled to the door where someone planted a boot in his backside.

"Go on, the rest of us want to hear," the sheriff said to a hundred seconds.

"What Ho is trying to tell you is bullets won't work. I know for a fact I hit that thing a dozen times myself. It's got to be silver or gold and it has got to stick in the wolfbat."

"Ah yes, must stick. Ho see wolfbat one time--very bad."

"Tell the rest Ho," Eddie said.

"Wolfbat not always kill. Sometime bite only. Wolfbat bite only--turn man into wolfbat."

"Jesus, Joseph and Mary," Ernie Carson said.

"Yeah," Eddie said. "Now, the really bad news."

"You mean it gets worse?" Carson asked.

"Afraid so. You see we…" Rich looked at his brother apparently out of steam.

"Jack wasn't all the way dead," Eddie blurted out. "He got away while we were trying to bury him."

"Take that, Avery Hawkins," Rich thought.

"You idiots," Zeke Tucker said.

Zeke made a grab for Eddie and found the barrel of Eddie's pistol pressed to his forehead. The click of the hammer could be heard across the room.

"You won't do it." Sweat ran down Zeke's temples.

Eddie smiled; his grip tightened on the trigger.

"Don't." Zeke croaked and backed away.

"That's better," Eddie said.

The sheriff broke the tension. "So you brought him here to tell us guns won't kill it and that Sandbar Jack has turned into a wolfbat?"

"That's about the size of it," Rich nodded.

"Ain't life grand?" the sheriff said.

"Ho said those things only come out at night. What if we find out where they hold up during the day?" Nate Johnson said.

"Wise man. Besta place look isa cave. Be sure look with nose."

"Look with nose? what's that supposed to mean?" Nate asked.

"Wolfbat smell very bad." Ho pinched his nose."

"There's dozens of caves in these hills not to mention all the mines," Carson said.

"There's only one that's been vacated recently," Eddie reminded him. " I'll bet that caves crawling with wolfbats. Remember how bad that bear smelled?"

"Okay, we know where to look. What about weapons?" Carson asked.

"Can't be bullets," Rich said. "Bullets pass right through."

"So what do we do?" Carson asked.

"Sling shots," Rich suggested.

"Sling shots?"

"You remember how to use one don't you, Ernie?"

The sheriff nodded. A murmur from bystanders said they were getting a handle on the situation.

"Where we gonna get enough silver and gold to kill God-knows-how-many wolfbats?" Bill Bentley asked.

A hush fell over the room. Everyone knew the answer.

"Ina my village, we round up, alla house," Ho said.

"Yeah, well this is America," Bentley pointed out.

"Right," the sheriff said. "So we're going to take up a collection and we better get enough in the plate the first time."

"Meeting adjourned," Eddie announced. "Drink up everybody."

Moses and children of Israel had nothing on the citizens of Missouri Flat. The exodus began the moment talk turned to confiscation. Miners and shopkeepers alike threw their possessions into wagons and hit the road. But, it was a long way to the promised land. Sheriff Carson was familiar with the story. Roadblocks were up before the first wagon was hitched. Folks were allowed to leave; silver and gold were not. A few well hidden ounces made it out Missouri Flat, but overall, the collection was nothing short of miraculous.

Most of the miners spent the night at the Red Dog. There was some talk of pulling out, but the majority decided to wait and see if the crazy idea of killing wolfbats with sling shots stood a Chinaman's chance.

Confident in his advice, Ho curled up on the bar and fell quickly to sleep. The Chinaman's snoring soon drown out conversation at the bar. Zeke poked Ho with a broom to try and to stop his snoring. Ho rolled over and broke wind.

"Lord have mercy Zeke, what did you do?" Rich said through his hand.

"It wasn't me." Zeke tried to wave the stench away. "It was that Chainman of yours."

"Good God, what do they eat?" Nate Johnson asked.

"I dunno, rice mostly." Rich shrugged.

"I can't breathe," Eddie said. "Let's go."

The miners gave Ho the bar. His snores were much preferred to the lingering odor emanating from the other end. At sun up, Zeke chased the miners from his saloon. He'd been on edge all night and decided to do something about it. He wasn't sure which frightened him more wolfbats or Eddie Powell. In the end, it didn't matter. Zeke was selling the Red Dog and getting out of Missouri Flat. Zeke already had a buyer in mind. He slipped out the back and made his way to the Lucky Strike. Avery Hawkins let him in.

"I need to talk to you," Zeke said.

"C'mon upstairs." Avery led the way. "Coffee?"

"No thanks. I'm pulling out. Between wolfbats and Eddie Powell, it ain't worth it."

"And you want me to buy you out?"

"I need a thousand."

Hawkins reached under his desk and spun a combination lock. He found the numbers he wanted and yanked open the door. Hawkins rifled through the contents.

"Can't do 'er, Zeke. Would you consider the $700 in cash and trying to sneak $300 in dust past Ernie?"

"Let me chew on it."

"Sure. Have you talked to Bentley?"

"No, and I ain't about to."

"Okay, okay. I was just asking. Let me know what you decide."

As Zeke rose to leave, Hawkins stopped him. Hawkins pressed a finger to his lips; drew a little hideout from his coat and tiptoed to the door. The bar looked empty. Avery was about to pull his head back into the office when he heard the faint click of the back door.

"We had company," Hawkins said. "You talked to anyone else about this?"

"No one. I didn't see anybody was following either."

"Be careful," Hawkins said.

Zeke nodded and slipped back to the Red Dog unseen. The Powells and Wei-Ho were sitting where he left them.

"Mornin' Zeke," Rich said.

Wei-Ho bowed. Eddie glared.

"We're leavin'. Thanks for lettin' us use your place," Rich said.

"Sure, Rich."

Ho followed Rich out. Eddie paused in the bat wings; pointed his forefinger and upraised thumb in Zeke's direction and dropped the hammer. Zeke knew what he had to do. He began packing.

When they were beyond eyesight and earshot of the Flat, Rich stepped down from his horse and handed the reins to Eddie.

"I'll meet you at the cabin. Have we got everything?" Rich asked.

"Yeah, I think so."

"Mista Rich be careful," Ho said

"Mista Rich gonna kick your butt."

"Ha ha, Mista Rich very funny."

Rich was back in the Flat just in time to see Zeke leave the Lucky Strike for the second time that day. Rich climbed the stairs and tapped lightly on the office door.

"C'mon in," Avery said.

"How'd it go?" Rich asked

"Slick as snot through a goose. Got it for $700 cash and three hundred in dust. I'll tell Ernie he's trying it sneak out of town. You can give it back later."

"Then we're square?"

"Almost."

"What do you mean, almost?"

"Just that--almost. I want Bentley's place too."

"That wasn't part of the deal."

"The deal has changed. I heard what you tried to pull in there. You try it again and you'll hang."

"Scotty's the one that shot Cletus. We didn't have nothing to do with that."

"You did everything but pull the trigger. This little scheme of yours was only fraud until Cletus. Now, its murder. Plans change. Deals change too."

"Okay, but while we're rememberin' poor old Cletus, you better remember what happened when he became a threat to his partner."

"Then you'll get Bentley to sell?"

"Yep. Then, we *are* done."

"Yeah, yeah. Get outta here."

"Whatsa matta Mista Rich?" Ho asked.

"Hawkins upped the ante. He wants Bentley too."

"Is that gonna be a problem?" Eddie asked.

"Not really. I just hate having the deal changed."

"Ho, think maybe wolfbat be ina town tonight."

"Me thinkee; Ho right." Eddie said.

"Let's get this wagon rollin." Rich began gathering supplies.

Sunday nights were not as raucous as Saturday, nevertheless, business was brisk. The regulars turned out as usual. Rich and Eddie skipped the Red Dog and showed up Bentley's Gold Nugget where they bought a round for the house and offered up a toast to ridding The Flat of wolfbats.

"Where's the Chinaman?" Bill Bentley asked after the grand toast.

"Back at camp. He's makin' some kind of silver blade," Rich said.

"Good. A saloon ain't no place for his kind. They're bad for business," Bentley said.

Eddie agreed. "You never know what that one's thinking. The Chinamen in Coloma swear he's some kind of medicine man."

"I hear they smoke stuff that makes 'em crazy."

"Opium," Rich said. "Rooms full a Chinamen layin' around smokin that stuff over there. It's no wonder they don't talk good."

"Woo-woo-woo-woof-wolfbat!"

Inside the Nugget; the music stopped. Words hung frozen in the smoky air; silence reigned---for exactly thirty seconds. Men began to scramble for cover in a flurry of movement which brought an obscene number of guns out of hiding.

"That sounded like it was right outside," Bentley said.

"Everybody keep still," Rich cautioned. "Bill, come with me."

With Bill and Eddie in tow, Rich peeked over the batwings.

"Get yer scattergun," he whispered to Bill.

Bill Bentley had a deep yearning to stay inside. He didn't want to see what was lurking outside. It preferred it stay a mystery. Rich had put him on the spot. Bill couldn't back down now. Curse his luck, he had to be standing next to the only men in Missouri Flat crazy enough to go chasing wolfbats.

"Let's go," Eddie said and nudged Bill forward.

The three men stepped out the door. The street was empty. Bill heaved a sigh and mopped his brow. He was sweating rivers.

"Which way?" Rich said.

"Towards the jail," Eddie answered.

Rich led the way through the shadows. Where the building gave onto a side street, Rich glanced around the corner. The gap was black as pitch.

"Too dark," Bill said.

"One at a time," Eddie whispered.

Rich nodded and plunged ahead. He picked his way across the void and waved for Bill to follow. Bill tried to swallow the lump in his throat, but his mouth was too dry to force it down. Whispering the Lord's Prayer, he stepped into the street. His hands wouldn't stop shaking. If only he could see…

"Wooo--wooo--wooo--woof--woofbat!"

Bill jumped as if he were shot. He wanted to run, but his feet refused to move. The wolfbat materialized out of the blackness. It came at Bill wings flapping in a crazy disjointed rhythm. Bill's feet came loose. He dropped his shotgun in the dust and ran. The creature charged after him. Bill turned to see if the creature gave chase. That was all the wolfbat needed. Bill went down--hard. Sharp claws raked his face. Bill's eyes filled with blood. He screamed, but the sound was lost in gunfire. From the head of the street, Rich and Eddie emptied their revolvers at the monster.

Rich dragged the blind Bentley to the safety of the saloon. Eddie reloaded and fired again at the slowly retreating wolfbat. A crush of miners pushed passed Rich and the wounded saloon owner. Flush with fresh liquid courage, they poured from the Nugget in time to see Eddie drop his guns back into their holsters.

"I got it," Eddie told them. "I know I got it. It just kept going."

Some of the drunker men pursued the wolfbat into the trees. The pursuit lasted until they came upon a patch of blood stained plaid material.

"It was Jack," Eddie said. "Let's get him."

But the chase was over.

"Not me," said Lefty.

"Me neither," Billy Johnson echoed.

"Why the heck not?"

"Wolfbat or Sandbar Jack, that thing's wounded and mean. I ain't about to go chasin' it through the dark," Lefty said.

"You got a point," Eddie conceded.

A bandaged Bill Bentley looked up into the faces of his customers. Bright fear stood front and center in their wide eyes. Faces turned quickly away from Bill's pleading gaze. He knew what they were thinking--he was thinking it too.

"He's bit," Lefty said what everyone knew.

The crowd inched away. Bentley touched his face. His hand came away sticky. The sight of his own blood filled him with panic.

"Help me," he pleaded. "Please, somebody do something."

"Ain't but one thing to do." Lefty drew his gun.

"No, not that." Bill tried to crawfish away. There was no place to go. "No, please don't."

"Got to Bill," Lefty cut off his retreat..

"Hold it right there." Ernie Carson stepped between Bill and Lefty. " Put that gun away." .

"Ernie, help me." Bill's eyes filled with tears.

"We all know it's got to be done," Lefty said.

"We don't know nothing of the kind." The sheriff lifted bill to his feet. "We ain't shootin' a man in cold blood on the say so of some Chinaman. He's coming with me. We'll keep him locked up until we do know."

Relief washed over Bentley's face.

"The sheriff's right," Rich said.

"But you're the one brought that Chinaman here," Lefty complained. "Who's side are you on?"

"I'm on the sheriff's side," Rich said. "I ain't shootin' nobody till I see the change with my own eyes."

"What about Jack?" Lefty persisted.

"You actually *see* Jack?"

"No, but..." Lefty wasn't getting any support.

"I ain't sayin' it wasn't Jack," Rich said. I'm saying none of us got close enough to say for sure."

A murmur of approval passed through the crowd.

"Come on Bill, we're getting out of here," Carson said.

"Drinks on the house," Bill announced. Ernie Carson never had a happier prisoner.

Chapter 4

Zeke Tucker was gone. Bill Bentley was history and everybody knew it. There was a fortune to be made by the man who outlasted the competition. The likelihood of dying in the process was growing, but there are always men willing to gamble their lives. Avery Hawkins was nothing if not a gambler.

The saloons were the only business in Missouri Flat not suffering from wolfbat mania. The general flight from The Flat cost the Fire Baptist Church most of all. Families left the morning after Wei-Ho's revelation that wolfbats carried off children. Bro. Ray's assurances weren't enough to hold them.

That it could boast a church only a month into its creation made Missouri Flat unique among California gold camps. It wasn't that folks drawn to the Flat were religious. The miners and misfits that made up the majority of the population were as immoral a bunch as there ever was. The Flat was destined to have a church boom or no boom. The reason was another of Missouri Flat's rather unique characters--The Reverend Raymond Powell.

Reverend Powell, Brother Ray to everyone on the Flat, was first cousin to the wayward Rich and Eddie Powell. He too cut his teeth on the lumber business. Ray abandoned the mill about the same time as his cousins, but Ray was not after gold. well, not directly. Ray had other plans. Those plans last all of one week. That was when Ray received "The Call."

Ray's call to the ministry came seconds after Grandma Powell heard Ray say he intended to open a saloon and be his own best customer. The Hand of God struck the aspiring drunk a dreadful blow. Ray recovered and spent three days locked grandma's in the root cellar repenting. Bro. Ray that emerged from that cellar a new creation blessed with the ability to call down fire and brimstone on the unrepentant. To say Ray put the fear of God into his hearers was like saying the ocean has a lot of water. The only ones Ray didn't frighten were little children and old women; they loved him. Grandma Powell saw to it her boys built Ray a real church house with polished pews and a bell to call worshippers to Sunday service. As shopkeepers and families moved in, the church grew as fast as the town. While miners were sloshing the waters of Shinbone Creek in their pans, Bro. Ray was busy using the same water to dunk sinners.

The coming of the wolfbat not only dried up the pool of repentant sinners, the saved began to seek safety elsewhere. Bro. Ray had to take drastic action to save his church. He decided to take his preaching to the people. Sinners were in abundance on the Flat. if they wouldn't come to him, Ray would go to them. On that particular day the largest gathering of lost souls happened to be was at the Gold Nugget. Thither went the Reverend determined to make the most of his situation.

Bro. Ray descended on the Nugget an hour after sunrise. The sight of miners littering the sawdust brought a smile to the preacher's face. Inspiration coursed through his veins pushing his volume to thunder. Bro. Ray stepped inside.

"Awake, you godless heathen!" Ray bellowed. the Sermon at the Nugget was underway.

Bleary eyed miners panicked by the sudden assault on their sin and senses scrabbled to pick themselves off the floor and flee. Ray blocked in the doorway. As the congregation stood, Ray clouted the nearest sinner with his Bible. The hapless miner hit the floor and scurried away on hands and knees. Ray followed him; sparing no one.

"Repent, sinners," he demanded. "This wolfbat is no Chinaman's monster. It is the Hand of God. Did you think God couldn't see your drunkenness? Did you think He would hold back judgment forever? No! God has seen your wickedness. Judgment is come. It is God who sent the wolfbat among you. Silver and gold cannot stay the hand of God. Vengeance is mine, I will repay, saith the Lord.

I tell you the wolfbat is come to root out; to pull down and to destroy this sin infested camp. Have you not seen how the wolfbat has chosen...yes, I say, chosen...to strike the most ungodly amongst you? Are there any bigger whiskey guzzling, blasphemous heathen than my own cousins and Sandbar Jack? No! Who shall be next among you?"

"You? Or you?" Ray stabbed a finger at the crowd.

Ray cornered his fleeing quarry. He bent to stare the sad creature in the eye.

"How about you?" he whispered. The next instant Ray was standing tall. "On your knees, sinners!"

Bro. Ray dunked forty new members that very afternoon. Rich and Eddie were not among the converted. The Sermon at the Nugget became local history and Bro. Ray proved himself a true prophet. The wolfbat descended on the camps with a vengeance.

Still, some did not believe.

***

Three nights holed up in their cabin was too much for Jeff Brown and Josh Robbins. They gave up hiding and moved outside. They sat beside an open fire, guns in hand, determined to drink their coffee under the stars.

"Dad gum, that was rank," Josh said.

"You should know; you done it." Jeff tried to wave the smell away.

"Did not. Now, move 'round down wind."

"I'm telling you, it wasn't me."

"Then who...Jesus, Joseph and Mary." Josh crossed himself.

"Woo-woo-woo-woof-woofbat." The monster came lumbering out of the trees.

"Run," Jeff screamed.

Josh was way ahead of his partner and the snarling, slobbering thing staggering along behind them. Neither man looked back until they reached the Fire Baptist Church. The two men hit the church doors screaming and hollering to be rescued. Bro. Ray's sleeping converts opened the door and let the frantic miners to squeeze inside. The lamps were lit to allow Jeff and Josh to find a place without stepping on anyone.

"What happened?"

"The wolfbat came after us. It came right into camp," Jeff said.

"Y'all saw the wolfbat?"

"It weren't exactly a wolfbat." Josh stared at his audience.

"It was Sandbar Jack," Jeff took over. "Only he ain't human no more."

Josh shivered. "He had wings sprouting outta his back."

"He didn't fly though," Jeff said. "Just kinda staggered; growlin' and slobberin' like an animal."

"Had wolf ears and hair everywhere, Josh said. "He smelt worse than Jeff after a week of beans."

Laughter rippled through the room.

"Reckon he's still out there?"

"Stick your head outside and see," Jeff dared.

Further discussion as to the wolfbat's whereabouts was cut short.

"Woooo-woooo-woooof-wooofbat." The cries circled the church twice before moving away towards town.

The next morning was Sunday. Missouri Flat spent the day divided between Bro. Ray's sermon and fashioning sling shots in a delicate balance between faith and a little extra security. The balance was upset later that day when Rich and Eddie showed up at evening service.

"Hallelujah and Amen," Eddie shouted from the door.

"What do you two want?" Ray demanded from the pulpit.

"A simple test of faith. I want you to show me your faith by your works."

"Thou shalt not tempt the Lord thy God." Ray lifted his Bible high.

"We ain't temptin' God, cousin. We're challenging you." Rich stabbed a finger at the preacher.

"You're spending a night on the creek," Eddie said.

"You can bring a gun if want," Rich added.

"The wolfbat is doing God's work. Why should I oppose God?"

"Because we ain't asking." Rich's gun was out. Eddie had two trained on the congregation.

Bro. Ray didn't believe his cousins would shoot him. He was not so sure they wouldn't shoot a member of the congregation. He consented to accompany them to their camp on Shinbone Creek.

"Is all this necessary?" Ray looked around his cousin's camp.

There was a small fire built about fifteen feet from the cabin door. A bedroll spread in anticipation lay near a pot of miner's coffee.

"Darn tootin'," Rich assured him. "You've had an awful lot to say about the wolfbat lately. We thought you ought to have a firsthand look."

"And if the wolfbat doesn't show, are we to do this every night?"

"Make yourself at home. Ho says the wolfbat is partial to preachers. We'll be watching from the cabin," Eddie said.

"Just in case your faith wavers," Rich plopped down a sling shot and three silver slugs.

Ray snorted and stretched out beside the fire. Minutes later, his snores reverberated in the dark with the same depth as his preaching.

"Is he that blasted sure of himself or is he just trying to hack me off?" Rich asked.

"A little of the first and whole lot of the second," Eddie answered.

Rich elbowed his brother in the ribs.

By the time the moon was directly overhead, only a few stubborn embers remained to warm the sleeping preacher. Ray's snores continued in raucous testimony that the Lord does, indeed, give His beloved sleep.

"Should be any minute now," Rich whispered.

"Wooo-wooo-wooo-wooof-woofbat!"

Gunfire exploded from the cabin. Ignoring the bullets whizzing overhead, Ray came off his bed in a single fluid motion. The wolfbat and the preacher advanced on one another.   "In the name of the Lord." Ray raised his Bible. "Back."

Ray stepped on a stick of kindling; his foot rolled forward and Ray crashed to the ground his Bible on his chest. The wolfbat kept coming. Ray rose to his knees. Moonlit reflected off silver shot. caught his eye. Ray dropped a shot into the sling and fired. The wolfbat howled in pain.

"Now!" Eddie yelled.

The net fell, but not on the wolfbat. Rich and Eddie captured only an angry preacher.

"I'm going after it," Eddie called over his shoulder.

"Get me out here." Ray thrashed around the ground trying to work himself free. he stopped long enough to notice his older cousin smiling down at him. "What are you smiling at?"

"You," Rich said. "You handled that slingshot pretty well."

"Oh shut up," Ray said.

"Ah, don't be mad, cousin." Rich untangled the preacher. You got the wolfbat."

"I did? Hey, I did."

"Yep. Now, help me with this net."

The cousins got the net stowed away. Rich stirred the embers and built up the fire.

"Eddie might need help. Ain't we going after him?" Ray moved closer to the fire.

"Eddie can take care of himself. He'll be okay as long as he doesn't lose sight of the varmint. Besides it's too dark to track. We'd best waiting until morning."

"Do you really think I hit it?" Rays eyes were dancing.

"You heard it holler." A smile crept over Rich's lips. "Dang right you got it. If what the Chinaman says is true and that shot sticks, we'll have ourselves another David."

"Where is the Chinaman?"

"Who knows?" Rich offered up a shrug.

Lost in their own thoughts, the two men stared at the fire. The silence soon weighed heavy on their eyelids. Their thoughts dull; sleep beaconed and they answered. For a time, wolfbats were forgotten.

Out in the dark east of Shinbone Creek Eddie Powell found the wolfbat. It was badly wounded, but not nearly dead.

"Dad blast it Eddie, your cousin shot me."

"Oh quit your whining," Eddie said.

Sandbar Jack pulled his pants down to get a look at his wound. Jack's right hip was black and swollen from beltline to buttocks. He gingerly touched the spreading bruise and grimaced in pain.

"By the way," Eddie said. "That was some wolfbat yelp you made when he hit you."

"Very funny. I ain't gonna be able to sit for a week."

The morning air said snow was not far off. Eddie turned up his collar to ward off the chill. Shinbone Creek was quiet. Most of the miners decided to stay in town until the threat of the wolfbat was ended. Eddie dropped his quarry in front of the cabin and went inside. A blast of cold air chased him through the door.

"Get up," Eddie said. "You two act like you get to see a wolfbat everyday."

Ray threw back the blankets and sat up. "You got it?"

"No, you got it. I just ran it down."

"Sweet Jesus," Ray said.

The preacher hopped through the door trying to get his boots on without falling. Rich was right behind him. At their feet lay a bloody wolf pelt; the cold was forgotten.

"Where's the wings?" Ray asked.

"Back with the carcass," Eddie said. "That thing weighed more'n a hundred pounds."

"I guess so." Ray's disappointment was palpable.

"You want the wings? go get 'em. They're in the abandoned cave on the west side of Forni Hill. Only you better take your slingshot with you. It ain't abandoned anymore. I counted a half dozen wolfbats flying around the entrance. No telling how many are inside."

"We need to get back to town," Ray said.

Rich and Eddie shared a smile.

"Right behind you cousin," Rich said.

"Shouldn't we find the Chinaman?" Ray asked.

"Don't worry," Rich assured him. "He'll find us."

Eddie hitched the team while the others loaded the wolfbat in the wagon. Rich and Eddie climbed into the seat. Ray stood over his trophy like a conquering hero. The killing of the wolfbat was announced with a volley of gunfire and a shout. Miners in all stages of undress turned out to hear the news and follow the wagon into town. More shots and shouts woke Missouri Flat to the biggest parade in the town's history. Everyone wanted to see the wolfbat.

Wei Ho appeared on the steps of the Fire Baptist Church to officially welcome the heroes and pronounce the pelt authentic wolfbat. According to Ho, the singed hair around the wound showed where silver touched wolfbat flesh.

"Why that ain't nothing but some mangy wolf hide," Lefty sneered. "Where's the wings? Where's the body?"

"Where were you when I had to carry the danged thing?" Eddie shot back.

"Take it easy." Rich laid a hand on his brother's shoulder. "The carcass is out on Forni Hill."

"Sheriff that cave is swarming with wolfbats," Eddie said. "You seen 'em?"

"Ah, what are you asking him for?" lefty groaned. "Ain't nobody seen a wolfbat 'cept them."

Eddie flew off the wagon and landed a solid straight right on Lefty's jaw before the other man could blink. Lefty went down, but came right back up swinging. He caught Eddie with a left hook that rocked the big man back on his heels. Eddie recovered and charged. The two men hit the dirt in a jumble of flying fists and boots.

"I got three ounces on Eddie," Nate Johnson offered.

"I'll take that."

"A hundred dollars on Lefty."

"I got fifty on Eddie."

The bets flew as fast as the punches. Eddie threw a roundhouse right. Lefty ducked and the blow struck squarely on the crown of his head. Eddie bellowed and grabbed his hand.

"I broke my danged hand." Eddie shook his hand trying to chase the pain away.

Lefty reeled backwards; dropped on the seat of his pants and promptly flopped over in a cloud of dust. Jeff Brown and Jeff Robbins jumped into the fray. Rich kicked Jeff's feet out from under him, but before Jeff hit the ground .45 caliber thunder called the fight and stilled the crowd.

"That's enough," Ernie Carson yelled. "Save it for the wolfbats."

"How much longer is that going to be, sheriff?" Bro. Ray asked.

"The shot will be ready this evening. The wolfbat hunt begins at daylight," Ernie told the crowd.

Three cheers followed the announcement. Ernie Carson waved Sam Colt's voice of reason and eloquently offered to shoot any jackass foolish enough to go near the cave before daylight.

The crowd, sensing the festivities were over took another look at the wolfbat and repaired to the closest saloon. Wolfbat hunting was bound to be thirsty work and there was nothing like getting an early start.

Around three that afternoon Rich and Eddie were standing outside the Red Dog when they saw the sheriff headed their way. Ernie wore a tight lipped frown and earlobes two shades of red brighter than normal.

"Oh, oh." Rich nodded toward the sheriff.

"Boys, I want to thank you for volunteering." Ernie's countenance brightened. He patted the brothers on the shoulder.

"But sheriff we..."Ernie's upraised palm stopped Rich.

"Sure you did." Ernie fixed his eyes on Rich.

"Yes, yes we did." Rich melted.

"I forgot though," Eddie said. "Remind me, what did we volunteer to do?"

"Raise your right hands. The other right, Eddie. I hereby deputize you to get your sorry behinds out to Forni Hill and make sure none of these other idiots do something foolish."

"I'll take that job." Eddie agreed with a smile.

"Sorry to disappoint you, but Lefty will not be one of the idiots to try. I plan on seeing to that personally."

"Darn it, Uncle Ernie." Eddie's smile was gone.

"Quit calling me that. I want one quiet night--just one. I'm tired. All I'm asking is for you to stay out of trouble for one night.

Stay away from the cave and make sure everyone else does to, got it?"

"You can count on us sheriff," Rich said.

"Oh, and take that spooky Chinaman with you." Ernie turned on his heels and went in search of Lefty Nickels.

"Go ahead," Rich told Eddie once the sheriff was out of range.

"Everything's set?" Eddie asked. "You have the stuff?"

Rich patted his coat pocket. "Gonna give old Uncle Ernie a very quiet night."

"Where's Ho?"

"At the Nugget. I'll send him along as soon as he's done there."

Bill Bentley strained to hear the news from his cell. He still didn't feel any different-- not yet. Of course, he didn't know how long it took to change into a wolfbat. He wished he had a mirror. Bill tried to walk of his anxiety, but pacing the cell made him think of caged animals. That was too close to home. He forced himself to sit. The sun went down and the noisy night of celebration never materialized. The Flat was quiet--too quiet for Bill Bentley's liking. He peered out the window at the empty street; even the saloons were dark.

"*Where is everybody? Am I all alone?*" Bill wondered.

Unable to keep still, he began to pace. The sound of his heels on the rough plank floor was the only sound he heard. The walls felt like they were closing in. Bill swallowed hard. Was he changing? He tried to think about something else; anything else. In the stillness, the doorknob rolled over with a faint click. Bill's heart jumped into his throat.

"Who's there?" Bill said.

The door swung open.

"Who's there? Ernie is that you?"

Through the open door, moonlight glistened on metal. something flew across the room and landed at his feet. Bill dropped the key twice before he got the door open. His black mare was tied outside. bill looked up and down the street--no one was there. Bill threw his leg over the saddle and was never seen in Missouri Flat again. He didn't bother to collect his things.

Two hours after sun up, Ernie woke with a throbbing headache. It couldn't be daylight already. He only had one drink. Ernie's head disagreed. He staggered to the door and looked outside.

"Where is everybody?" His own whisper boomed in his head.

He dressed as fast as his aching head allowed and made his way to the jail. The front door was wide open as was the cell that once held Bill Bentley. His first thought was that the miners had strung up Bill and went to slay wolfbats. The sacks of shot still locked in the adjoining cell told a different story; one that Ernie wasn't sure he understood.

"What's going on around here?" he asked.

"Good question sheriff."

"Not so loud, Bro. Ray." Ernie pressed his fingers against the bass drums pounding in his temples.

Ray Powel, dressed in his Sunday preaching suit, stood in the door his Bible in one hand and a sling shot in the other. The preacher looked as perplexed as the sheriff.

"Where is everybody?" Ernie asked.

"Still passed out in their favorite dens of inequity."

"Everyone?"

"Everyone. Everyone except the few God-fearing at the church."

The sheriff nodded and stepped into the street.

"God, help me," he prayed and fired three shots into the air.

The hung over mob that responded made him wish he'd let them go after the wolfbats the night before. The opium powder Rich and Ho slipped into the liquor supply had an extremely deleterious effect on the wolfbat hunters.

It was noon before the Great Wolfbat Hunt got under way. Bro. Ray took point and led the sober marchers in singing "Onward Christian Soldiers." The hung over stayed as far back from the sound as possible. The sheriff took up the drag and kept the back of the pack moving. It was slow going. The pace quickened when a shriek rang out near the head of the column. The stragglers rushed to see what all the shouting was about. They found a crowd huddled around a jumping, swearing Jonas Everwhite.

"What happened?" Carson shouted.

"Dewey shot me in the butt," Jonas roared.

" I knew it. I just knew it. It had to happen." Ernie bit his lip. He tried to hold it--God, how he tried.

Laughter exploded from the sheriff. Once loose, the laughter could not be contained. It infected the whole crowd. Josh Robbins' queasy, hung-over stomach couldn't take it bouncing with laughter. Josh collided with Jeff and puked rancid whiskey down his partner's arm onto the sheriff's boots. Ernie's sense of humor departed. He kicked Josh in the seat of the pants and the brawl was on.

Order was restore a half hour later. the survivors limped on towards Forni Hill. The wounded and plain lazy lay where they fell.

"I ain't seen a fight like that in years." Jeff crowed.

"You ain't gonna be seeing much for a day or two," Josh said.

"I kin see good enough to wonder where your front tooth went."

"And I kin fix that for you too."

"Shut up and keep moving," Lefty said.

A sullen quiet descended on the wolfbat hunters. Bro. Ray's bunch quit singing. They traveled the final mile in silence. Halfway up Forni Hill smoke billowed from a stand of manzanita. The hunters gravitated towards the spot.

"Rich! Eddie! Ray called ahead.

"C'mon up," Eddie waved the hunters on.

"Where's the Chinaman?" Ernie asked when they reached the Boys.

Eddie pointed up at the mine.

"What's he doing up there?" Ernie asked.

Eddie gave him a silent shrug.

"Never mind. Ray have the men fan out below those rocks," the sheriff ordered. "It'll be getting dark soon."

The western sun was sitting on the treetops. Time was running out. Ray got the men positioned. Ernie prevented Lefty's group from rushing the mine by threatening to shoot anyone not waiting for orders.

"You see wolfbats yet?" Ernie asked.

"Not since daylight," Rich said. "What took you so long?"

"Bad night," was all Ernie had to say.

The men positioned, Ray joined the group around the fire. "Everyone's ready. How many wolfbats are up there?"

"We counted six this morning," Eddie told him.

"What about Jack?"

"If he's there," Eddie pointed up the hill. "He's gone completely wolfbat or is staying inside."

"Maybe Wei Ho can tell us. He went up to try and get a count before they stir," Rich said.

"I don't think that was a good idea," the sheriff said.

"Me neither." Eddie shook his head. "But you can't tell that Chinaman nothing."

As if summoned by name, Wei Ho appeared at the cave entrance. His return confirmed the sheriff's notion and upset everyone's plans.

"Wolfbat…Aaaheee," Ho screamed.

A huge wolfbat clung to Ho's back; its jaws around his neck. Covered with blood, Ho twirled in tight panic driven circles trying to shake the wolfbat. Ho screamed and fell to the ground. The mine entrance was suddenly alive with wolfbats.

"Fire!" Ernie screamed.

His voice jolted the wolfbat hunters into action. Fifty scared miners and shopkeepers jumped to their feet as one man and launched a wild barrage of silver and gold shot. Holes opened in the wings of the wolfbats; the two biggest ones went down. Spurred by the effect of their shot, the hunters left their concealment and advanced on the wolfbats.

Ho was back on his feet. The wolfbat was still clinging to his back, but looked to be short a wing. Running under the hail of flying shot, Eddie charged; Ernie and the others followed. The hunters covered twenty yards before skidding to an abrupt halt. Their blood ran cold. Ho held a lighted stick of dynamite. There were cases of the stuff littering the cave opening. Men scattered. They plunged down the hillside putting distance between themselves and the coming blast.

"Take cover," Carson ordered. He could have saved his breath.

The rumble started deep in the ground working its way up through the hunters' shoes. Forni Hill shook and the sky exploded into a cloud of red dust. Rock and timber rained down on the wolfbat hunters. Already battered bodies took on more bumps and bruises. It was a minute or two before dust covered heads emerged from hiding.

"Ho's been blowed clean back to China," Rich said.

"At least he's buried proper." Ernie nodded towards the cave. "Must be a ton of rock blocking that hole."

"I don't see any wolfbats," Rich climbed into a small oak for a better look.

"Think we got 'em all?" Ernie brushed dirt from his hair.

"Let's make sure," Lefty said.

"I ain't going up there." Eddie shook his head.

"Those wolfbats are dead or sealed up. Leave it alone." Ray insisted.

"I'm for that," the sheriff agreed. He turned to face the hunters regrouping under a stand of pines. "Everybody, off this hill."

"You've got to be kidding." Lefty stepped up to face the sheriff. "There's got to be twenty thousand dollars buried up there."

"I made it closer to thirty," Ernie said.

"We can't just leave it," Lefty shrieked.

"Anybody got anymore shot?" Ernie asked. "No? Didn't think so."

As arranged beforehand deputies at the foot of Forni Hill were checking the hunters for unfired shot.

"Anything down there?" Ernie yelled down to his men.

"One or two."

Ernie turned back to Lefty. "The cave stays closed."

"But Sheriff," Lefty tried.

"In a week or two, when we're sure the wolfbats are dead, we'll all go in together." Ernie promised.

"You can't guard this hill day and night," Lefty protested.

"Don't plan to." Ernie bit off a fresh plug.

"What?" Lefty's voice cracked as it jumped up the scale.

"Me and my deputies will patrol it. Meanwhile, we find it open or anybody starts spending too freely, we shake down the whole town. Anybody trying to grab and run won't get far. Oh, and sorry Boys, but you'll have to stop cutting wood up here until then."

"We'll just see about this," Lefty said.

"You do that." Ernie drilled his finger into Lefty's chest. "While you're doing it, I'll kill anyone caught prowling around this hill--and I mean anyone."

The sheriff's warning was passed throughout the hunting party. Only Lefty seemed disappointed with the decision. The rest of the men were swept up by a celebratory spirit. The hunters marched back to town hell bent on a wild night of drinking and self-congratulations.

The hunting party returned to find all the saloons locked up. Zeke Tucker was long gone. Bill Bentley had escaped to God knows where. Avery Hawkins ought to have had the bars open, but no one seemed to know where Avery was. He hadn't joined the hunters or been seen in town all day. The crowd, being in no mood to bother looking, kicked open the doors to all three saloons and the whiskey began to flow.

"Drink up boys," Eddie told the regulars at the Red Dog. "It's on the house."

Ernie Carson sat on the porch at the Sheriff's Office and watched the celebration get underway. He sighed and rubbed his aching back. It had been one long day. It looked to be an even longer night.

"Oh no, what now?"

Lefty Nickels was headed toward the jail. He got right to the point.

"Avery's gone," Lefty announced. "His safe's standing open and his horse isn't at the livery."

When no more seemed forthcoming, the sheriff spit and looked up at Lefty.

"Avery's a smart man," Ernie said, wishing he'd left town himself.

"Well, ain't you going to do something?"

The nasally whine in Lefty's voice pushed Ernie to a decision about his course of action for the night.

"Yes," the sheriff said and stood to his feet. "Yes, I am going to do something, by God. I'm going to bed and may the Lord have mercy on the fool who disturbs me before morning. The drunks can tear the town down for all I care. As for you Lefty, you can go straight to...well...you can just go."

Lefty hauled his jaw back into place. He started to argue. Ernie could hear the wheels turning in Lefty's head. Lefty's mouth opened; closed again and he walked away.

"Guess he's not a *complete* idiot after all," Ernie said.

Lefty left the sheriff, but he didn't return to join the festivities rocking the Flat. Instead, he gathered up a protesting Jeff Brown and Josh Robbins. After a short, animated discussion, the three of them slipped out of town.

It was dark out on Forni Hill. Lefty and company didn't need much light. Lefty thought horses tied out near the cave would be too easy to spot and convinced the others to walk the four miles for the third time that day. Their picks and shovels were heavier than sling shots and Lefty's partner reminded him of the fact every few minutes.

They began digging by the light of the rising moon.

Dawn turned the sky behind Forni Hill a deep violet. Lefty, Jeff and Josh were still digging. There was in fact a ton of dirt in the entrance.

"Ernie will skin us if he catches us," Jeff said.

"He ain't gonna catch us. I got that from the horse's mouth." Lefty tossed a shovelful of dirt over his shoulder. "I'm through. Dig boys, dig."

The hole widened quickly as the three men began to shovel furiously. They could smell easy money. Lefty was the first to squeeze through. The charge had been well placed. Only the cave entrance had been covered by the blast. Inside, the cave walls were intact.

"I knew it," Lefty said. "We've been had."

An intricate maze of wires, pulleys and counterweights was suspended from the roof of the cave. The floor was littered with wolf pelts; some still connected to the strange apparatus. The pelts were used to cover slabs of thick leather tied around wooden frames. The pelts, leather, walls and ceiling were pocked by shot.

"That's how they made them fly," Lefty threw down his shovel in disgust.

"I found the one who was flying them," Jeff said.

A few feet deeper into the cave, tangled in wire, his hands on a series of levers, was Avery Hawkins.

"Avery? I coulda swore..." Lefty scratched his head.

"You can't trust nobody no more," Josh said.

"Where's all the gold and silver?" Jeff asked.

"Gone, that's where. That yellow devil blowed the cave on purpose." Lefty rolled Avery over. "Then, knifed his partner in the back. There's got to be another way out. C'mon."

The three men plunged deeper following a series of turns until they came to fork.

"Daylight." Josh pointed to the right.

The passage narrowed as it sloped upwards towards the light. The men were forced to crawl on hands and knees as the light grew brighter. They wiggled through the exit into a stand of oaks atop Forni Hill entirely concealed from the trail below.

"Well, I'll be," Jeff said.

"He had a horse waiting." Josh pointed out the fresh tracks.

"Nope, two horses," Lefty corrected. "Headed southeast, probably three or four hours ago."

"What'll we do?" Jeff asked.

"Ain't nothing to do," Lefty conceded. "We'll never catch 'em now. That Chinaman circled the Flat and is on his way to San Francisco by now. I'd lay money on it."

"I think we all did," Josh said.

Ten miles southeast of Missouri Flat two riders met on the road to Plymouth.

"Mista Rich lookee hung ova."

"Shut up Jack."

"Ah, Rich. You ain't no fun no more."

"Yeah, that's what Eddie says too."

"Where is Eddie?" Jack handed Rich a heavy pair of saddlebags.

"He's minding the store. The Lucky Strike is an abandoned claim. Eddie's sitting on it until the Red Dog and the Gold Nugget go up for sale."

"You two are going to have to watch out for Grandma."

"How much did we get?"

"Twenty, thirty thousand. It's hard to tell exactly. Either way it's more than we had a week ago."

"Amen to that."

Jack and Rich turned in unison. They weren't alone.

"Don't panic," the third man held his hands up.

"What are you doing here?" Jack asked.

"Ray, you scared ten years off my life," Rich said.

"I hope not. I'm praying you live a long and very prosperous life."

"Why is that?" Jack asked.

"Because I meant it when I said the wolfbat was sent by God. Don't look so puzzled---partners." A broad smile overwhelmed the preacher's face.

"Cousin," Rich gasped. "Blackmail's a sin."

"And you a preacher," Jack added.

"I am. And as pastor of a growing flock, it's my duty to see to their welfare. That's where you and the wolfbat come in. Only it's not blackmail. As you pointed out, blackmail is a sin. It is also illegal. Besides, the money's not for me."

"You want..." Rich started.

"Tithes." Ray finished for him. "Yes, indeed cousin. I want the Lord's ten percent. I want it now *and* as long as this money keeps making money. You'll square it with Eddie for me won't you?"

Rich and Jack looked at each other too stunned to speak. But, they could laugh. Ray joined them.

"How did you know?" Jack asked when the laughter faded.

"You three aren't as smart as you think," Ray said. "Besides there's nothing covered that shall not be revealed."

"Does that mean you're turning us in?" Jack wanted to know.

"No, I," Ray assured him. "Your sins will find you out.

"You got us cousin," Rich said. "I'm in; Eddie too. Jack?"

"Sure, why not."

"The Lord will surely bless you," Ray promised.

"Consider the work of God: for who can make that straight, which He hath made crooked." Ecclesiates 7:13

Marie Theridide

The folks on Bonaire Bayou guard their secrets. No one in the parish guarded theirs better than Marie Theridide. Still, secrets have a way of escaping. Marie's secret got away one day and a fellow by the name of Octavo Blackmon found it out.

Polite folks on the bayou said Octavo was simple minded. The plain truth was the boy was a snail in a town not known for its speed. Which is why Octavo still lived at home with his Mama long after his brothers and sisters moved on to lives of their own. There were times even Mama Blackmon despaired Octavo would never leave.

"If only he would find that special someone and settle down," she told her neighbors.

Mama Blackmon would never admit it, but she was partially to blame for the boy's backward ways. She was the one who filled Octavo's empty head with tragic tales of innocent young boys trapped in the web of a wily female. Octavo learned slowly, but he learned well. Once an idea set up in that concrete thinking of his there wasn't much hope of changing his mind.

To be sure, Octavo had his intellectual shortcomings. The Lord, being the merciful sort He is, made up for Octavo's lack in other ways. Octavo was one good looking hunk of maleness. His café-au-lait skin and dark black eyes made gals take a second look just to take it all in. Yes sir, he was fine. Octavo didn't lack for pretty, young things offering promises of sinful pleasures. Hardly a day passed that some flirtatious filly didn't try to lure Octavo away with them. They would whisper his name and stretch their long legs his way. It was all to no avail. Just as it looked like they might draw him aside, Mama's warnings would echo in Octavo's head and he'd hot foot it home.

All that changed the day Octavo first caught sight of Marie Theridide. Marie was older than Octavo, but she had it all--and then some. Her ebony legs went on forever and were so smooth they fairly well shined. Her narrow waist flowed into a round, curvaceous body that set hearts pounding. Her eyes were deep pools from which there was no escape.   Marie wasn't a bit shy about showing it all off and in all fairness to Octavo, he wasn't the first guy blindsided by her charms. True, she was a widow, but it was well known on Bonaire Bayou that her husband died a very, very happy fellow. Anyway, Octavo got one peek at Marie and forgot everything his Mama ever told him.

Besides being attractive as they come, Marie knew a thing or two about the male of the species. She'd get one chance to catch Octavo Blackmon; she planned to make it count. Marie had an affinity for the cool evening breeze. It just so happened that the breeze was best every day right about the time Octavo made his way past her place. Marie never seemed to notice his passing. She was way too busy stretching her legs and holding her head up in the cool air. Her feigned indifference ended the day he nearly ran head on into a boulder. She giggled a little girl giggle at his confusion and came his way. Octavo was having trouble breathing.

"Why you're Octavo Blackmon, aren't you?" Marie lightly touched his arm.

Octavo's mouth was too dry to answer. He managed a blushing nod. Marie leaned closer.

"I do hope y'all will come see," she whispered.

It took Octavo three days to work up the nerve to act on the invitation. He primped and preened for an hour before setting out for Marie's place. He spent another hour pacing up and down outside working up the courage to knock. At last, unable to resist another minute, he walked up and tapped gently.

Octavo could see her inside tiding up. But, Marie pretended not to know he was there. She heard him knock all right. Would he tap a little louder and linger a little longer? She was not disappointed. Desire eating a hole in him; he went to pounding.

Marie finally let him in. She had her desires too. She stopped him before he could speak and snuggled up close. One of her soft hands caressed his face. Marie let one of her long legs brush Octavo. It was like being swaddled in silk. Octavo forgot he had a Mama.

Marie was kindled fire of black lust. Words were not needed. Octavo caressed her legs and followed them up her body. Tentative, at first, he grew bolder; surer of himself. Their bodies met. Their legs intertwined. They became one. It was divine rapture. Octavo abandoned all restraint.

Afterward, spent and exhilarated at the same time, he rolled slowly aside unable to do other than bask in the glow that enveloped him.

"Octavo, do you what happens…" Mama's voice jolted Octavo back to reality. It was only in his head, but it seemed so real.

He looked over at Marie. Mama was wrong. He never knew it could be like this. Marie moved astride him; her legs encircled his body. Her eyes were alive with ravenous hunger.

"Marie…Marie?" Octavo's voice broke.

That hunger in her eyes was not passion. Terror gripped his heart. Panic swept him. Marie, more than twice his size, pinned Octavo to her web. Her fangs dug into his abdomen. There was no physical pain; just a warm sensation spreading over him. The sweet bitterness of betrayal was a grievous wound.

Marie's soft belly floated before his eyes. Had he really found that red hourglass tattoo sexy? She slipped a fine thread of silk around Octavo, but there was no need. Her venom hit his brain and Octavo's muscles seized. He tried desperately to move, to cry out, but he couldn't; his tissues had begun to liquefy. Marie slowly started to eat him.

"Mama!" Octavo's voice echoed down a long corridor in his head.

Octavo was still.

Marie savored her prize. The male isn't always eaten, but Marie savors very bit of her romances. After all, males are the ultimate repast of the black widow.

"Her house is the way to hell, going down to the chambers of death."
Proverbs 7:27

Mesmer's Door

Ever been hypnotized? I have---once. Believe me, once was enough. Supposedly, under hypnosis, people won't do anything that violates their moral code. That may be true. My experience doesn't allow me to say more or less with any certainty. I do know that no hypnotist knows for sure what lies under the veneer of respectability we wear. Beneath our skin, in the private haven of the soul, there are things we don't, or can't, talk about. They are secret sins, as yet unborn, but alive and waiting to devour.

Taboo 101 isn't formally listed in any high school curriculum, but that doesn't mean its study is not part of the education mill. Critical thinking, experimentation, exploring your inner self, thinking outside the box, call it what you like. It's all stepping over the line and seeing if you can get back alive. Hypnotism is taking the trip with a somnambulist at the wheel.

September had just rounded the corner into October my senior year when Scott Thornton, Dave Ryan, Buddy Pilkinton, and I decided to spend the weekend camping. There wasn't anything unusual about that. We did a lot of hiking and camping together. This trip was special because stowed in the trunk of Dave's old Chevy were two cases of that magical mixture of grains and Rocky Mountain spring water loved by high schoolers everywhere. Best of all, we got the beer for free.

The week before our trip some less than cautious classmates of ours had been bragging about a party they were throwing. The party was to take place on the site of a new housing development with heavily wooded lots and gravel streets. The spot had a growing reputation as place to hang out. It was outside the city limits and police jurisdiction. The sheriff's deputies, spread thin over the county weren't likely to show up unbidden.

Buddy, put out at not being invited, decided to give the partygoers a little scare. His dad was a mechanic for the county garage and there happened to be a couple of police cars in the shop for the weekend. Buddy and I slipped into the shop and borrowed a light bar from one of the squad cars. Scott rigged the lights to a switch in Dave's old Chevy and we stashed the lights in the back seat.

Dave killed the headlights and we coasted to a stop the entrance to the subdivision. Buddy and Scott pulled out the light bar; leaned out the Chevy's back windows and held it on top of the car. Dave hit switch; then the gas. Under a halo of flashing red and blue, the Chevy threw gravel as it raced toward the party. The tipsy celebrants heard squealing tires; saw flashing lights; and knew they were busted. They pitched their beer into a nearby ditch and hauled ass. By the time we reached the scene, two unopened cases of abandoned the beer was all that was left. Fearing for the brew's safety, we took it into custody.

Monday we listened to the ever growing exploits of the daring partygoers. It turns out they eluded the police following a high speed chase over the county's back roads. It was the heady stuff of high school legend. We nodded and grinned at the telling and retelling of the tale. *That* beer was going to go down smooth.
***

We arranged to leave for our camping trip after school on Friday and be home sometime Sunday. It was a practiced routine and the folks were cool with it. We really did like to camp; the beer was a bonus. Dave picked everybody up on that morning and we loaded his trunk with sleeping bags and camping gear. Neatly tucked away under all the gear was the purloined brew.

I have to admit, sneaking around to drink beer sounds kind of lame these days. But back when Nixon moved into the White House, it was still a big deal to a bunch of seventeen year old kids.

"We're old enough to die for our country," was the mantra back then used to justify all manner of indiscretions. We played it

to the hilt and the idiots in the legislature bought it. I think the best and brightest gave up serving in government about the same time they ditched powdered wigs.

Anyway, we cut out of school Friday afternoon and headed up into the hills. It didn't take long to set up camp. While the beer was cooling in the stream, we gathered firewood for the night and scarfed down a huge pot of beanie weenie. After a couple of cold beers, the farts and lies began to fly.

I don't remember how the subject of hypnosis came up. I do remember it was Buddy who started spouting about hypnotized people having surgery without anesthesia, being cured of diseases…you know, all that happy kind of stuff. We all started ribbing him pretty hard.

Out of the blue he says: "I can hypnotize people."

Once the laughter died down, Buddy laid down his challenge. We were cowards unless one of us let him hypnotize us.

"Who wants to prove me wrong?" Buddy figured he had us. That cheese eating grim of his took over his face.

"What the hell," I said. "Show us what you got."

Buddy pulled his chair over so we were sitting nose to nose. He told me close my eyes and concentrate on his voice. It was tough at first to get by his beer and bean breath. He kept up a real monotone.

"You're relaxed; you're getting sleepy, sliding down to sleep."

He kept it up until I lost track of what he was saying. There was just his voice. I did feel kind of relaxed; like I was floating.

"You're fast asleep," Buddy said. "You can't open your eyes. I'm going to count to three. When I say three, I want you to try and open your eyes."

That's when Buddy, the camp, the beer, everything vanished.

I was in an old house. Light filtered through windows scarred by boys with rocks. A breeze ruffled the weathered curtains liberating years of dust that sparkled as it danced on the air. The room was alive with it. The weight of my steps on the rotten floor made no sound. The crystal pendants on the chandelier swayed in silence. No rats stirred or scurried within the walls. I could not hear myself breathe; nothing but the quiet work of decay.

Moth eaten furnishings undisturbed for years testified of inhabitants long dead. Cobwebs filled the corners once haunted by bits of conversation. I wandered from room to room, not looking for anything in particular- just looking. Wherever my eye went the same forsaken scene followed.

A door leading from the parlor caught my attention. Set into an interior wall, it seemed to go nowhere. I tried the knob. The door opened noiselessly onto a flight of stairs leading up to a second floor. I climbed the stairs and found myself wandering in an underground passage. Yeah, I know--weird.

Rock hewn walls lit with flickering torches stretched out for miles. I could hear water dripping somewhere. My breathing, audible once more, was accompanied by plumes that hung on the cold, damp air. The cavern began to wind in serpentine coils going nowhere until, at length, opening up into a large underground room.

The room was empty--almost. There was a single large stone near the point where the passage exited through the far wall. At the foot of the stone a hint of reflected fire light shone from the floor. Atop the stone was a pair of crossed poles. I moved in for a closer look. The poles uncrossed; the stone was alive.

Leather skin filled with pulsating arteries stretched taunt over bone unfolded. The poles became wings. Beneath the open wings was a creature of bone covered with the same leather skin. It sat on deformed haunches, its head tucked between gnarled knees. Clawed hands lay folded across its face. The hands opened as the creature's head rose. I did not want to see that monstrosity's face, but my eyes that moments ago would not open, refused to close. I was paralyzed. The creature's head turned toward me on cracking arthritic joints.

There was not a trace of humanity in that face. Feral eyes aflame with hatred burned within the avian skull. Its feline ears were notched and torn from many battles. It drooled uncontrollably from a hooked beak of a mouth that was packed tight with rows of misaligned teeth. The beak snapped open and closed chewing some savory unseen morsel.

Wings held wide, the creature raised itself upright on the rock. The beak snapped inches from my face. The hollow sound of bone on bone carried the rotten egg scent of sulfur. It struck again. I was beyond its reach.

Stalemate.

I couldn't move, but neither could the creature leave its perch. Head turned skyward the creature loosed a screech that set my teeth on edge and ice down my spine. A wave of pleasure washed over the grotesque face that turned my way. The ground began to move. I was being carried to the creature. The beak opened. The smell of rotting flesh wafted from the thing's mouth as a leering collection of digested flesh and bone crawled up from the thing's gullet.

"One...two...three."

A door slammed. I was sitting beside the campfire looking at Buddy.

"Told you," Scott laughed.

"Buddy the Magnificent," Dave crowed. "Hypnotist extraordinaire."

"What happened?" I asked.

"Not a thing," Dave said. "You closed your eyes; Buzzard-breath rambled; counted to three and you opened your eyes."

"You went under though," Buddy said. He was still looking me in the eye.

"No way," I pushed my chair back.

"You're lying," Buddy fired back.

"Screw you," I tried to sound indignant.

It worked well enough. We laughed it off and got rip roaring drunk. Sometime later, I passed out.

"So, what do you think, Doc?"

"I'm more interested in what you think," Dr. Pappas said.

"You're the shrink."

"Psychologist." The doctor leaned back in his chair. "I think you already know the answer."

"You think I'm lying too."

"Tell me, Arthur, who was the creature?" He slid the recorder closer.

"Not _was_, Doc, _is_."

"Okay, who _is_ it, then?"

"It's a guardian; a kind of sentry."

"Did your friends trespass? Is that why it killed them?"

"The police say I killed them."

"I've read their report. But we're talking about what you think, remember?" The doctor fixed his eyes on mine. "What's your sentry guarding?"

"I can't say for sure."

"Arthur, Arthur, we were doing so well." Dr. Pappas shook his head. "You must let go of it. You're safe here at Green Mountain. Once the truth's out in the light of day, your fears will not seem so overwhelming."

"It's guarding the path to Hell. There, I said it out loud." My heart was hammering in my chest.

"And how do you feel about that?"

"I'm afraid to close my eyes at night."

"What would it take to ally your fear?"

"I think I'd sleep better if I knew two things."

"What two things might that be Arthur?"

"If I knew whether I was coming or going on that walk through hell."

"And the second thing?"

"Was that thing crawling in the creature's throat really me?"

"Know ye not, that to whom ye yield yourself servants to obey, his servants ye are..." Romans 6:16

Let Them Eat Cake

Whitmore High Class of '93 toasted its ten-year reunion in the Waverly Grand Ballroom. Senior class president, Jim Abernathy, reached deep into his own pockets to see that the two hundred and seventy-eight graduates who turned out in evening gowns and tuxedos weren't disappointed. The Times sent society columnist Cindy Hunter to report on Abernathy's self-proclaimed affair to remember. The headlines came later.

Inside the Waverly, the Blue Suede Jazz Quintet laid down a smooth blanket of cool over catered tables, ice sculptures and flowing rivers of champagne. Most of the guests never strayed far beyond the city limits. A few like Ed Ritchie, the Air Force's youngest ever full colonel, and Nick Jackson, a fifth round draft pick of the Dodgers, were real celebrities. Glasses clinked, smiles flashed and glad hands moved through the crowd. Under it all, a whispered secret passed.

Amid the music and the mingling, a tinny ring tone blasted out Bad to The Bone bringing groans from those standing nearby. There's always somebody who can't live without one for a night. Tonight, that somebody was Ray Duncan.

Ray didn't belong at Whitmore in '93. It seemed he was still having trouble. Ray came from Winlen Street. His father drove a grader for the county road department and his mom took in laundry from uptown. Ray was an average student headed for a blue collar existence until his parents splurged to buy him a week at Camp Oswego. At camp, only a week before two-a-days began at Whitmore, Ray had the extreme good fortune to beat Jim Abernathy in both the 100 yard dash and the anchor leg of the 4x100 relay. The next September, Ray Duncan had a newly created scholarship and was the starting wide receiver for the Whitmore Eagles.

Ray's trip uptown to Whitmore was a bumpy ride. His quiet nature mixed with an awareness of all the eyes watching his every move made him appear awkward. Financial shortcomings put many of Whitmore's social events beyond Ray's reach. Nevertheless, his six feet of granite good looks, dark chestnut hair and smoldering green eyes went a long way to smoothing the way. To everyone's surprise, given a road that led somewhere, Ray turned out to be exceptionally bright. He was an All State academic as well as All State wide receiver. In his four years at Whitmore, the only thing Ray failed at was Kerrie Stinnet. Kerrie was high society incarnate. She could see Winlen Street all over him. Ray found that money talks; bull walks; and he was a pedestrian.

Ray sailed over the rough spots at Whitmore by culturing a "tortured bad boy" image that paid huge dividends, especially with the girls. It was an easy role. When you're a pivotal piece of consecutive State Football Championships, you can play any role you want--no matter what side of town you come from.

Ray no longer lived on Winlen Street. His uptown office at Howard, Fine and Howard looked out over the park, buy Ray still played the part. You stick with what works. Ray flipped open the phone with a practiced hand and held it to his ear.

"Hello," he said.

"Hey, Ray, old buddy," Jim Abernathy said. "How's it hanging?"

"Jimbo! Where are you?"

"Unavoidably detained. I just called to see how the party's going."

"Absolutely great. You did an amazing job putting this thing together. Where did you find that band?"

"They were playing a little club downtown. A place called the Tempest. You know the place? (Go ahead, lie to me.)."

"Yeah, it's down in The District; on Ringgold, right?"

"That's the one. (As if you didn't know. Were you too busy with my wife to notice?). They had an open night. For the right amount of cash, they decided a class reunion wasn't so hokey after all."

"Way to go, Jimbo."

"So, how does everybody look? (See any wives you want to screw around with?)."

"At least twenty pounds heavier and dressed to kill. Wait until you see the amazing set of implants Mary Hill bought herself."

"Impressive, eh? (You freakin' puke.) Ray, have you seen Kerrie around there anywhere? She's not answering her phone (He...he...he)."

"Kerrie's here?"

"Yeah, someplace. (You won't believe where.) The evening wouldn't be the same without her. She's the star tonight."

"The star?"

"Yeah. We got a special surprise cooked up; sort of a big finish on the night."

"Then the rumor's true?"

"What rumor would that be?

"That your former prom queen wife and lustful fantasy of every guy at Whitmore, is gonna jump out of a huge cake wearing nothing but a smile."

"I don't know much about the fantasy part. (No telling how many of you guys she was really screwing.), but the rest is one hundred per cent."

"And you're okay with that?"

"Sure, it's just a little harmless fun. It's not like other guys haven't seen her naked. Right? (Here's your chance to come clean.). It's just a quick flash and dash."

"I don't know, man. I wouldn't want my wife popping out of a cake."

"But, Ray," Jim's voice took on a harsh edge. You don't have a wife."

"True, but still..."

"That is unless you want to count my wife. You might as well the way the two of you have been playing house behind your best friend's back. Ain't that right old buddy?"

"Huh? Jim, no. I..."

"Skip the wounded denials. I know, Ray. I've known for months. What? You think I'm an idiot?"

"No. Look, Jimbo, I'm sorry...I don't know...it just sort of happened...you know?"

"Don't Jimbo me. Got that, Ray? Sure, I know. Kerrie made sure I knew."

"Jim, I..."

"Forget it, Ray; water under the bridge; spilled milk and all that happy stuff. As of tonight she's all yours. I'm leaving. I'm leaving her. I'm leaving town. I'm outta here. So, in a way, old buddy, it's your wife popping out of that cake. That is, unless you want to stop her."

"But, I swear, Jim she ain't here."

"Trust me on this one; she's there. She's probably hiding out until her big entrance. You will say good-bye to her for me, won't you Ray?"

"Jim, wait."

"So long, Ray."

The song of the broken connection assaulted Ray's ear. He stared stupidly at the phone's glittering LCD display.

Call ended.

Ray snapped the phone closed.

"What's she done now?" he muttered.

Until that moment, Ray hadn't considered what would happen if Jim found out. His only considerations were Kerrie's soft, willing body and his own lust. Ray supposed, if he dug down into the unexplored depths of his psyche, a small tree of revenge grew there; kept alive by a bright little glow of satisfaction in knowing Abernathy's club wasn't as exclusive as he thought. What Ray didn't see while he was exploring was that betrayal and vengeance carry a weighty price tag.

Now, the bill had come due. Ray's long friendship with Jim Abernathy was just the first installment. He had to find Kerrie and sort this out. Jim seemed so sure Kerrie was at the party. Ray's eyes scanned the room until he hit on a familiar face.

"Jana!" Ray waved and moved toward a shapely brunette.

Jana Grimes and Kerrie, close in school, kept in touch through the years. Jana would know if Kerrie was around. Smokey eyes looked Ray over before giving way to a sly smile.

"Jana." Ray sighed catching his breath. "Have you seen Kerrie tonight?"

"No, but she promised me she'd be here." Her pout didn't carry much disappointment. "Bill Jackson was talking like he thought she was here."

Jana gave the room a quick look before focusing on Ray again.

"Come to think of it, I haven't seen Jim either. How about you?"

"I just spoke with him on the phone." Ray glanced at the floor. "He said Kerrie was already here. I've got to find her."

"I'll tell her you're looking." Jana laid a hand on his arm.

Ray turned back to the crowd. Kerrie was here; he was sure of it. Ray was no good at reading faces, but even he could see Jana's smile was laced with secrets. Was Kerrie avoiding him? Was she afraid he would disapprove of her juvenile prank? Of course he disapproved, but that hardly seemed to matter. At last, she had told Jim. They had a future together. Why hide now?

Picking up the only clue he had, Ray weaved his way through the room searching for Bill Jackson. On his second circuit, he spotted a small group of people going in and out a side door.

Not much had changed since school. He found Jackson, a dedicated Marlboro Man, outside among the smokers. Bill was still a head taller than the rest of the crowd and just as loud. Ray caught him by the elbow and steered Bill away from the carcinogenic cloud.

"Have you seen Kerrie Stinett?" Ray asked.

"No…at least not yet." Bill gave Ray a shot in the ribs to go with his ridiculous wink. "I hear we'll all see her real soon though."

"You mean you haven't heard?" Kurt Reno broke in.

"Heard what?" Ray said.

"Kerrie's going to be the star of tonight's show." Bill said. "Guess things don't change much."

"We heard she's jumping out of the cake," Reno interrupted again.

"And you believe it?" Ray asked.

"Hell, yeah. I got the word from Jim himself," Jackson said. "Why else do you think all these guys showed up?"

"Where's the cake now?" Ray was already moving.

"Kitchen," Bill called after him. "First door left of the bandstand."

"Hey, they're bringing in the cake," someone said from the doorway.

Cigarettes forgotten, there was a mad rush for the door. Ray was swept back into the ballroom on the tide in time to see a seven foot pillar of elaborate icing gently wheeled into the ballroom. It took four of the caterer's assistants to maneuver the massive cake through the doors. Their efforts were rewarded with a standing ovation.

"Time to get this party started," Bill said as he pushed by Ray.

The applause wound down quickly, but the jostling for position continued until Jana Grimes stepped up to the microphone.

"May I have your attention please," Jana took her position next to the cake. "Your attention please."

A wave of restless quiet rolled over the undercurrent of anticipation. All eyes were on Jana.

"Are we having fun yet?' Jana shouted and the quiet disappeared.

"Well, the fun is just starting."

The crowd roared its approval.

"Jim Abernathy called me moments ago," Jana let the cheers die again. "He sends warmest regards to the Class of '93 and wishes me to convey his regrets. He can't be here tonight, but..."

"We heard he left us a surprise," a voice shouted from the back of the room.

Laughter and whistles greeted the friendly interruption. Jana held up a hand for quiet.

"C'mon Jana, you know what we want to see," the heckler called again.

Jana flashed the crowd a glimpse of one long, slender leg. More cheers, whistles and calls to "take it off" followed.

"She's in on this," Ray thought.

"I'm sure I don't know what you're talking about." Jana smiled and winked at the front row. "As I was saying, Jim sends his best. He also asked me to introduce a unique addition to tonight's celebration."

"Let's hear it for Jim!" the voice in the back said.

"Ray Duncan, will you please step forward," Jana said when the cheers died.

The spotlight found Ray and the crowd parted to let him through. He felt suddenly naked; an uneasiness spidered its way through his center. Bright lights and attention never bothered him. Ray thrived on it. There was something wrong with all this, but no time to worry about that now. The crowd was propelling him toward the stage.

Jana was holding a small black box in her hand and smiling at him. The flatness in her eyes said that smile was a lie.

"Since Jim couldn't be here tonight," she gave Ray a sly wink. "He asked that Ray do the honors. I'm going to leave this to Ray; any cake with a remote control has got to be a guy thing."

Cheers went up around the room as Ray took the box from Jana and stepped to the microphone.

"I don't know what to say," Ray said.

"Don't say anything. Shut up and cut the cake," said the voice from the back.

"Cut the cake...cut the cake...cut the cake," the chant grew irresistible as it enveloped the room.

"Okay, okay," Ray said.

He pointed the control at the cake and pushed the button. Small pops accompanied by bursts of flying frosting sent happy cheers through the spectators. Everyone leaned closer for a better look. Slowly, deliberately, the cake came apart. Ray bent to look inside the opening cake.

Kerrie Abernathy didn't exactly *jump* from the cake. The cake opened and she kind of oozed out. The rumors were true. She was naked; was posed for all to see. No longer supported by cake, a pair of heavy garden shears dropped from the remains of her throat. Kerrie Abernathy, Whitmore's prom queen...bloated, maggot-riddled Kerrie Abernathy had become the creamy confection at the center of a mountain of sweet frosting.

The smell made an immediate impression on the crowd. Bill Jackson turned into a baptismal fount of hot, partly digested caviar and sour champagne. Those christened by Bill became a gagging, stampeding herd. The Waverly Ballroom emptied quicker than any practiced drill. Ray staggered from the bandstand unable to take his eyes from the decomposing horror inside the cake. He recognized the shears imbedded in his lover's neck. He'd been looking for them all week. Freed from layers of cake, Kerrie's head dropped to her bare chest with a loud click of teeth.

77

Ray began to scream.

American Airlines Flight 972 from New York to Rio touched down while Ray was being questioned by police. An hour later, Jim Abernathy's phone rang.

"Perfect. I'll pick you up tomorrow." Jim couldn't suppress the smile that lit his face. "Yeah, I'm at the hotel. Good. Bye, baby."

Jim Abernethy snapped his phone closed and dropped his bags.

"I have a reservation." He slid his credit card to the dark skinned desk clerk.

"Good evening," the clerk looked at the card, "Mr. Traber. Welcome to the Hilton.

Hell to Pay

"Someone has to pay". The words weren't only printed on Rick Stuart's business cards. They were imprinted on his soul. Richard Harold Stuart, Esquire, attorney at law, personal liability lawyer, ambulance chaser, crooked shyster; take your pick—semantics didn't matter as long as somebody paid. Rick made a living seeing to it the high, the mighty, and the well insured paid; and paid dearly. If that made Rick a slimy bottom feeder, so be it. As long as the settlements and the scope of what constituted injury continued to grow, he was a happy man. Rick made no bones about the delight winning gave him. His joy showed in his downtown loft, the sleek black Ferrari parked at the courthouse and the tailored suits he wore.

The glitter of his success produced a steady flow of clients sure Rick could wring riches from bosses, landlords and negligent business owners. It also drew the vocal condemnation of his peers. But, what really galled Rick's critics was the simple, undisputable fact that he was the best lawyer in town. According to Judge Bancroft, Rick was the ultimate waste of talent.

Rick's new gold mine was an unemployed, undocumented petty thief named George Mendez. George was the latest in a long string of victims of Sparky, the cat from hell. Sparky belonged to Mildred Wylie, reclusive heiress of the Wylie Oil fortune. The cat had a nasty habit of biting and scratching anyone who dared venture near the widow's door. Rumor had it the widow was not above using similar tactics on those who crossed her. Until now, no one cared to press the matter of Sparky's attacks.

After slipping over the widow's back fence with a crowbar, George made the mistake of attempting to move the hissing, spitting feline with his bare hands. George fled the scene leaving his tools and his desire for the widow's silver. He took with him multiple lacerations. Those on the back of his right hand became infected when George failed to seek medical treatment. A week later a cousin found George unconscious and septic. The cousin dumped George at the local emergency room. George subsequently had the ring and pinky fingers of his right hand amputated.

When George came out of anesthesia he was represented by the best injury lawyer in Clarkston County. Rick Stuart cared a great deal about pressing the matter of Sparky's violent proclivities. In situations such as this; somebody has to pay.

It made no difference to Rick that good old George scaled Mildred's eight foot tall back fence with a crowbar in one hand and a pair of bolt cutters in the other. It did not matter that Mildred had "Keep Out" signs posted every six feet along the fence. What mattered was that all the signs were in English. What mattered was that Mrs. Wylie allowed her vicious cat to roam free. It mattered that Mildred Wylie threatened everyone who came near her house. All that mattered a great deal. But what mattered most of all was that George Mendez was seriously injured and someone had to pay.

Juries wanted to know who must pay and Rick always had the right answer. In this case the answer was clear. George Mendez, couldn't read English. The pittance he drew from SSI couldn't be called a living wage. George's only crime had been trying to prevent injury to Sparky by moving him aside. He had been rewarded with pain, suffering and permanent disfigurement.

Should the hard working taxpayers (and jury members) be forced to pay for Georges medical treatment? No. Should the people working at Clarkston Hospital go unpaid? Of course not.

But, *some*one had to pay.

That left Sparky and his evil mistress, Mildred Wylie. The rich widow could afford it. Of course she could and she deserved to pay. Rich people like Mildred Wylie kept the Georges of the world poor and helpless. Rick would be sure the jury knew there was just one language Mildred Wylie understood--money. Rick would ask the jury to speak loud and clear.

Mildred Wylie must pay.

Rick could hardly wait to serve this juicy tidbit to a jury; not that it was going to happen. Al Jantz, who was defending the widow, would never let this go to a jury. Jantz and his client would settle. The only question was how far could they be pushed? Rick smelled eight figures.

The scent grew stronger when Rick's secretary announced Mildred Wylie was waiting to see him. The widow wasn't the pitiful bag of wrinkles and potential jury sympathy Rick expected. Mildred Wylie was five feet-three inches of New Hampshire granite chipped into human form by Lizzie Borden. Her white hair pulled back in a tight bun lent an added sharpness to her angular features and thin, down-turned lips. Her dress, complete with high collar and long sleeves, had to have come from the Carrie Nation catalogue. Rick made a mental note not to offer her water—at least until the case was settled.

"Thank you for seeing me without an appointment." Bright blue eyes sparkled with undisguised intelligence from behind her wire rim glasses.

Rick started to close the door; decided something was missing and looked back down the empty hall.

"I'm afraid Mr. Jantz will not be coming today," she said.

"Mrs. Wylie, I must insist your attorney be present during any…"

She cut him off with a wave of her hand.

"Mr. Jantz no longer represents me." She flashed Rick a disarming smile and took a chair across from his. "I shall be conducting my own affairs from this point on."

81

"Mrs. Wylie, I don't think that's wise," Rick warned. "This is an important matter. You should have legal representation. Why don't we postpone until you've had a chance to find someone else."

"No need, Mr. Stuart." There was that smile again. "I am perfectly capable of representing myself."

Rick smelled blood. He'd given her a chance. He circled in for the kill.

"Very well, if you're sure?" A toothy smile spread across his face.

"Oh yes, quite sure." Mildred smiled in turn.

"You must know liability in this case..."

"Mr. Stuart," she cut him off, "let me make this easy. I've written a figure on this piece of paper. It's my one and only, final offer."

"Really, Mrs. Wylie, ultimatums are a bit premature." Rick leaned back in his chair. "However, I'll be glad to look at any offer you care to make. We only want what's fair for George."

"We'll see." She pushed the slip of paper across the desk.

Rick looked at the figure printed in her neat hand; blinked; swallowed hard and looked again. His eyes rose to meet those of Mildred Wylie.

"Well?" she asked.

"It's a very generous offer, but I'll have to speak with my client before I can give a firm answer."

"You do that." She gathered herself to go. "There is one condition. You and your *client*..."

Rick thought it strange how the words "your client" could come from such dainty lips and yet sound so repulsive at the same time.

"...must be at my house this evening at eight o'clock. I shall have your money ready--in cash. It shall pass from my hand to yours with no one the wiser. I want this over."

"You have that much cash on hand?"

"It will be arranged. Tell your client, for once in his life, not to be late. This offer expires at 8:02. After that, as you lawyers are so fond of saying, I'll see you in court."

Without waiting for an answer, she stepped to the door.

"Mrs. Wylie," Rick called after her.

"Eight o'clock, Mr. Stuart," she said and was gone.

Rick phoned George Mendez and arranged to pick him up at a quarter to eight. His calls to confirm with Mildred Wylie went unanswered. Rick was a bit put out with her arrogance, but for the money she was shelling out, he'd play along.

George was standing at the curb when Rick arrived. The ecstasy of new found wealth glowed on George's face and nervous excitement—or body lice had his limbs in constant motion. Rick was glad he drove the Caddy. Before getting out at the Wylie place, Rick decided to go over it with his client once more.

"Georgie, your job is to keep your mouth shut and let me handle this. You do that and you'll walk away from here tonight with more money than you've ever seen. Comprende?"

"I understand."

"Good. And you understand our arrangement?"

"Si. We split the cash. I get my $50,000 and none of this ever happened."

"Good man, Georgie. You're going to do just fine."

"But why does the senora want us to come here in the night?"

"Because George, in cases like this, somebody has to pay. Senora Wylie understands that. She wants to avoid a big embarrassing scene in court with everybody in town knowing her business and to do that she is willing to pay up front in cash."

"If you say so. I still feel funny about this."

"That's just the feeling of money, George; lots and lots of money."

Rick heard the widow kept her fortune well hidden behind a veneer of cobwebs and mildew. Where those kind of stories start was anybody's guess. It sure didn't show from the curb. The Wyllie House was a three story Victorian jewel resplendent with gingerbread trim and twin turrets. The walk up to the hand carved oak doors had him salivating with avarice.

Rick and George were met at the front door by a brown skinned beauty with long black hair that cascaded over bare shoulders and dark eyes that shone from beneath the flutter of long lashes. The neckline of the woman's gown plunged into a depth sure to invoke the widow's ire. Shimmering silk clung to her curves in rich, emerald folds.

"Buenas noches, Senors," she purred.

"We are here to see Mrs. Wylie," Rick added.

"Of course, this way please."

Her walk had the intoxicating sway of palms in a tropical breeze. Her heels clicked on the red tile floors as she led them to a sitting room just off the entrance. Rick loosened his collar to let the heat escape.

"Please, gentlemen, be seated. Senora Wylie will be with you in a moment."

"The transformation is remarkable," Rick said.

"How is that, Senor?"

"The outside of the house is, excuse my bluntness, so spinster Victorian. Inside--we could be in Taos or Santa Fe."

"What makes you think you are not, Senor Stuart?" The shadow of a smile lengthened along her lips. "The truth, as you know, is pliable. It may be fashioned to our purposes without breaking its integrity. Isn't that so?"

"Yes, I suppose it is." A knot of uncertainty tightened in his gut.

The widow did her homework and unlike, <u>Legal Today</u>, she'd managed to quote him correctly. Rick was impressed. Maybe she could handle her own affairs.

"Please help yourself to some wine. Senora Wylie will be right with you."

George filled a glass and settled back into a large leather chair.

"I could get used to this," he said.

"And so you shall, Georgie. So you shall."

"You really should try the wine, Senor Rick. It is excellent."

George couldn't tell sangria from Ripple, but Rick decided to taste it anyway. He was surprised--again. The wine was an excellent Montebuena. The fruity taste lead to a warm glow with a subtle hint of a sweet aftertaste Rick found unusual.

"The taste of easy money," he told himself.

The taste soon soured. The few minutes became twenty. Rick's inner thermostat climbed as the minutes ticked by. He wasn't very good at waiting and had no sympathy for those who forced him into it.

If the old lady was looking for a fight, she was well on her way to one. Rick loosened his tie and slowed his breathing. He tried to remind himself how much money was at stake. He needed calm, but the pounding in his temples refused to allow it. Rick's building choler ratcheted his jaws together. His eyes slowly turned into cruel slits unable to disguise the fire beneath them.

"Old woman you don't know who you're messing with." The words forced from between clenched teeth sent Rick's rage spiraling.

"Are you okay?" George asked.

Rick ignored him and began to pace. Every muscle in Rick's body was turning to steel. He was definitely *not* okay; not at all.

"We're leaving." Rick announced.

"But, the money," George pleaded.

"Don't worry about the money." A lipless smile stretched over teeth poised to bite and tear. "She's gonna pay alright. God help me she is really gonna pay. C'mon."

Rick was at the door before George could move. The growl from the lawyer's throat froze George in his seat. An inhuman rictus of rage speared George with a savage stare.

"Locked! That old…" Rick searched in vain for words. "She's locked the…the gall…she's gonna try and…on *me*!" Rick bellowed.

George jumped from his seat. He knew that look. Things were about to start getting smashed. George had learned as a young boy it was good to avoid being one of those things. He slowly retreated. A hand closed on his shoulder and George screamed.

"Sorry, for the wait," a female voice said. "M'lady was detained, but she will see you gents now. If you would be so kind as to follow me."

The voice belonged to a dark haired, middle aged maid. At least Rick supposed her a maid. The woman looked more like a retired linebacker. She had a thick body and bowed legs that had only the most fleeting of acquaintances with a razor. Her heavy arms ended in hairy fists bunched against her hips. The woman looked more like a merry Popeye than Mary Poppins.

"It's about time," Rick hissed.

The appearance of someone to vent on eased the internal pressure slowly deflating his anger. Rick and Wylie's maid exchanged glares before donning professional smiles and getting back to the business at hand. The apron wearing mountain led them through the door behind her to the foot of a grand staircase. The ornate Victorian decor Rick expected swallowed them up.

"What happened to Santa Fe?" Rick asked.

"Santa Fe, luv? Whatever do you mean?"

"The Southwest; like in this ro…" Rick looked back into a thoroughly Victorian parlor.

"Something the matter?" she asked.

"Hell yes, something's the matter. We were just sitting in…oh, never mind," Rick said. "Let's get this over with."

"Very good, luv. This way then."

Rick and George were ushered into a small office at the top of the stairs. Inside, Mildred Wylie, her hands folded primly in front of her, sat behind a massive mahogany desk.

"That will be all for now Mrs. Harrington." The widow smiled and waved the maid away.

"I am deeply sorry for the delay, gentlemen." She turned to peer over her glasses at Rick. "I hope you weren't too uncomfortable. Mrs. Harrington had such a difficult time bringing up your money. Such a sum is a trifle heavy."

Rick and George's eyes were drawn to a pair of identical dark blue foot lockers with RAF stenciled in large black letters on the top.

"I'm afraid the sum we agreed upon is rather bulky as well," she nodded at the foot lockers. "All arranged as you specified, Mr. Stuart. Now, before we sign the final agreement, I have three small provisos."

"Now wait a minute, Mrs. Wylie," Rick said.

"Oh bother, Mr. Stuart hear an old woman out. You shall have your money. I only wish to ask a few simple questions; for my own peace of mind, you see. I'm paying a rather large sum of money. You could do me the courtesy of hearing them, can't you?"

"Of course, Mrs. Wylie, my apologies. Ask your questions," Rick said.

"The first question is for you Mr. Stuart."

Rick nodded for her to proceed.

"Do you believe in accidents, Mr. Stuart?"

"I'm assuming that by accident you mean an unforeseen occurrence for which no one is responsible. Am I correct?"

"You are."

"Then, my answer is: "No". Every effect has a cause. Every cause is initiated by a personal action. Regardless of intent, that person is responsible for the cause and the effect. I believe it was Sir John Davies that said:

"Much like a subtle spider which doth sit
In middle of her web, which spreadeth wide;
If aught do touch the utmost thread of it,
She feels it instantly on every side."

That's very much our world. You may touch the web inadvertently, but that doesn't matter to the spider. That's why, Mrs. Wylie, in cases like these somebody always has to pay."

"Last week I read in the papers about a golfer that was struck by lightning. Do you mean to tell me the golfer is responsible?"

"No, indeed. The responsible party is the golf course operator who let that man out to play with a thunderstorm approaching."

"You're incredible, Mr. Stuart. So, the golfer has no responsibility to himself?"

"I don't see your point. The golfer is an innocent bystander just out to enjoy his leisure time. What exactly would you have him be responsible for?"

"Is he not to blame for his own blind action?"

"Not blind--innocent. He is not to blame for wanting a few moments relaxation. Don't *you* expect to be safe when you pursue your pastimes?"

"So, someone else is always to blame for our misfortune?"

"Misfortune is made possible only by negligence. Absolutely, Mrs. Wylie, somebody always has to pay."

"I thought as much. What about Job, Mr. Stuart?"

"Job?"

"Yes, the man from the Bible? The man with all the patience?"

"I know the story."

"Well, Job was an innocent man, pursuing his leisure, as you would tell it. God struck him with disaster after disaster, even physical pain and suffering. Who is to blame? God?"

"Actually, I believe it was the Devil that did the striking."

"So it was, Mr. Stuart. Shall we blame the Devil?"

"I suppose we could if any of these things actually happened or any of these characters existed."

"When you blame the Devil; won't there be Hell to pay?"

Rick shrugged and smiled. "I suppose so."

The widow turned her attention to George.

"Very well. Mr. Mendez, my second question is for you. I want you to answer freely, no matter what Mr. Stuart has told you. This case is already decided. You shall have your money regardless of your answer. Do you understand?"

"I understand."

"What were you doing in my backyard, Mr. Mendez?"

George began to fidget. He was unsure what to do with his hands or if his hair was in place. He opened his mouth to speak and abruptly changed his mind.

"Mrs. Wylie, really, it doesn't matter," Rick said.

"It matters to me!" Mildred screamed.

Her eyes blazed from their sockets as she jumped to her feet and leaned across the desk. Rick could see the blood pulse in her temples and the cords stand out on her neck. Gradually, the arterial beat slowed and the flush ebbed from Mildred's face. She sat; smoothed the wrinkles from her lap and began again.

"Let's just say I have millions of reasons for wanting Mr. Mendez's answer. You came here to rob an old woman, didn't you? Well, you're leaving with my money; be man enough to answer."

It was George's turn to brighten with anger. He swallowed hard.

"Yes, I came here to steal from you," George said stiffly. "And now; I will go."

George stood and hauled the footlocker up on his shoulder. "I think it would be best if we both left," Rick agreed.

Carrying the heavy chests reduced their pace to a slow waddle, but as far as they were concerned the interview was over. Mildred Wylie was not to be deterred. She stuck her head out of the office and called after the two men.

"Aren't you gentlemen interested in my third question?"

"No, not really," Rick answered.

"But it's an ever so amusing question. Are you sure you wouldn't like to hear it?

"Oh, very well. Ask it quickly," Rick said.

"My third question, for the both of you, is this: just how you plan to get out of here alive?"

The room swam wildly out of focus. Rick wasn't sure if it was his head or the room that began to spin. Whichever it was, he stomach lurched threatening to lose its contents. Rick leaned against the wall to steady himself.

George was not so lucky. The banister he grabbed for support gave way. He lost his balance and tumbled down the stairs amid a series of thumps and wounded curses. Bone exploded with a sound like snapping lumber leaving George, both legs bent at impossible angles, moaning at the foot of the stairs. Dry rot, and decay raised by George's fall rushed up to meet Rick. Dust stung his eyes and unleashed a flood of tears. Rick blinked away the water from his eyes to clear his vision.

The house changed again.

The draperies lay in tatters over boarded windows. The stray shafts of light that found the cracks in walls spotlighted torn wallpaper and moth eaten furniture. Cobwebs hung from every corner. Bare light fixtures with broken bulbs testified that light had lost the battle for this house long ago. The floors were bare and scarred except were George's blood formed in pools.

The house was not all that had changed. Mildred Wylie tottered from her office on ancient joints that popped and cracked with each step. The old crone Rick first imagined had come to life. Her face, yellowed with age and creased by innumerable crevices, offered him a toothless smile. She hooked an arthritic finger at Rick. His sudden terror produced a cackle of delight.

Below him, George screamed in fresh pain. The mange pocked Sparky stood on George's chest and raked his face. Blood and gore from George's right eye streamed from between his fingers. Sparky hissed at the vain attempt to stop his onslaught. His teeth fastened on George ripping away the tip of the bleeding man's nose.

"My dear, Mr. Stuart." Mildred croaked and tapped his shoulder with a fungus infested nail. "Looks like there may be Hell to pay after all."

Mildred hooked her nails into Rick's shoulder tearing through his coat. The terrified lawyer bolted down the stairs still clinging to his new found riches. Midway down, a tread buckled beneath Rick's feet sending him through the rotten wood to his waist. The RAF footlocker slipped from his grasp. The treasure bounced down the steps littering them with $100 bills and coming to rest on George's broken right leg. Rick struggled to free himself. Rusted nails and jagged planks dug into the flesh of his stomach. Blood tickled down his legs into the dark realms under the stairs.

Sparky continued to bite and claw at the shredded mass of flesh that was the remnant of George's face. When George was still, Sparky settled down to lick the blood from his coat.

"Hell to pay, Mr. Stuart," Mildred reminded him. "It's time to pay up, Dearie."

Rick groaned. He'd heard the sound before-- from his opponents. Until now, he never appreciated their pain. He'd never negotiated from defeat before, but he knew the litany. He wasn't sure which hurt worse the wood digging into his flesh or the rotten taste of defeat he was choking on.

"What will it take to settle this?" he said with a sigh.

George was beyond caring, the thing to do now was to

extricate himself as painlessly as possible.

The answer was a soft laugh and Mildred's voice calling: "Here kitty, kitty, kitty.

"Agree with thine adversary quickly, whiles thou art in the way with him…Thou shalt by no means come out thence, till thou hast paid the uttermost farthing." Matthew 5:25-26

Shock Theater

It was a perfect night. Lengthening moon shadow and a warm breeze sloughing through the branches urged the moon higher. The silver clad sidewalks were empty. Along Winslow Street, the twin rows of red brick ranch houses were dark; all except number nine hundred.

Ten fifty-five...five minutes to go.

The unmistakable buttery aroma of popping corn wafted through the house. Lucy took a quick sip of Pepsi and rushed back to the kitchen. With the thin wire handle, she began to slide the pan back and forth over the glowing surface.

"Hurry up, hurry up," she pleaded.

The commercial for Excedrin headache #24 wound down. Risking her fingers, Lucy tore open the aluminum bubble that and dumped the contents into a bowl. The theme music for Shock Theater started. She whisked the bowl of popcorn from the counter and dashed for the sofa.

On screen a coffin opened on rusty hinges. Lucy dropped down on the couch trembling with anticipation. A finely manicure hand appeared. Lucy's breath caught in her throat. Six feet of dreamy white skin and wavy dark hair in a tailored tuxedo rose from the coffin.

A squeal, high on teen delight, escaped the hand covering Lucy's mouth.

Count Stephan was the sexiest man alive. The camera moved closer to those chiseled cheeks; that sculpted aristocratic nose, that unbelievable dimpled chin. His dark eyes, almost without irises, searched for his biggest fan. Lucy melted.

She saw Count Stephan in person a year ago at the Downtown Halloween Festival. She was seventeen then. Old enough to drive, but her mother insisted on going along. Seeing Stephan up close made up for everything. When their eyes met; she nearly fainted right there.

A deep sigh unleashed a wave of heat through her.

Besides being the heartthrob of every teen female in Braxton, Count Stephan, was the host of Channel 13's Shock Theater. Every Saturday night at eleven o'clock he emerged from his coffin on the fog shrouded set and for the next four hours treated his audience to a double feature of Hollywood's finest (and not so fine) horror movies. The highlight of every episode was Count Stephan's "Midnight Snack". Shock Theater fans couldn't get enough.

At midnight Count Stephan would appear beside a scantily clad girl. He would sweep the transfixed maiden off her feet and into his coffin. Then, Count Stephan followed her inside! The flimsy gown went flying into the air. The movie returned to the screen with the girl's screams and the sounds of Stephan feasting. The Count reappeared later covered with fake blood and picking his teeth. He always had the cleverest puns about how "tasty" his latest snack had been. It was so sexy.

The girl in the scene was someone different each week. The casting calls sometimes erupted into brawls as girls duked it out for the chance to climb into Stephan's coffin. Lucy turned eighteen next week. She thought it might be embarrassing to wear that sheer gown on television, but she planned to join the battle. She had fallen asleep during many a "B" movie fantasizing about being in the box with Count Stephan. She blushed at the thought of how his kisses would feel on her skin and where he might kiss her.

Frankenstein Meets The Wolf Man brought her back to reality. Lucy loved this movie. Bela Lugosi and Lon Chaney Jr. what could be better? She drew her bare feet up under her and moved the glass of Pepsi closer. Lon Chaney was about to sit down with the Baroness Frankenstein.

A knock on the door. Lucy inclined her ear and listened.

94

Poe's tapping, tapping, gentle rapping came again. Youth's sense of indestructibility is a wonderful gift. Lucy opened the door to pale skin and raven eyes. Her jaw fell. A chill wind swirled around her bare legs. She was so cold. Drawn deeper and deeper down the crystalline caverns of Stephan's eyes, Lucy shivered and slipped into darkness.

Light returned with a vengeance. Lucy blinked against the harsh glare. In stolen glimpses, silhouetted figures moved behind the lights. Lucy tried to lift a hand to shield her eyes. The hand twitched, but wouldn't obey.

"Who's there?" Unmoving lips sent the words echoing through her mind.

"You do not know me, my dear?"

Lucy turned toward the voice. Freed from the direct light, her vision cleared. Count Stephan smiled and stroked her hair.

"So young, so beautiful," he said.

His lips didn't move how she could hear him? He lifted her face towards his. The want in his eyes sent her pulse racing. Passion warmed blood sent a flush of color and warmth surging through her. Despite the heat, her arms were covered with gooseflesh.

"Soon, my love," he promised.

"And we're back in three...two..." said a voice from beyond the lights.

Count Stephan's eyes turned away. He began speaking to people Lucy couldn't see. His abandonment left her desolate. She felt as if she were falling into eternal emptiness. His voice faded to a whisper.

Stephan reached for her; found her and Lucy was back. He lifted her hand to his lips.

"Isn't she lovely? He asked the camera.

Shimmering gossamer slid down Lucy's arm to pool at the elbow. The gown she dreamed of wearing floated around her; clinging to her curves.

"Oh my God. I can see right through it," she thought.

She wasn't embarrassed by her thinly veiled nakedness. Stephan was beside her; looking at her. He was so handsome. The hunger in his eyes was all she needed. The cold fled before the fire Stephan kindled inside her. Want beyond possibility flooded Lucy. She must have him.

"Lucy, my love," he said.

"Stephan," she whispered.

"Come to me," he commanded.

Lucy could move again. She melted into arms that swept her up. He was so strong. Lucy burned with his touch; ached for him. His eyes held her as red silk walls grew up around them. Lucy slipped the gown from her body. The silk against her bare skin did not cool her boiling blood. Her naked body brought a lascivious smile to Stephan's lips. His smile opened over sharp canines. His dark eyes turned to orbs of fire. Lost forever, Lucy held out her arms to him. A wisp of wind passed over her. Cold lips closed on her neck. The audience of Shock Theater heard Lucy scream. Was her very last sound agony or ecstasy?

Until next week.

SUNDOWNERS

Brianne stared across the street at the rambling old mansion searching for the courage to open the door of her battered Pinto. Her fingers drummed the wheel which her hands refused to leave.

"Five minutes." She reminded herself.

She could drive away. She could blame the missed appointment on car trouble. Lord knows that happened often enough. But...

"Missed interviews don't get you hired. And they sure don't pay the bills." The sound of her own voice returned some of the confidence she felt before pulling up in from of Sunset Retirement Center.

What's the big deal?" she asked.

Brianne's bravado withered as soon as her eyes returned to the mansion. The heavy oak gates were open. Yuccas wearing clusters of white, bell shaped flowers ringed the courtyard and peered over the low wall surrounding it. She could see a tiled fountain bubbling just beyond the gates, the sounds of its gentle waters drowned by the surf crashing far below. It was the perfect invitation to step back into Old California.

Perfect, except for the cold sweat tracing its way down her spine. She could do this. She *had* to do this. Brianne took a deep breath and stepped out onto Pasco Del Mar. The salty breeze ruffled her auburn hair wrapping it around her face.

"Another day in paradise." She pushed the hair back and started across the street.

Brianne had grown up in San Pedro; spent her summers tanning at Cabrillo beach and her nights watching the submarine races off Point Fermin. She didn't remember the old adobe mansion on the cliffs. That wasn't surprising; over the last two years Kyle's fists had taken more than her dignity.

A pair of passing surfers eyed Brianne with undisguised appreciation.

"Damaged goods boys, keep on driving."
Battling the breeze, she tugged at the hem of her skirt and hurried through the gate. Inside the courtyard, Brianne lingered by the fountain. She told herself she was taking time to smell the flowers, but the nagging uncertainty eating at her resolve said otherwise. Despite her attempts to banish it her unease flittered just beyond reach. Brianne flipped a penny into the fountain.

There was no bell near the weathered doors. An engraved bronze plaque instructed visitors to Knock and Wait. Brianne knocked and waited. Welcome relief washed over her when a second knock went unanswered. She turned to go.
Movement caught her eye. Her heart froze as the doors swung slowly open. A pallid scarecrow dressed in black suit stared down at Brianne. A thin hand rose to shield eyes unaccustomed to the daylight. The man's down turned mouth made Brianne wonder if she smelled bad.

"I'm Brianne Christopher." Her words failed to crack the man's stony affect. "Mr. Zanna is expecting me."

The scarecrow nodded. His lips returned to neutral and a sweep of his hand bid her enter. The large foyer was adorned with ornate crosses lit by rows of candles. The room reminded Brianne of a small church. Crosses carved into the heavy doors convinced her it was true. The thought lasted for the millisecond it took for a spark of recognition to jump to life.

"No, it wasn't a church. It was…a…a…funeral home."
Bugs crawled over Brianne's arms. She swallowed hard and hurried after the scarecrow. The clack of her heels on the tile floor drew a disapproving glance from a housekeeper. Brianne ignored the look and followed her guide down a dark hall. The man stopped before an unmarked door; opened it without knocking

and motioned her inside.

Edison Zanna, the administrator of Sunset Home, was a trim fifty-something with a trace of gray gathering at his temples. Zanna's dark hair and charcoal Armani were a sharp contrast to his smooth skin which appeared as unfamiliar with the sun as that of the scarecrow guide.

"Welcome to Sunset," Zanna's baritone voice was as rich as his coffee-colored eyes. "I've been looking forward to meeting you."

The manicured hand he extended to Brianne was soft only on the surface. She could feel steel lurking just below the surface.

"Please, sit down Ms. Christopher." Zanna's eyes held hers a moment beyond comfort. "Your resume is very impressive. I'm wondering if Sunset may not be too tame after five years in the ER."

The administrator smiled as he leaned closer. His nostrils flared just enough for Brianne to notice. The hair at the back of her neck stood at attention. Did he see her anxiety; smell it rolling off her?

"Actually, I'm looking for a change of pace." She hoped that didn't sound too eager.

Zanna's smile disappeared.

"I'm going to be frank with you." He leaned back and folded his hands on the desk. "I don't wish to waste your time or mine. Employment here at Sunset is not for everybody." He held up a hand against any protest. "No, please, let me finish. We pay extremely well. The money attracts a lot of interest from some very talented people, but we're looking for more than skills. We're looking for a commitment to the unique needs of our residents that money can't buy that. So, tell me, why are you here?"

Brianne shrank into her chair. The old tide of insecurity, the one that carried all the flotsam of the last two years, began to rise.

Yesterday she told the social worker at the shelter that her days of being beaten were over. But were they?

"Knuckle time," Kyle's voice whispered in her head.

Brianne fought off a surge of panic. She wiped her palms on her skirt and shifted in her seat. She was about to violate the rules of a successful interview, but at the moment, she didn't care.

"No more covering up the bruises." She promised.

"I'll be equally honesty," she began. "I need a fresh start. I'm going through a divorce and I'm living at the women's shelter. I need the money, but I need more too. I need a chance to care about people again."

Zanna's eyes softened. "Our residents can be challenging."

"Between Kyle Christopher and the Emergency Room, I'm accustomed to challenges." On firmer ground, Brianne straightened in her chair. "Getting to know people I can invest my heart in again would be as therapeutic for me as my patients."

"Have you heard of Sundowner's Syndrome?"

"I've heard of it." Red flags went up poles along Brianne's neural pathways.

"Here it comes."

"All the residents here are afflicted with a peculiar form of that malady. As such, they require special attention. We have very strict rules concerning their care."

"I'm not chasing crazies all night; I don't care what it pays."

"Do they wander?" she asked aloud.

"No." Zanna fumbled his pen. "No, we have measures in place to prevent that. They get a little restless to be sure, but they're lucid and pleasant. They simply refuse to sleep at night and, at their age, I feel they should be allowed to do as they please; within reason, of course."

"Of course." Brianne nodded. The red flags in her mind were snapping in the wind.

"It's not like that," Zanna said. "Sunset is a privately funded facility. Unlike at nursing homes, *our* residents are expected to abide by the rules. Nevertheless, they need independence. Surely, you understand?"

"Yes, I do." Brianne couldn't suppress the smile working at her lips. "What exactly would I be doing here?"

"Direct care of the residents is handled by Anna, our night attendant. Anna has been with us forever. She's a wonderful woman and a conscientious worker, but human compassion is not her forte. I'll be counting on you to supply that."

Brianne's eyes misted. "When can I start?"

An hour later, Brianne left Sunset fingering a new name badge and battling an intense craving for pizza.

"Extra garlic, please."

The small smile that began earlier had spread over her entire face. She had a new job; a new life—and Hallelujah, the Pinto started on the first try. A celebration was in order. Brianne made a left onto Gaffey and headed for Buono's Pizzeria to spend the last of her cash.

At three in the afternoon traffic in Buono's was light. Brianne found a table with a view of the front door. Back to the wall, like a nervous gunfighter, she ordered a Special. Two minutes later she called the waiter back. She decided to get the extra garlic after all. Except for a couple of overweight tourists and the Buono family taking a break before the evening crowd started coming in; the restaurant was empty. Frank Buono would shudder at the thought, but Brianne liked it that way. She no longer went out at regular mealtimes or during the daily commutes. There were things worse than eating alone--much worse.

"Knuckle time." She could still hear the sick delight in Kyle's voice.

She told herself again that she wasn't going to become one of those women cowering in fear downtown at the shelter. She refused. She'd die first. Gooseflesh spread along her arms ahead of a sudden chill. It was the first time she agreed with Kyle in years. The pizza came and Brianne pushed the thought aside. This was a celebration. The world couldn't help but look brighter through layers of mozzarella, provolone, tomatoes and garlic. No doubt about it, pizza is comfort food. She felt better already.

An hour later, Brianne dropped the box containing the remnants of her pizza on the passenger's seat and slipped behind the wheel.

"God, pleeease let this thing start." She crossed herself; anything to keep the car running another day.

The engine ground hopelessly. Brianne released the key; added a few more "pleases" to her prayer and tried again with the same results. Before desperate anger could catch her, terror pumped ice water through her veins. Brianne gasped. She dropped behind the dash searching for the ability to breathe. She found it in time to get a good look at the black pickup with a leering skull in the back window. Kyle's truck rolled slowly past the restaurant.

Knuckle time was looking for a place to happen. The Pinto's engine ground and refused to fire. Red lights flared in the corner of Brianne's eye--brake lights.

"Oh, God." There was no time or strength for more than that.

Brianne twisted the key again. The engine coughed; backfired and came to life. She threw the car in gear; stomped the accelerator and bounced between parked cars into the street. Her sanity returned somewhere north of the Pacific Coast Highway. Brianne made a series of turns to make sure she wasn't followed and retreated to the shelter. Locked away behind steel reinforced doors and the off duty cop at the desk, Brianne buried her face in a pillow and sobbed.

The close encounter with her soon to be ex-husband scared the hell out of Brianne. She was not as ready for a new life as she imagined. She was still Kyle's captive.

"When does it end?" she asked the God of "get me out of this" and car starts.

Brianne couldn't be sure she was ever answered. Nevertheless, she took the growing steel that welled up in her for one. For the first night in years, she slept in peace.

Brianne called it conserving her new strength. The irritating voice of her conscious said she could call it what she liked, but it amounted to hiding. Brianne didn't care which it was; she stayed inside the shelter until time for work. Being free doesn't require being a fool.

Sue, the nurse who gave Brianne a tour of Sunset the day before, was waiting in the Nurse's Office. One of the great things about being a nurse was how the off-going shift was always so glad to see you. Sue, filled with the wondrous vision of getting out of her shoes, met Brianne with a glance at her watch and a huge smile.

"You're early," Sue said. "I like you better all the time."

"I have a thing about being late." Brianne put her purse on the desk.

"Did you bring a book? Oh, no matter, there's a library down the hall." Sue gathered her things.

"What about the patients?"

"We call them residents, honey," Sue reminded. "Anna will take care of them. Sit back, read a book, enjoy life."

"Anything else?" Brianne asked.

Sue's face turned to stone. "Don't ask too many questions and always, always wear your name tag."

Brianne was able to stand the quiet, encroaching walls of the office for all of fifteen minutes. Sunset was quiet as a tomb. Given the place's history, it was the last stop for many before that final destination.

"Probably still is," she whispered.

Brianne decided to do a little exploring. There were always things they didn't show you on the tour. She left the office and made her way to the patient…

103

"Resident's"

wing of the building. The squeaking of her Reeboks on the worn tile was only sound along the entire length of the hall. Fearing all her charges wiped out in a single mass heart attack, Brianne tried one of the doors. It was locked.

"What am I supposed to do peek through the keyholes?" The old fashion locks were meant for a bulky skeleton key. The keyholes were certainly large enough for peeking. Brianne lowered an eye to the door.

"Our residents value their privacy."

Brianne clamped a hand over her mouth to keep the scream and her hammering heart inside her chest. "You...you scared...scared the...you scared me," she told the old woman.

"I'm Anna." The woman offered Brianne a knobby, arthritic hand. "Don't worry they're all fine."

"How can you be so sure? The doors are locked."

"Yes, m'am, locked from the inside." Anna nodded. "The residents insist on it."

"But what if something happens to them?" Brianne realized she was letting her inner nurse take over and ignoring Sue's advice.

"Not to be unkind, but they're better off dead," Anna said. "Don't worry, they'll find you later this evening."

Anna walked away leaving Brianne to wrestle with the truth she just heard. "Better off dead" was a truth Brianne knew well. She had said the same herself and never doubted the truth of it. There were days she felt the prognosis fit her. Patience was not one of Brianne's virtues, but she gave in to it. She decided to end her exploration in favor of waiting for the residents to show themselves.

At half past nine laughter drew Brianne from her office. The long residential wing was alive with silver haired people. Brianne was surprised; there was not a single cane or walker in sight. The impeccably dressed group descended the hall with heads erect;

shoulders straight and a bounce in their step. They were immediately drawn to the new nurse. A tall, thin man with intense blue eyes stepped forward to meet her. Introductions were short and confined to first names.

The tall man introduced himself as Max. He claimed to be a German film director back in the 20's who came to America to escape the Nazis. Brianne smiled and nodded agreement with his imaginative story. On Max's arm was a regal beauty with a Slavic accent whose name was Elizabeth. Her erect carriage and haughty manner almost persuaded Brianne to believe Elizabeth's claim of royalty. Mercy and Simon were clearly the New Englanders they said they were. They came west after losing children to a strange illness that frightened their puritanical neighbors. Michelle was drawn to the glamour of Hollywood in the 40's. Richard, a loner with a feral smile, grew up in Sacramento and came south after some trouble with the local police.

The group was more eager to hear about Brianne than to talk about themselves. They were full of questions about her life and loves. Their unabashed interest melted her heart. Brianne was swept along with the group to an inner courtyard where silver moonlight shone through a high glass ceiling onto an eclectic collection of furnishings. The group gravitated toward favorite seats. Brianne learned the chairs were last personal possessions left to the residents of Sunset.

"I love the star light, don't you?" Mercy swept a hand skyward.

Before Brianne could answer, Mercy was off to join Simon and Michelle rifling through a stack of old records. The trio settled on Glen Miller and the room was filled with Big Band bounce. A bit of Brianne's blues fell away as the music transported her imagination to a happier, more romantic time. She slid across the room to join the others at a table near the windows.

"Do you play cards?" Richard asked.

"Not very well; perhaps one of the others." Brianne nodded towards the group by the phonograph.

"They won't play," Richard groused. "They're prisoners of a puritanical upbringing. Cards are the Devil's game and all that sort of nonsense. "

Richard fanned the cards and vanished the deck with a turn of his hand. The cards appeared in his other hand and he began to shuffle. While Richard's hands deftly worked the deck, his eyes never left Brianne.

"I've been warned about you," she said with a wink.

"Lies, all lies," Richard assured her. The impish mischief in his eyes made her smile.

"You can be Richard's partner." Elizabeth offered the chair opposite Richard. "Max and I are wise to him."

"Ruffs and Honours?" Max asked.

"Of course." Richard began to deal.

Cards turned to the making and taking of bids; big bands belted out boogie and tales of days long past consumed the night. The moon vanished and the sky turned a deep violet that too soon gave way to indigo. Anna began lowering shades over the windows and closing the retractable cover overhead.

"I'm done in," Richard said. He stifled a yawn. "Think I'll go to bed."

"Will you come again tomorrow night?" Elizabeth asked.

"Of course, I will." Brianne laid a hand on Elizabeth's shoulder.

Elizabeth's pale skin felt cold even through her dress. Brianne jumped.

"Are you alright, dear?" A cloud passed over Elizabeth's face.

"I'm fine," Brianne said. "It's been a long night."

"Come along, Madame Elizabeth," Anna said. "It's time for bed."

Anna steered Elizabeth down the hall. Elizabeth stopped outside her door to glance back at Brianne and wave. Further down the hall the other residents parted company; women to the left; men to the right. Doors closed and silence descended on Sunset Retirement Home.

***

"I see you survived the night," Sue said. "How was it?"

"Great. They're absolutely lovely." Brianne was beaming. "I may like being a nurse again."

"Yeah, well be careful," Sue warned. "Those lovely old souls have fangs."

Brianne couldn't help but laugh. So, it was true. It was possible to become cynical no matter where you worked.

Brianne blinked back the morning sun that sat atop Point Fermin Lighthouse. Out in the harbor the Pacific dressed in shimmering gold gently rocked a tanker awaiting the pilot boat. Brianne drank in the new day watching the surf beat against the rocks and fill the air with the salty tang of the ocean. The morning chill sent shivers along her arms that forced her to retreat to the warmth of her car. The Pinto started on the first try. Brianne was jazzed. She whistled "In The Mood" and tapped the steering wheel in time. In a week she'd be free of the shelter and tooling around town in a new convertible. She didn't notice the black Ford pull out into the traffic behind her.

A good day's sleep returned a measure of rational thinking. On her way to work Brianne remembered to watch her mirrors and weave her way through town. The old Spanish mansion seemed to have lost its eerie pall. She bounced inside eager to spend another night with "her" residents. It was silly to think of them that way so soon, but her heart had a mind all its own.

The residents appeared as they had the night before. Brianne joined them beneath the stars where Anna had set a table with champagne and finger food.

"The residents wanted to give you a special welcome. Looks like you made quite an impression," Anna explained.

"It's lovely of you. Thank you." Brianne was smiling, but only to hold back the tears. It had been a long time since she felt truly wanted.

Explaining she was on duty, Brianne declined the champagne over the group's protests and settled for tea. She was not an adventurous eater, but gave in to their urging to sample a delicacy called Black Sausage. Surprised by the delightful taste, she helped herself to dishes she to which she could only guess at the name. Laden with food and drink, Brianne and the card players gathered at their table while the others were off to their music.

Two hands into the game, Anna appeared phone in hand.

"A call for you, Ms. Christopher." She looked like she sipped rancid milk.

'Who would be...calling...me?" Before he spoke; she knew. The color drained from Brianne's face; her lip quivered and her eyes grew wide. Brianne clamped a hand over her mouth allowing only a tiny whimper to seep through her fingers.

"Nice place." Kyle voice sloshed over the words. "I'll be picking you up in the morning. I suggest you spare the old folks and come along nicely."

The line went dead. Brianne wished for the same fate. This was never going to end. Lacking means and opportunity to do the deed immediately, she decided on a slower yet equally effective means. She needed a drink.

"Knuckle time; he doesn't even have to say it anymore. Oh, God why now? Why?"

The first drink was lost by her trembling hands. Champagne spilled down the front of her blouse. The second drink reached its destination safely but couldn't stall the tears of frustration and despair that coursed down Brianne's cheeks. Mercy took the empty glass from Brianne's hand and tried to steady her.

"Let me help." Elizabeth tipped Brianne's face up to hers.

Brianne tried to look away. Something moved in Elizabeth's eyes. Impossible, but there it was again. Brianne leaned closer. A single, white feather, like the ones from Grandma's pillows, floated on a soft breeze. Brianne felt the wind on her face and in her hair. She was floating.

"Enough of that Elizabeth," Max ordered.

Elizabeth released her. Brianne floated into herself again and looked into the worried faces surrounding her. She had seen the look before; seen it on her coworker's faces in the ER. She'd seen it on the faces of cops trying to convince her to file charges. She wasn't bloody and battered—not yet, but the looks were already there. She had to get away. Brianne bolted from the room. In the staff restroom the tears came on unchecked. Brianne was certain this time they would never stop. But life goes on; the tears dry up and life goes on mindless of the lingering pain. Brianne looked in the mirror. Despite the snot and her leaking, swollen eyes she did not see the ugly creature Kyle said lived in her skin. Neither did she see the lost little girl she knew lived there. Behind the mucous and tears was a woman; delicate as a flower or-- perhaps a feather.

Brianne blew her nose; wiped her eyes; and splashed water on her face. The cold sent some of the redness and swelling packing. She would be almost presentable in a few minutes.

"Brianne, I have a dry scrub top," Anna said through the door.

Brianne slipped a hand into the hall to collect the dry top. She didn't want anyone to see her just yet. The old scrub top was worn, but serviceable. It wasn't the first time she'd been forced to change at work. However, the resultant splash was usually something far more disgusting than champagne. She was moving up after all. The thought produced a flash of smile. Brianne washed her wet blouse out in the sink and hung it to dry. She was ready to go out and face the questions. She'd done it before.

Simon sniffed the air. The salty, iron-rich scent was intoxicating. He had to hurry; the others had the scent too. Spittle ran down Richard's chin. Mercy's head was up sucking down deep drafts of air. Elizabeth licked her lips. Max was already up. The residents of Sunset broke for the door. Their shroud of civility gone, they clawed, scratched and bit desperate to be first. The residents, lips drawn back; fangs bared and eyes burning with bloodlust closed on Brianne like starving wolves. The stunned nurse froze waiting for Death.

A hand seized Brianne. She was jerked off her feet and thrown to the floor, but not by the onrushing demons.

"No!" Anna, an uplifted crucifix in one tiny hand, stepped between Brianne and the advancing terror. "For God's sake, get in there and get your name badge on."

Brianne scrambled into the restroom where her name badge hung from her dripping blouse. Brianne snatched the badge; pulled the lanyard over her head and collapsed near the sink.

"*Oh God...Oh God...Oh God...*" the thought played like a mantra through her brain.

A knock on the door brought the walls closing in. There was no place left to hide. Brianne screamed and wedged herself tighter into the corner.

"Ms. Christopher...Brianne," Anna called.

A small squeak escaped Brianne's throat.

"Everything's alright now," Anna assured her. "I'm coming in."

The door opened just wide enough for Anna to slip inside. She was alone. The elderly aide's knees popped as she was seated next to Brianne on the floor. Anna put an arm around Brianne and drew the nurse to her. Brianne's breathing slowly returned to normal as Anna's voice, soft and warm, whispered in her ear. Zanna was wrong. Anna was a master of comfort. Brianne sat silently soaking in Anna's words.

Once the existence of vampires is accepted, it's easy to believe the strengths and weaknesses that make them almost human. Vampires exist for a long, long time, but not forever. Intemperance is the first step on the undead road to dementia. Vampires sent into an uncontrolled frenzy by the mere scent of a human are a danger to everyone. A refurbished funeral parlor made into a vampire retirement home made sense; in a twisted sort of way.

"The view here is lovely," Anna said. "But we really should get back to work."

"I suppose so." Brianne sighed and helped Anna to her feet.

In the parlor, the monsters were gone. In their place sat six contrite senior citizens with heads hung like guilty children.

"We're sorry," Max confessed. There were tears in his eyes.

"Don't leave us Brianne," Elizabeth pleaded.

"Please," Mercy chimed in. "It won't happen again."

Tears flowed around the room until a quiet peace settled into place. Brianne surrendered to an ironic acceptance that her inhuman charges were more human than diabolical. She knew the devilish nature of men firsthand. There was nothing new under the sun and no sense in raging against nature.

"Who was that on the phone, dear?" Mercy asked at last.

"The man I'm divorcing." It was Brianne's turn to hang her head.

Simon place a finger under Brianne's chin and lifted her eyes to his. "Has he been mean to you dear?"

Brianne nodded unable to speak.

"There is a way to end all that. There's a way to be free." Simon pushed the phone towards Brianne.

The group was smiling at her. There was a twinkle in Simon's eye.

"Why give him a call. You could invite him over to work things out."

It took a moment for what Simon was saying to sink in. When it did, a smile crept onto Brianne's lips and slowly blossomed across her face.

The Strange Dream of Ben Eli

Ben Eli closed his eyes and hoped the dream would return. Dreams were such fickle things; they visited when they would only to flee at the slightest turning. The dream he longed for now was an old friend. It often came to him in times of bitter trial. This was such a time. He'd been in the fever's grip for days. He wished only to be free. He was so tired. The dream comforted him; renewed him somehow.

Ben Eli closed his eyes against the fire that raged within him. Sleep gently lowered him into the realm of dreams. His old friend came to him. Somewhere, far above, a smile touched his lips.

The dream was always the same. Ben Eli followed the river through a steep valley. At one point, high walls blocked the light turning the path into a land of shadows. The dark held no fear for Ben Eli; he knew the way. He also knew the valley was short. He could see light ahead. The light came from the place where the valley opened onto a wide meadow.

Across the lush green, the river fell from the sky. Or so it seemed to him. The river actually cascaded down an escarpment of stone. In his dream, Ben Eli climbed the rock; disappeared into the mists and, at last, hauled himself over the top. He always awakened at the top--always. But not before catching the shadow of a glimpse of the land beyond from the corner of his eye.

Once, he thought he saw a city. Most other times, he believed it was a mountain. Ben Eli liked to believe it was the Mount of God. That kind of thinking was sacrilegious, but in his heart, he couldn't help dreaming it was so.

As he had so many times before, Ben Eli followed the river through the valley, across the meadow, to the rock and climbed towards the sky. Near the top, he carefully worked his bare foot into a crease in the rock and pushed up to the next hand-hold. He knew every inch of the rock by heart. His fingers closed around damp stone. The mist covered the rock; clung to his clothes and beaded on his skin refreshing him like the morning dew. Climbing made him feel young again. Of all the dream's wonders, he enjoyed that most.

The top was only a few feet away. He could hear the waters gurgling around the stones sharing the secret of their descent. The smell of myrrh on the breeze from above teased his nose. One last step with his right foot; a final push and he was over the top. Ben Eli scrambled to his feet. He was eager to awake to the new day and warm bread.

Something was wrong. There came no rattling of pots to his ears. No tantalizing scent of bread pulled hot from the oven to welcome him from his bed. Ben Eli opened his eyes. He blinked three times. It couldn't be—it must be; he was still dreaming.

"Always with your head in the clouds," his father's voice sounded in his head. Memories of the wizened old man blossomed into a smile.

"But, Papa, you should see this," he whispered.

He dared not move. Lest he wake, only his eyes wandered. A green plain stretched to the horizon broken only by the trees along the crystal waters of the river.

"Rivers," he said.

The sound of his own voice broke his self-imposed stillness. Ben Eli stepped onto the plain. Warm grass, soft beneath his feet greeted him and seemed to infuse his tired old joints with strength. He quickened his step. He found his sudden revelation was right. He counted four rivers that rolled through the plain. The cloudless day danced upon their waters reflecting jeweled light skyward and crowning the mighty mountain rising from their confluence.

As a boy, Ben Eli had seen Mount Hermon. He marveled at the snow far above the brown valley below. The sense of wonder he felt that day came back; doubled, and then multiplied a hundred fold. The towering rock before him touched the heavens. The mountain was unmarred by time. It looked like a single stone new from the Lord's creation. The breath caught in Ben Eli's throat. The air, resplendent with cassia, filled his lungs and coursed through his body.

"Like Paradise." Ben Eli breathed.

He stared upstream. The trees lined the river path. Their boughs heavy with fruit bowed to offer their wares. As long as he was dreaming, he thought it was only right to enjoy himself. As he walked; he ate. The fruit burst between his teeth showering his tongue with sweetness beyond honey. The juices ran down his chin and disappeared leaving his beard dry and his robe unstained.

"Well, it is a dream," he told himself.

This also explained the curious planting. Many of the trees bore more than one kind of fruit. But, every third tree bore a single, curious bread-like fruit. The round little fruit of those trees tasted like a honey wafer kissed with coriander. Ben Eli wondered what it could be. As he wondered, he ate, and as he ate, he walked.

He walked all morning long until he was certain it must be time to wake up. He looked upward a found another cause for wonder. Though he felt warmed and the way was well lit, he could not see the sun. Ben Eli supposed that was not a strange thing. He couldn't remember ever seeing the sun in a dream. Though he was not tired, he sat in the shade of a tree and watched the still waters flow. There seemed no need to hurry. The sturdy trunk seemed to just fit his back. He might have slept were it not for the glorious world before his eyes--and the arrival of guests.

The pair came from the direction of the mountain and as they drew closer he could
see it was a man and a woman. The couple waved and seemed as if to pass on their way.
Ben Eli returned the gesture and motioned for them to join him. The pair altered course to
meet him.

They were young, not more than children really. A score of years, if that, he
decided. They approached arm in arm, laughing and quite obviously in love. Ben Eli remembered the wife of his own youth. What joy Abigail had given him. The approach of the young couple drew his thoughts away. He couldn't help thinking he had seen them
before. There was something in the curve of her face, but the hair was all wrong. The
man's walk--something almost remembered. The notion flew away as quickly as it came.

"You look very familiar," Ben Eli said. "Have we met before?"

"Oh, yes." The voice was unmistakable. The young man smiled as recognition dawned on Ben Eli's face.

"It's not possible. You're...I'm..." Ben Eli's voice faded to a whisper.
"You are not dreaming," his father finished for him.
"The Messiah...Jesus...then the Kingdom has come?"

Before his father could answer, the ground began to tremble. The air rippled with power. The heavens split, pushed open by the voice of a thousand thunders. Ben Eli's name trumpeted in his ears.

"LAZARUS,"

Lazarus Ben Eli was lifted skyward on the single word he heard.

Through a rift in the heavens, blackness swallowed him. Time ripped a jagged path across his consciousness. Pain slammed his body. Shards of ice pierced every joint. His eyes flew open and Lazarus screamed.

The scent of myrrh and aloes mingled with decay filled his nose. He blinked against the spicy glue that filled his eyes. Lazarus tried to claw away the blindfold, but his hands were bound. He couldn't move his feet. He was helpless in a world of cold and black.

The voice boomed again.

"COME FORTH."

Lazarus was seized by a surge of unspeakable power. A huge, throbbing, fist closed around his body propelling him through the air. Warmth touched him. Sunlight filtered through the layers of ointment and cloth covering his face. His feet settled onto solid ground once more. Sweat beaded on his skin and ran down his body. People were shouting and weeping. A voice cut through the clamor; softer now, but still filled with power.

"Loose him and let him go," the voice commanded.

Hands tore the grave clothes from Lazarus' arms and legs. Mary and Martha threw themselves upon him heedless of the pungent aroma that still clung to him. He embraced them, kissed their cheeks. Loss and glad reunion wrapped his heart against the surge emotion flooding it. Lifted by his sisters' unfeigned love, he sighed.

When Lazarus looked up from his embrace, the eyes of Jesus captured his. The voice spoke again. The words were for Lazarus alone. They filled his head with joy and the only consolation that would soften his resurrection.

"Well done, good and faithful servant."

Exhuming Angels

Michael looked down from Pisgah. A single word slipped from his lips: "Hephzibah".

My delight, the land that stretched below him to the sea was well named. It was hard to look away. A tear welled up in Michael's eye. He was used to difficult tasks, that is why he was chosen. But for a man to stand on this mountain; take in this view and be turned back? Perhaps, it was well he died.

With a slight turn Michael exchanged his view of the blessed land for one of the cursed. His eye traced a path into the Valley of Moab and his destination--the House of Peor. The thought of entering canted, foul Peor was grievous, but he had a duty to perform there. Michael sighed and started down the mountain.

In silence Michael wound his way through a garden of stones bleached white by millennia in the desert sun. Contrasted against the cloudless sky they seemed almost alive. The decision to walk had been his. The gentle rhythm of creation breathing life around him in such a solitary place was refreshing.

The sun was directly overhead when he reached the track of sand and shrub that was the Valley of Moab. The heat was oppressive. The dark soil of the valley reflected the down turn in Michael's mood. His eyes fell. He was content to watch the little clouds of dust rise from the road and cling to his clothes and feet. The people of Moab bore a grievous curse, but there was a stark, almost reluctant, beauty to the land itself. The mystery of beauty interwoven with cursing couldn't distract Michael from the heaviness within him. Michael wet his lips with tip of his tongue. His destination was still miles away.

Not far from Peor, Michael stopped to rest in the shade of a single defiant palm that grew beside the road. He had never been on a mission quite like this before. Given the entire world, why had his father picked this lonely place?

"Father has his own ways." Michael confessed.

That was fine by Michael. He always found father's ways pleasing. He smiled and pushed on. His duty was clear. He was to bring the body home. His father's friend was not to remain buried in Peor where enemies might rob his grave. The thought of the body in the possession of rebellious idolaters made Michael physically ill. Should the body fall into evil hands, the nation would not survive. It had happened before.

The stench of the House of Peor rose up to greet him. The scent of charred flesh was unmistakable. The god of Moab exacted a terrible price from his followers, but there was no mourning for their sacrificed children--only the lingering smell. The Moabites loved Chemosh and casting their children into the flames. But there was more on the air than burned flesh.

Michael felt an evil turbulence that had little to do with idols. Perhaps, just this once, his senses were wrong. There was much to do and hoped to be gone before trouble found him. His eyes walked over the land searching for a sign.

"It's just there. Do you see it?" a small voice whispered.

"Yes, " Michael said. "I see."

A mile off the road, in a grove of palms, three stones reflected the afternoon light. In the bright sun they appeared made of gold. It was the place he sought. This was place his father buried the body. Michael hastened his steps.

Michael fell to his knees and pushed away the stones. He thanked God digging in the loose sand was easy. Michael worked quickly. Two feet down he found it. The man's face, visible through the delicate wrappings was untouched by the heat or decay. He appeared to be sleeping.

"Hello, Michael," a familiar voice said. "I'll take that now."

Michael closed his eyes and sighed. It was not going to be easy after all.

"I think not," Michael said. "The body belongs to my father."

"Does it? Your father kills his favorites and plants them in a forsaken strip of sand? Doesn't sound to me like he wants that body."

"Father has his own way of doing things."

"Yes, yes, and they are all *sooooo* beyond finding out. I'm sick of hearing it. Can't you come up with something original now and then?"

"He's your father too."

"Makes you wonder, doesn't it? But, that's beside the point. Give me the body."

"No." Michael drew his sword.

"I'm afraid that will never do. Your bravado is duly noted and completely unnecessary. You remember Meribah, don't you? A little matter of disobedience? That gives me a right the body. Any of this sound familiar to you, Michael?"

"My memory is quite good."

"Then why all the fuss over a worthless bag of bones?"

"You never were a good storyteller. You left out the best part. The part where your claim was abrogated."

"Abrogated? Michael, I expected better of you. I can't be put off with lofty sounding words. We go too far back for that."

"You broke our fellowship."

"Not broke, Michael--altered. You may join me in fellowship anytime. But enough of old times, we have business to conclude. Sheath your sword and stand back."

"It's not going to be that easy."

"Don't provoke me, Michael. This is *my* kingdom. No more talk. The body is mine and I will have it. Wipe that smile off your face or I'll do it for you."

"Provoke you? God forbid. I was wondering, do you remember the song he sang at Nebo?

"Give ear, O ye heavens, and I will speak; and hear, O earth, the words of my mouth. My doctrine shall drop as the rain, my speech shall distil as the dew, as the small rain upon the tender herb, and as the showers upon the grass: Because I will publish the name of the LORD: ascribe ye greatness unto our God. He is the Rock, his work is perfect: for all his ways are judgment: a God of truth and without iniquity, just and right is he."

"Oh, stop...stop! You never could carry a tune. A poorly sung song? Is that all you have with which to challenge the Prince of this World? Enough foolishness; put down the sword and give me what is mine."

"As you wish." Michael lowered his sword.

Satan smiled. He was already enjoying his new possession. The fun was just beginning.

"Michael? You're not smiling."

"The Lord rebuke thee," Michael said. It was enough.

Lucifer fled leaving Michael alone in the House of Peor. Michael cradled the body in his arms. The gossamer shroud became a robe of shimmering light. Michael, the archangel, looked down into the face and smiled.

"Moses, you're going home."

Yet Michael the archangel, when contending with the devil he disputed about the body of Moses, durst not bring against him a railing accusation, but said, The Lord rebuke thee. Jude, verse 9.

Code Friends

A couple of years ago my nursing career took a sharp turn off the healthcare superhighway and I found myself bumping along the dusty back roads of rural medicine. I thought I was ready for anything. Boy was I wrong.

Littman County sits slightly west of the geographic center of nowhere. This little corner of the universe has three seasons: hot, cold and tornado. Sometimes all three seasons visited in a single day. To balance the volatile weather Littman County has two constants; the people and the wind.

The wind comes sweeping down the plain just like in the Rogers and Hammerstein song. When it does, the sky turns a washed out red and every horizontal surface wears a dust coat. The farmers in Littman County don't worry much about erosion because the wind quickly changes direction and blows everything back where it belongs.

As for the people? The only changes that take place in Littman County are puberty and menopause. They are a steadfast lot to say the least. A preacher once said God picked Israel as His Chosen people because while God was able to part the Red Sea, He wasn't sure He could get the folks in Littman County to try something as novel as walking across on dry ground. You love these people—or hate them. There doesn't seem to be any in between.

Into the world of Littman County; enter Alan Crowder. That's me. After years traveling the country working in hospitals big and small, I finally settled down in my wife's tiny hometown. I hired on at Littman County Hospital the one and only healthcare facility for twenty miles in any direction. Flexibility is the key to travel nursing and I found "doing it their way" worked especially well in Littman County.

Rural nursing often lacks the division of labor found in the big city. At Littman County two nurses cover the hospital ward, the Emergency Room and serve as the hospital switchboard. For twelve hours each night we contend with the constipated, the inebriated, and the opinionated. Generally speaking they all have the same problem. While we're not "big city", our little staff gets the job done as well as anybody.

There isn't always a doctor on hand out here in the sticks and sometimes things get serious in a hurry. Until a doctor arrives, it's just the two of us, the EMT's and some poor soul in a heap of trouble. The first time things got truly serious for me, the ambulance rolled up to our door with a fifty-five year old gent in cardiac arrest. His name was Harlan Kaufman. We did it all for Harlan. We stuck needles, lines and tubes in every orifice. We pounded mercilessly on his chest. When that didn't work we pumped him full of drugs and shocked him God knows how many times. Despite our efforts, Harlan died leaving all of us physically and emotionally spent. That, my friends, is life in the ER.

A few hours later, Harlan rode off with the undertaker and I headed home. I was driving along a stretch of open highway where nothing taller than cotton stood between the horizons. Suddenly, I couldn't escape the feeling of being watched. I told myself the bugs crawling over my skin were only a mild case of stress induced psychosis or, perhaps, numbing exhaustion. I turned the radio on and cranked up the air conditioning. When that didn't help I tried my version of whistling past the graveyard; I hummed; anything to take my mind off that crawling sensation on the back of my neck.

Well, almost anything. I refused to look in the rearview mirror. A quick upward shift of the eyes and all my fears would be put to rest, except I wasn't about to look up into that mirror. I knew what I would see—eyes; dead eyes peering through a milky haze, eyes that looked at me, but didn't see.

"That's ridiculous," I said.

123

Ridiculous or not, I didn't look back.

"Trust your gut," the voice of reason reminded me. "Don't look."

Self control has never been my strong suit. I looked.

A pair of eyes met mine. The sclera weren't the sick ivory that I imagined. They were a muddy yellow color set deep into violet skin.

The car slipped onto the shoulder and began walking sideways. I steered into the slide; brought the car back under control. Which is more than I could say for my heart.

"Watch it kid. You want to get us killed?" Harlan said.

I eased the car to a stop. Whatever kind of insanity this was—he had a point. I turned in my seat. Right behind me sat the newly deceased Harlan Kaufman. He was smiling. In fact, he looked down right chipper for someone who just died. I couldn't help but stare.

"What?" he asked.

"You're…you're dead."

"Yeah, pretty much."

"What are you doing in my car?"

"Well, I was drifting towards this bright light." Harlan suppressed a chuckle. "Only
kidding. I saw you driving along and thought I'd drop in."

"I'm not keeping you from something important, am I?"

"Nah, no hurry. I got plenty of time." Harlan waved his mottled hand.

"But...but?"

"Close your mouth kid," Harlan said. "You look silly with it hanging open like that."

"You're not real."

Harlan laid his hand on my arm. He was solid and very, very cold. Cold as the grave you might say. I shivered involuntarily.

"Real enough for you?"

"Okay, but I don't under…"

"Hey, me neither, kid."

"What do you want?"

"I want to know you did everything you could back there. I want to hear it from you."

"To tell the truth, I don't know. I did everything I knew to do. Did I do enough? Was I fast enough? Who's to say?"

"I think that would be me," Harlan said.

"Yeah, and you're dead."

"Don't take it so hard. There's worse things than dead."

"Then you're not---mad?"

"Who me? Nah, y'all looked real professional. I got to tell you though, that thing with the catheter, that hurt."

"Sorry."

"Forget it kid. Just do me one favor, eh?"

"What's that?"

"Don't forget me."

Harlan's gone now. I'm still a nurse. I'm still at Littman County and, yes, I still remember Harlan. I don't think you ever forget those who die under your care. Thinking about Harlan still scares the heck out of me, but in a good way. His memory is more like an old friend or as I prefer to think of Harlan—a code friend.

"And whatsoever ye do, do it heartily, as to the Lord, and not unto men." Colossians 3:23

Home For Christmas

Bill turned up the collar of his jacket. The chill wind that swept the concrete valley called Cherry Street carried the salty tang of the ocean and the dirty smell of exhaust. Except for his solitary figure beneath the cone of yellow light the street was empty. It was Christmas Eve.

There was no family to rush home to; no crackling fire waiting; no sweetheart beneath the mistletoe. Whether it was the tug of Christmas or only the desire for a hot cup of coffee, Bill was eager to get home. It never really seemed like Christmas in Southern California; not like when Bill was growing up in Wisconsin. Sometimes he missed building snowmen and shoveling the drive.

"Suck it up, Slick. Get used to it," Sgt. Torres always said.

The Sarge was right; he was always right. Bill got used to it. He even got used to palm trees wearing Christmas lights. But, tonight was colder somehow. He felt it in his bones. Bill drew his jacket a little tighter and silently thanked God he wasn't still in Wisconsin… or Nam. He shivered involuntarily.

"Goose walked across your grave," a woman's voice said.

Bill looked up into the face of a tall, willowy woman dressed all in white. The glow of the streetlight diffused through the mist and wrapped her head in a halo of soft light. She looked like an angel. The woman stepped toward Bill and her halo became a white cap pinned neatly in steel gray hair.

"Not an angel - a nurse," Bill thought.

Bill had difficulty distinguishing between the two of late. This one confused the issue even more when she smiled at him. She was older than Bill, but not grandmotherly by any stretch of the imagination. The years had been kind to her. Her skin was smooth and clear with only the very beginning of soft wrinkles around the corners of her dark eyes. Her smile sparkled brighter than the Christmas lights draped from the rooftops. She clutched a small black purse in dainty hands held together at her waist.

"How's that?" Bill asked.

"It's an old saying, you shiver like that; it's supposed to mean a goose walked across your grave. Mind if I sit next to you? My bus should be along soon," she said.

"What? Oh no, please, sit down."

Bill slid over to make room on the bench for her. Was he waiting for the bus too? He wasn't sure, but he must be because he was going home -- and obviously he was sitting at the bus stop.

As if she read his thoughts, she said, "Are you going home?"

Bill nodded.

"Did you just get out of the hospital?" she asked with a glance back at the building behind them where twin trees decked out for the season flanked the entrance to the Veterans Hospital.

Memory came crashing back. Bill had been in the hospital. He'd been there for quiet sometime. Rehabilitation the doctor's called it. Bill didn't quite see how teaching a high school dropout and sometimes grunt to maneuver on steel shins and fake shoes amounted to anything worth calling rehabilitation, but he was feeling better and going home at last.

"Yep," he said. "Glad to be getting out of that place. Oh, sorry, no offense. I just meant..."

"I know." she laughed. "I feel the same way every night. I'm Emma."

"Bill," he said.

They shook hands; his rough and worn; hers soft and smooth. They touched and walls came down between them. In a moment they were old friends.

"Was it Vietnam?" she asked.

"Yeah, Da Nang about six months ago. I stepped on a mine and lost both legs. They finished patching me up in Hawaii, then sent me here to rehab. Do you work here?"

"The three to eleven shift, but I got off early tonight."

Emma glanced at her watch just as the big clock in the hospital tower tolled eleven times. The sound was muffled by the fog that rolled moved in off the harbor. The fog was getting thicker drawing the edges of their world closer and quietly enfolding them in its embrace.

"Although, I'm a vet too," Emma said.

"Really? You were in Nam?"

"Oh no, she laughed."But it is sweet of you to say so. I was an army nurse in the Pacific. I've been working here at the VA since my discharge. Guess, I just couldn't give up on my GI's."

"Well, thanks on behalf of all us guys," Bill grinned.

"Thank you. I don't hear that very often anymore," she said.

"Yeah, hell of a world ain't it? All those hippies spouting about love and peace when all they really care about is themselves."

"You're awful young to be so cynical."

"It doesn't take long nowadays."

"I guess not. I'm afraid you boys haven't been treated very well."

"That's putting it mildly," Bill said. "But, what the hell, right? I didn't ask to go and I ain't asking for no gratitude either."

"Still, a "thank you" would be nice. I work for a paycheck, but it's the occasional "thank you" that keeps me coming in to work every day."

"Yeah, I suppose you're right. Whatever may happen back here in the "world", it's better than getting shot at. I can say "thank you, very much" to that any day."

"I know what you mean. We're understaffed, underpaid, and over worked on the wards, but it's a picnic compared to a Japanese POW camp."

"POW? You? Really?"

"Yes indeed. When the Japanese took the Philippines back

in '42, I was stranded on Bataan. Later, I was moved to Corregidor. When the island surrendered the nurses were sent to a camp in Manila. The soldiers, well, I'd rather not think about that," Emma's voice trailed away to a whisper.

She didn't have to say it. The words; "Death march" crowded into Bill's consciousness and refused to go away. A long silence stole over them as the dogs of war ran riot through their minds.

"You ever see anybody you knew from back then?" Bill asked.

"A few. It's sad to say, but after a while the faces all seem to run together. Then came Korea and Viet Nam. I've seen a lot of dead and dying young men in my time."

Bill nodded and the silence crept back in. The faces and the names never went away and the dead never slept.

The cold wind blew itself out and the fog crept a little closer. The bells of the harbor buoys clanged in the distance and a foghorn blew its mournful song. At times it seemed the faces took on flesh and peered out of the fog at them. Bill's hand closed over Emma's. She welcomed his touch with a warm smile, but there was sadness in her eyes Bill had not seen earlier. Emma moved closer to him and leaned her head on his shoulder. Bill felt time slip; catch and slip away again. He felt as if he could sit here with her like this forever. When Bill finally opened his eyes he could just make out the faint outline of buildings across Cherry Street.

"You ever miss the old days?" Bill asked. "Not all the fighting and dying, but you know, the people?"

"Every day."

"Yeah," Bill agreed. "It would be nice to see the guys again. Maybe someday, huh?"

"I'm sure of it," she said.

"Do you have any family?" he asked.

"No, I never married. I was always too busy working I guess. How about you?"

"No, never really got that serious?"

Their conversation was interrupted by the sound of the tower bell high overhead tolling twelve. Emma heaved a heavy sigh.

"It's Christmas," she said.

"Christmas," Bill repeated and looked into Emma's eyes. "There's no bus coming tonight is there?

"No, not tonight," Emma sighed again.

"It's cold out here," Bill said at last.

"Want to come with me? There's a wing across the street for all the soldiers who don't have any place to go. There's supposed to be a party tonight."

"Sure, why not."

Emma led Bill by the hand. They crossed the street and climbed the stone steps. "Hospital Entrance" was written in large block letters above the glass doors.

"Before they built the one across the street this was the main hospital," Emma explained.

The entry way of the hospital looked dark and deserted, but Bill could see a light burning down the hall. He hesitated for a moment.

"Something wrong?" Emma asked

"No, let's go."

The waiting room just inside the doors was dusty and unused. The entryway was dark, but Bill found he could see well enough to navigate down the hall. Emma led him down the main hall towards the light up ahead. Bill noticed there were pictures along both sides of the wide hall. Pictures of men and women with proud smiles and dressed in their best uniforms. Atop each frame the inscription read "Employee of the Year". Bill stopped suddenly to stare at the last picture on his left. He stepped closer to look at the smiling face and read the name twice.

"In loving memory, Emma Faith. Employee of the Year. 1955," he read aloud.

A single tear coursed down Emma's cheek. Bill brushed it away.

"Are you dead?" he asked.

"Yes Bill," she answered.

"Then, I'm...?"

"Yes, Bill, but it's going to be all right, you'll see.

They continued down the hall and entered a large open ward. Suddenly, the old VA Hospital was neither dark nor abandoned. The room was decorated with garland and tinsel that glittered in the bright lights. An enormous Christmas tree stood in the far corner all decked out in silver and gold. Men and women in dress uniforms danced in the center of the room while others stood around laughing and joking with one another. Emma bent and tugged on Bill's pants.

Bill saw his blue dress pants with their bright red stripes once again went all the way to the floor. His face was reflected back at him from the tips of his shined shoes and new pink flesh rose up from above the tops his socks.

"Merry Christmas, Bill."

"Merry Christmas, Emma."

"Blessed are they that mourn: for they shall be comforted."
Matthew 5:4

Last Christmas

Stars. Trees. Blackness.

Jared forced his eyes open. The blur above him congealed into vague shapes that smelled of disinfectant. Hospital; the word floated behind his eyes and the shapes became tubes and wires that bound him to machines. Jared's throat was on fire. He tried to swallow, but his mouth was too dry.

"What happened?" he whispered in a ragged voice.

No one answered.

"Nurse!" he yelled.

Pain responded in an instant. No nurse came.

Far down the hall, Dr. Johnson heard the scream. He pushed the drawer closed with a sigh and turned toward Intensive Care.

"You're awake," he greeted Jared.

Jared rubbed his eyes trying to focus.

"The nurses put ointment in your eyes," Dr. Johnson explained.

"Where am I?" Jared croaked.

"Platt County Hospital. I'm Dr. Johnson. Do you remember what happened?"

"I…we…oh God, where's Annie? Is she all right?"

"Calm down. She's here…in another room."

"Can I see her?"

"Not just yet. Tell me what happened."

"We spent Thanksgiving with Annie's parents. I had…that is…we started home. I don't remember. I guess we had an accident."

"You're lucky to be alive."

Jared didn't feel lucky. He felt like he had been ripped apart and glued back together. Dr. Johnson's deep, warm seemed to soothe the aching places and shattered nerves. Jared drifted on that voice. Treatments, medicines and machines; none of which he understood, floated past.

Jared jumped at a sudden chill.

"Sorry," Dr. Johnson said. "Cold hands, warm heart."

Dr. Johnson poked, prodded and he hurried away as doctors have a habit of doing. Jared slept. In his dreams strange words rolled across the sky.

Anoxia. Electroencephalogram. Decorticate rigidity.

Time vanished. There was no light or dark. Dr. Johnson appeared; said a lot of nothing in his rich voice and vanished again. Jared wished for a clear look at Dr. Johnson.

"Doc, what's a full code," Jared asked during one of the doctor's visits.

"A full code is when we do all life saving measures."

"Am I a full code?"

"Why do you ask?"

"I heard someone say it was a shame to keep someone like me a full code."

"Yes, well, they shouldn't be discussing such things in your hearing."

"Doc?"

"Yes, Jared."

"Level with me, how's Annie?"

"Annie's dead."

"She died in the crash, didn't she?"

"Yes. I'm sorry I didn't tell you sooner. I wanted you to get stronger."

"It's okay. I think I always knew."

During the doctor's next visit, Jared remained stone-faced. Dr. Johnson sat on the bed and waited.

"Please clean this crap out of my eyes," Jared said at last.

Dr. Johnson swabbed away the ointment. The doctor's short black hair and moustache made his thin, pale features jump from his face.

"Disappointed?" Johnson asked.

"No, relieved. I was beginning to wonder if you were real." Jared turned his face toward an insistent beeping. "What *is* that noise?"

"Just a wonder of modern technology making a nuisance of itself. Those blessed machines are always making noise. Want to get away? I brought a wheelchair. How about I take you for a ride?"

"You're a saint, Doc."

Jared sat up sending the room spinning out of control.

"Steady," Dr. Johnson caught him. "It will pass."

When the room stood still, Dr. Johnson lifted him to the wheelchair. Vertigo swept over Jared again. The doctor waited for it to pass.

"Where are we going?" Jared asked.

Dr. Johnson nodded at the hall decked with lighted garland and doors wrapped to look like enormous gifts. Jared could see a huge Christmas tree in the lobby.

"Merry Christmas," Dr. Johnson said.

"Christmas? God, I've lost a month."

"More or less. How would you like a chance to get out of here?"

"Really? Doc, you're the greatest." Jared smiled up at the doctor. "No kidding."

However, Jared's enthusiasm died as quickly as it was born. Annie was gone. There would be no Christmas together; not this one or any other--ever.

"What's the point," Jared's chin fell to his chest. "Take me back."

"I want to show you one more thing."

Dr. Johnson turned down a short hall and stopped before a door covered with toy trains. A big blue ribbon and bow covered the door. The doctor rapped on the door and wheeled Jared inside. In the bed a small boy with coffee skin and curly hair played with a toy steam engine. The boy had dark hollows under his eyes and labored to breathe despite the oxygen mask. He smiled and waved at Dr Johnson. Jared looked at the doctor in time to see a single tear slip from Johnson's eye. Dr. Johnson quickly wheeled the chair around. Before Jared could speak, they were out of the room.

"What was that all about?" Jared asked.

Dr. Johnson studied the ceiling. "That was about an eight year old boy who won't see the new year without a heart."

"Geez, Doc that's some holiday cheer."

"It can be," Dr Johnson said. "That's up to you."

"Me?"

They were back at the ICU. Dr Johnson pointed to Bed 3. Though Jared had seen that face in the mirror every time he shaved, he had trouble recognizing the man. A dark haired nurse pumped furiously on his chest. The rest of those crowded around were occupied with instruments and medicines.

CPR. Shock. Full Code.

"Your choice. Go back to bed; maybe live another month or…" Dr. Johnson's voice traveled away.

"That's some choice."

"You've done it before." Dr. Johnson's dark eyes burned into Jared. "You decided for Annie."

Jared was silent a moment. "I only had one…"

"You were drunk," Dr Johnson snapped.

"Where will I go from here?" Jared hung his head.

"That's not up to me."

***

Eight year old Tommy Gebhart looked up at all the red and pink hearts. He was on his way home at last--and just in time for Valentine's Day.

"You be careful out there," the nurse said. "Don't let some little girl break that new heart of yours."

"I won't," Tommy promised.

He could see his father's Honda through the automatic glass doors. His mom was holding the car door for him. Tommy stepped from his wheelchair into the backseat. His chest didn't hurt anymore.

"Would you do one more thing for me?" Tommy asked.

"Sure kiddo." The nurse ruffled his hair. "What is it?"

"Tell Dr Johnson 'Thank you'," Tommy said.

The nurse, her face colorless, raised a hand to cover her mouth open.

"Something wrong?" the father asked.

The nurse looked at her shoes and shook her head.

"It's just that, we don't see Dr Johnson very often anymore. He's sort of...uh...retired." she finally managed.

"But Tommy said he was a young man," the senior Gebhart replied.

"Yes. Some say, tragically young, but believe me he's older than he appears."

The Ninth Life of Sandbar Jack

Prologue

"You awake?" Charli asked.

"No, go back to sleep," Jay answered.

"What was that?"

"Nothing. Go back to …" Jay froze.

A loose floorboard groaned. Footsteps moved up the stairs. Charli caught Jay's arm in a viselike grip. He didn't notice. The footfalls stopped on the landing. Jay could feel the presence in the hall.

The door exploded. Fragments of the door and frame sprayed across the room. Moonlight glinted on steel. The shotgun belched fire and thunder. Jay fell to the floor. Enveloping blackness and impending death never came. Jay explored his chest; no blood, no gaping hole, no pain, nothing. He pulled himself onto the bed. Charli's head was on her chest; she wasn't moving. Jay touched her shoulder.

Charli's scream ripped through the hotel. Bleary eyed vacationers stumbled into the hall. A medical supply salesman from Paducah brandishing a mean looking .357 bolted through Jay and Charli's open door. The terrified couple and gun wielding salesman exchanged stares.

"Okay folks, everybody back to bed. That's it move along," ordered a voice in the hall.

Seth Winters, owner of the Rio Rosa, pushed his way through the bystanders. His joints creaked and popped as walked, but his voice had the strength of one used to giving orders. The crowd dispersed. That's when Seth saw the gun.

"Put that thing away, you fool," he growled. "Better yet, give it here."

The salesman bowed his head. He handed the weapon to Seth who stuck the pistol in his belt and turned to the couple cowering on the bed.

"Sorry, about all this folks," he offered. "You okay?"

"No, we're not," Jay shouted. "What the hell's going on?"

"Bad dream," Seth explained.

"Bad dream! Somebody just kicked in our door and took a shot at us."

"This door?" Seth asked swinging the still intact door on its hinges.

"What about the shot," Charli protested. "Surely to God you heard the shot."

"Only sound I heard was an ear splittin' scream. I'm pretty sure, if you check with your neighbors, they'll tell you the same thing."

Seth's calm certainty grated on Jay's shattered nerves.

"Looks like you folks got your money's worth," Seth said.

"Say what?" Jay asked.

"You know, the most bang for the buck, so to speak. Ain't that why you came?"

"I don't know what you're talking about," Charli said.

"Look here, I'm old…not stupid. It happens now and then. Folks wanting a scare or a thrill check out 'haunted travel' on the web and if they scroll down far enough they find us. We're inexpensive. We have some good reviews to boot."

"Okay, so you got us, but that doesn't explain what happened."

"You're a smart young fella, take a wild guess."

"That was Sandbar Jack?"

"Give that man a cigar!"

"So the story's true?"

"Of course it's true. My grandpa was there; saw the whole thing. He even wrote it down."

"There's a book?"

"Not for the public. However, it's always been my policy to let anyone Jack calls on read the story. Stop by my office when you feel up to it."

"How about now?"

"Why not? I'm a bit of a night owl. I'll make coffee."

Jay and Charli followed the ancient innkeeper down the stairs to a cluttered cubbyhole behind the front desk. Glossy copies of *Cowboys and Indians*, and *American West* covered the top of every horizontal surface. Bookshelves stuffed with the likes of Louis L'Amour, Zane Gray and Larry McMurtry covered two walls. Photographs turned yellow with age took up the remaining wall space. Atop a weathered pine desk, the latest model from Dell poked through the Wild West memorabilia. Seth pulled a leather bound book from one of the shelves.

"This is it. Gramps wrote it a short time before he passed away. Help yourself. There are a couple nice chairs through that door. I'll be along later. I got foxy lady on the chat-- I could get lucky."

Jay and Charli carried the book to the loveseat in Seth Winters apartment. Tooled into the leather cover was the date: 1888.

Chapter 1

1888 was one heck of a year. Not many people know it, but I made a small fortune that year. All the excitement stirred up by Sandbar Jack kind of covered my tracks. That's fine by me. This is the story of how I made that fortune. It's also the story of how Rio Rosa became a ghost town.

Business, like everything else, in Rio Rosa started off slow that year. Mine was slower than usual. The first couple of months passed without a single customer which pleased everyone in town. I didn't mind myself. The desert was in bloom and the hills were covered with Mexican poppies. I spent my mornings out walking;

glad to be out of the shop. Nothing ever seemed to change in Rio Rosa. That was the way of things back then.

One April morning, I was sitting in front of the Sheriff's Office with Tinker Larribee. Tink had been sheriff about a year and was working on making himself a name. It was thirsty work. We were working our way through a second bucket of beer when Billy Rubin came running down Main Street like his hair was on fire.

"Sheriff, Sandbar Jack just bought a shotgun," Billy huffed.

Tink leaned forward waiting. "Uh huh, and...?"

"Pardon, Sheriff, but ...but," Billy sputtered.

"So, the man bought a shotgun? Every man in town has one."

"Yes sir, but, not Sandbar Jack," Billy replied. "He ain't ever owned a gun. I tell you sheriff something's up."

"Maybe; maybe not. One thing's certain; it ain't against the law to own a gun. Jack can carry it down Main Street at high noon if he likes. There's nothing I can do about that. But seeing as you're sure he's up to something, I want you keep an eye on ole Jack."

Billy nodded and set off on the trail of Sandbar Jack. Tink poured another beer. We drank in silence until I decided Tink wasn't going to say anything more.

"He's right, you know," I said. "About Sandbar Jack, that is. The man hasn't touched a gun as long as I've known him."

Tink continued to study the street. He let go a stream of tobacco; rocked his chair down on all four legs and stared me in the eye.

"You know more about this than you're letting on," I said.

" CJ, I may be new to this job, but I ain't stupid. Jack's up to something all right. Buying a shotgun means it's a little more serious than I figured, but, like I told Billy, there's not a dang thing I can do. He ain't broke the law.... yet. When he does, Rio Rosa is going to have one less whiskey peddling, pimp."

140

Chapter 2

Later that evening, I got to ruminating on Larribee's attitude towards Sandbar Jack. It didn't come as a surprise. I'd just never given it any thought. Sandbar Jack had a genuine gift for grating on a great many people. It was a kind of family tradition. Jack told me once that his Pa was a Cajun from Louisiana whose business it was to relieve riverboat travelers of their hard earned pay in games of chance. I got the impression the travelers were the only ones taking a chance. When that happens it's just a matter of time before disagreements arise as to the fairness of play and someone gets killed. Jack's Pa won a good many arguments. But, you only get to lose once.

Jack inherited the family business and did rather well. When gold was discovered out in California, Jack pulled up stakes and headed west. He had his Pa's knack for trouble and left the gold fields in somewhat of a hurry before he settled in Rio Rosa. He had a sharp wit, a head for business and a good deal of money; all of which galled folks around here. Jack has to share the blame for what happened. He was not content to let folks stew. He had an irresistible urge to stir the pot.

Jack bought an empty hotel and turned it into the Trails End, Rio Rosa's one and only saloon. He sold whiskey to the Indians, ran a whore house, gambled, swore, kept a Rebel flag, and anything else he found would irritate his neighbors. Several attempts were made at driving Jack out of business. All of them failed miserably. The Trails End did a vigorous trade from the town and drew the copper miners in on Saturdays. I couldn't complain, the Trail's End sent more business my way than all the other places in town put together.

Success accorded Jack a kind of begrudging respect. This is not to say, he was well liked. I knew the feeling. My own business had a tendency to put people off. It was only natural the two of us hit it off. I became a regular at the Trails End. I played cards on occasion, but most of the time I sat and chewed the fat with Sandbar Jack. Jack wasn't generally known as a conversationalist. He didn't say much to say to those he didn't trust. I'm not sure why Jack trusted me. Nevertheless I was glad to have his companionship.

I couldn't help but wonder why Sandbar Jack, who kept a saloon full of rowdy, drunken, copper miners in line without ever resorting to firearms, now felt the need to buy a shotgun. Thinking about it made me thirsty. I decided to wander over to the Trails End.

The light from the batwings of the Trails End made it easy to find my way. Rio Rosa's storefronts were dark except for the sheriff's office. Tink Larribee was working late. I stopped to peek in the window and found the sheriff in conversation with Rev. Fellows. The preacher was a thin drink of water with a booming voice, which, I suppose, came in handy in his line of work. Anyway, I didn't have to eavesdrop to hear what he had to say. I just kind of loitered.

Judging by the look on the sheriff's face, Rev. Fellowes was the last person Tink Larribee wanted to see before closing for the night. The preacher was an arrogant fool, but, then, aren't they all? They all want to change people. Tinker was a firm believer that people don't change. He was happy if they just saw things his way. Of course, Tinker's way had six revolving chambers.

"The safety of the townsfolk is a concern we share," Fellowes was saying. "You look after their physical safety and I their spiritual well being. The people of this town are in danger every moment that Sandbar Jack is allowed to operate that den of inequity. Whiskey steals a man's soul and opens the door to every kind of evil. The people of Rio Rosa have a right to a peaceful life."

"I agree, Reverend. But what can I do? Jack's saloon may be immoral, but it's not illegal. The law is what I have to work with and everyone gets its full protection. Sandbar Jack has the right to run his business."

"Which brings me to why I'm here. The town council meets next week and the Church has decided to propose a ban on saloons and selling whisky within the city limits. Most of the council members are also church members, so I feel confident the measure will pass, but I'd feel better knowing that we had the support of the sheriff. After all, it will be up to you to enforce the ordinance and close down Sandbar Jack."

"Whoa preacher, Sandbar Jack's not the only one that will be unhappy if you go pushing that. There are a lot of men who won't be happy losing their whiskey."

"I'm sure you're right. That's why the ban is only to be on saloons and sales. Unfortunately, it will still be legal to drink."

"I hate to say it, but not everyone will see it that way. There's the financial impact to consider. Most of the shops in town count on the miners Jack's place draws into town."

"Surely you don't mean to oppose the Church and the Council on this?"

"I didn't say that. I'm just saying this is going to ruffle people's feathers. But, like you said, my duty is to enforce the law. You get it passed. I'll see it's enforced."

"That you would do your duty, I had no doubt," Fellows said. "I wanted to be sure your heart would be in it as well, Sheriff."

"My heart is sworn to uphold the law. You can count on that, Reverend."

"I am, as is all the Church," Fellows beamed. "We are firmly behind you sheriff."

Tink returned the preacher's smile and offered the preacher his hand. "I'm counting on that. Rio Rosa's a decent town we want to keep it that way."

"Indeed we do," said the preacher. "God is counting on you to do your duty."

"To everything there is a season, Preacher. It will all come right in time."

"You know he bought a gun today, don't you?" Fellowes asked.

"I do and I mean to see it comes to no more than that. If Jack gets rash, you may not need your ordinance."

I stepped into the shadows as the two parted. Tink went back into his office and I waited for the click of the lock before walking to the saloon.

Chapter 3

My arrival at the Trails End made it official. The "usual" Monday night crowd was present. Billy Rubin was at the bar nursing a beer. Andy Byrd was dealing draw poker to Heck Mason, Zeke Morrow and a couple of drifters. Sandbar Jack was sitting in his corner absorbed in a game of solitaire. I usually make the rounds at the Trails End and decided to start tonight seeing what I could find out about Jack's recent purchase.

"Mind if I join you, Jack?" I asked.

"Nope, knock yourself out," Jack motioned me to an empty chair and waved to Clyde Bristow for a bottle of Jack's private stock.

"Whisky?" Jack asked.

"That's why I'm here," I replied.

"Hmmm," Jack said, "and I thought you came for the fine upstanding company we provide."

"Oh, yeah, that too." I took a shot of the whisky Jack poured and then helped myself to a second to sip.

"How's business?" Jack asked.

"Dead," I answered.

It was an old joke, well rehearsed and still appreciated. Nothing much changes in Rio Rosa.

"How about you?" I ventured.

"This is Rio Rosa, business as usual," Jack said.

"Not what I hear."

"Oh, and what do you hear?'

"I hear Sandbar Jack bought a shotgun."

Jack downed a shot and studied the bottom of his empty glass.

"Let's talk about this shotgun, Jack"

"Ain't much to talk about."

"C'mon, Jack. You haven't owned a gun in all the time I've known you. Why now?"

"Well, just to set your mind at ease, I've always owned a gun. I have a Colt hanging next to my bed. From time to time I even carry a little hide out. So, you see, nothing to worry over."

"Why the new addition?"

"You know how shotguns impress people"

"Who are you trying to impress? You could care less what people think."

"You got me there. Tell you what just be around when the Temperance Society comes calling."

"The Temperance Society? You can't be serious…using a shotgun on those sweet, little old ladies?"

"Now CJ, you know those ladies are neither sweet nor little. Be that as it may, I have no intention of harming them. My recent purchase is for the benefit of dear Rev. Fellowes. I hear he's planning to deliver a sermon on "Demon Whiskey" from my steps. If he does I plan to deliver a load of rock salt to the reverend's well used backside."

"You're bluffing."

"Guess we'll have to wait and see how the cards are played," Jack said.

"Thanks for putting my mind at ease."

"Glad to be of service. Do me a favor and let the news slip to Billy. Maybe he'll quit following me everywhere."

I delivered Jack's message before drifting over to join the boys playing poker. Jack went back to his solitaire. I made my way home around midnight and fell asleep wondering what Jack really intended to do with his shotgun.

Chapter 4

Less enigmatic than Sandbar Jack's shotgun, was Tinker Larribee. Tink was a bulldog of a man. He was six feet four inches of solid muscle. His huge biceps bowed his arms around his frame to match the bow of his legs. Green eyes cut from stone sat above his heavy jowls and perpetual scowl. Larribee was a formidable presence and he knew it. He enjoyed the respect the town accorded him. More than that, he needed it. That respect was the garden that grew the power he fed on.

Tinker had his own way of looking at things and it never occurred to him any other way existed. When he set his mind to something there was no changing him and no chance of him letting go of it. Tinker considered Sandbar Jack a thorn in his side and his chief competitor for the admiration of Rio Rosa.

The Trails End did a vigorous business that it shared with the rest of the town. It didn't buy the love of Rio Rosa; it did buy Jack a grudging acceptance. Merchants like John Honeywell and Luke Jamison considered Jack a necessary evil. They even help thwart some of the attempts to put Jack out of business. This was before Larribee's time, but Tink understood well enough. It was all well and good for Rev. Fellowes to invoke the name of God to such men. Tinker held elective office.

Sandbar Jack was the theological enemy of the preacher. He posed a real threat to Larribee's. Could Jack buy the Sheriff's office next election? Larribee thought he could. The preacher's plan to outlaw the saloon was doomed to failure. Rio Rosa needed its saloon and the miners it drew. Larribee believed the town didn't need was Sandbar Jack.

Chapter 5

The ladies of the Rio Rosa Temperance Society were the town's most ignored citizens. However, in the fall of '87 they found themselves the fire-breathing preacher, Rev. Alistair Fellowes. Fellowes actually took them seriously. Fellowes was more than vocal--he was an organizer. Fellowes transformed the Temperance Society into more than a church bound nuisance. With the wives of the town council and half the merchants in Rio Rosa behind him, Fellowes was determined to see Rio Rosa saved. That salvation was to begin with the destruction of Sandbar Jack and the Trails End. This became the Temperance Society's sworn mission.

For the most part, the fight between the Temperance Society and Sandbar Jack remained one sided. The preacher fired a steady barrage of words trying to move his congregation into action and Jack continued to ignore them. The battle intensified when Clara Ann, one of the saloon girls, got religion. At Fellowes suggestion, she moved out of the Trails End and into the sheltering arms of the ladies of the Temperance Society. In Clara's newfound zeal for God and desire to impress her benefactors, she was not the least bit shy about laying the blame for her life of sin at the feet of their favorite devil. Her story was believable enough for church folk. Clara, on the other hand, knew better.

The truth was Jack was just the landlord for the business operated in Trails End's upstairs rooms. He was never an active party to their activities. As far as I know, he never ascended the stairs of the Trails End, which made him unique among the male population of Rio Rosa. The real operator was Aggie Winslow. Aggie took a hands-on approach to management that made her look like just another "one of the girls". Aggie could always muster up some muscle when the situation called for it while quietly remaining in the background. She and Jack were content to let people think whatever they wanted. It was a decision Sandbar Jack would live long enough to regret.

His regrets began the first Sunday afternoon in May. Fellowes said his "Amen"; wives awakened their husbands; and the congregation poured from the church into the street. Husbands were sent ahead with their buggies while preacher and congregation paraded down Main Street singing "Rock of Ages". Stirred by the unusual racket, bleary eyed denizens of Rio Rosa peered out their windows and doors. Clara Ann flanked by Rev. Fellowes and Ginny Honeywell; the President of the Temperance Society led the march. The group stopped outside the Trails End for a rousing rendition of "He Set Me Free". Those who expected a confrontation with Sandbar Jack were disappointed. Not to be denied, Rev Fellowes mounted the steps of the Trails End.

"Behold, beloved, the devil has no answer to the power of God!" shouted Fellowes. "God has delivered our sister, Clara from his clutches and there is nothing the powers of hell can do. We shall be His instrument to deliver every soul in Rio Rosa from the bonds of the whiskey demon!"

Silence.

Fellowes shook the doors of the Trails End. "Come out demon!" he demanded. "In the name of Christ come out and see how God has freed your prisoner."

Only silence.

"Let us continue to the river saints of God. This devil has no answer."

The congregation resumed their march to the San Pedro. There was a spring in their step and their singing filled the air. Clara Ann was baptized in San Pedro Creek amid a flourish of praise from the faithful. Rev. Fellowes thanked the church for their courage then gave center stage to the lovely, redeemed Clara Ann. Clara, her hair dripping from the plunge beneath the waters of the San Pedro, told how drink led her away from a loving home and down the road of drunken prostitution. Tears streamed down her cheek as she told of the many attempts to free herself from the clutches of sin. Attempts forever foiled by Sandbar Jack and the whiskey he peddled. The preacher wept as well but he was smiling through his tears.

Chapter 6

Rev. Fellowes swam up out of sleep. The room was silent but the preacher's nerves were singing. He was not alone. Cold steel pressed against his eyes.

"Hello, Reverend," whispered Sandbar Jack. "Keep your mouth shut and you'll live to see dawn. You could be dead right about now. You understand? Nod your little head."

Fellowes complied. Jack lifted the shotgun from the preacher's face.

"Good," Jack continued. "I don't want you thinking you had any divine protection this morning. I let you have your little moment. It won't happen again. The next time you try that I'll kill you. You'll find martyrs don't change much in Rio Rosa."

"I'm leaving now. You're going to be tempted to go whining to the sheriff. Go right ahead. A half dozen folks are lining up to swear I never left the Trails End. One beautiful lady will testify to having carnal knowledge of my whereabouts all night long. The sheriff may believe you but he won't be able to prove your story. What he can prove is what Larribee is going to be concerned with. So, Reverend, turn back over and bury your face in that pillow. Stay just like you are and you'll stay alive."

Chapter 7

The morning air was clean and sweet possessed of rare late spring mildness. It put Larribee in a foul mood. The sheriff had a real disdain for wasting time on a fool's errand. Rev. Fellowes was a fool and this was his errand. At first light Fellowes made a beeline for the sheriff's office with his tale of Sandbar Jack's nocturnal visit. Larribee had no doubt the preacher's story was true. He was just as sure Jack would have an ironclad alibi.

The sheriff found Sandbar Jack and Clyde standing at the bar sipping coffee. They were waiting for him.

"Why, Sheriff, what an unexpected pleasure," Jack said. "Join us for some coffee?"

"I doubt it's either one," Larribee answered. "But I'll take the coffee just the same."

Clyde poured; Larribee took a sip and managed a small smile. The morning was getting brighter. He wasn't likely to get a confession from Sandbar Jack but the coffee would help make up for it.

"Mighty fine coffee, Clyde," Larribee said. "Especially after the chill in the air last night. I'd have hated to be out wandering about. How about you, Jack?"

"Way too chilly for me Sheriff," Jack replied.

"If you don't mind my asking, just how did you pass the night?"

"Right here all night Sheriff. Why?"

"The preacher was by to see me this morning. He says you showed up at his place last night and stuck that new shotgun in his face."

"I know he's a preacher and all Sheriff, but you know that can't be true."

"And how's that?"

"He walked into your office this morning, that's how," Jack said.

"Anybody see you here after closing?"

"Clyde," Jack jerked a thumb at his barkeeper.

"What about it, Clyde? Was your boss here all night?"

"Sure was Sheriff. My room's under the stairs. I sleep light and no one crosses those stairs and I don't know it," Clyde answered. "But to tell you the truth, the whole truth, and nothing but the truth, Sheriff, he didn't stay in his room all night."

"Oh?" Larribee said. He held up a burly hand to stop Jack's interruption.

"Believe I heard him tiptoe a couple of doors down the hall in the wee hours," Clyde said with a smirk.

"Dang it, Clyde," Jack said with a flush of his cheeks. "Must you tell everything you know?"

Clyde chuckled through a wide possum grin.

"I see," said Larribee. "What about the preacher?"

"Must have been dreaming," Jack offered. "Strange I should be on his mind day and night. He so rarely crosses mine."

"Okay, guess that's it then. Clyde thanks for the coffee. Jack, do I need to tell you I'll be keeping a closer eye on you?"

"Consider me warned, Sheriff," Jack smiled.

Chapter 8

When he had delayed as long as he could, Tink Larribee returned to his office and his waiting guest. His next conversation with the Reverend Fellowes went about as Larribee expected-- badly. Larribee was on his feet; face bright red and jaws locked down tight.

"Preacher, no disrespect intended, but, I'm no Job. My patience has a limit. I'm telling you for the last time. It doesn't matter what I *believe*. It's what I can *prove* that matters. I'm sure everything happened just like you said. Given Jack's demeanor this morning I'm certain of it. The Law requires proof. You say Jack was at your place. His people swear he was at the Trails End all night. Are they lying? Sure, they are, but unless I can prove that with some hard evidence, there's nothing more I can do. Do you understand?"

There was going to be hell to pay in Rio Rosa today. Larribee's bite was worse than his bark and he was set to tear into someone. At that moment I would have given the Preacher and Sandbar Jack even odds.

"I'm sorry Sheriff," Fellowes retreated. "I'm still a bit shaken from having a shotgun held to my head. I know you're doing everything you can."

The color receded from Larribee's face. Tink settled back into his seat.

"Look, Reverend," he began. "This doesn't mean I'm going to do nothing. I just don't have enough of a case to arrest the man. Still, he took a big chance to threaten you like that. A man taking chances like that is going to slip sooner or later. I'm putting a tail on Jack day and night."

"Do you think Sandbar Jack is the type to make idle threats?' Fellowes asked.

"Not on your life, Preacher. So you be careful and keep away from Jack and the Trails End."

"I'm not sure how to do that. Faith without works is dead."

"What are you getting at Preacher?"

"Just this Sheriff," Fellowes answered. "Sandbar Jack's snapping and growling like a dog about to lose his bone. He's not so sure his saloon is indispensable to Rio Rosa. That means we've struck a blow for temperance and godliness. We've won a battle. We can't quit now; we must take action."

"This is not a game Preacher. Don't trifle with Sandbar Jack."

"No it's not. It's a deadly struggle with evil. An evil, I'm sure, is not content with threats. You can't be neutral anymore Sheriff. No one can stand in the Light and Darkness at the same time. That's God's Law."

Rev. Fellowes rose and let himself out. I had the feeling his leaving did not make Tink Larribee feel any better.

Chapter 9

My job brought me into frequent contact with Rev. Fellowes. However, he had never been to see me unannounced. Given Rio Rosa's propensity for routine, I was startled to see him come through my door.

"Reverend," I said. "So good to see you. Everything okay?"

"Oh yes. This is more of a social call really."

"Then I'm especially glad to see you." I shook the preacher's hand and directed him to a seat in my parlor. "May I get you something? Lemonade, perhaps?"

"No, thank you Mr. Winters."

"CJ, please Reverend, just plain ole CJ will do."

"CJ. Actually, I came to see you to talk about whiskey," Fellowes replied.

"Whiskey? Now I'm really lost Reverend."

"Let me explain," Fellowes chuckled. "I'm told you have a certain rapport with Sandbar Jack. I'm also told that Jack has a … what shall we call it? … an open door policy. That is, any one may enter his saloon."

"Well, yes, I suppose that's true on both counts. I've known Jack a long time and I've never seen him refuse anybody who was behaving themselves."

"Exactly." Fellowes smiled. "And he never varies from this policy?"

"I wouldn't actually call it a policy. But this *is* Rio Rosa; not much changes around here, not even Sandbar Jack."

"Except for the recent purchase of a shotgun? Or so I'm told."

"Biggest change in Rio Rosa since Arizona became a territory."

"Mr. Winters … CJ," Fellowes began. "May I ask you one last question in the strictest confidence?"

"Sure, Reverend. I can keep a secret."

"Excellent. Suppose that I was to go into the Trails End and just sit at one of the tables. Would Sandbar Jack throw me out?"

"Are you serious?"

"Absolutely, serious Mr. Winters," Fellowes said.

His eyes searched mine. He was sizing me up; waiting to see if I would I tell him the truth. The man may have been soft on the outside, but there was a glint of steel in his eyes. He was very serious.

"Will Sandbar Jack resort to violence without provocation?' Fellowes pressed.

I decided the truth here would be safer for everyone. "I don't think so preacher, but isn't your being there a bit of provocation?" I asked.

"We shall see." Fellowes nodded. "We shall see."

Chapter 10

Rio Rosa always came to life on Saturday night when the miners rode in from the Lavender and the Big Queen mines. The mines were closer to Bisbee, but Sandbar Jack was an exceptional host. He never interfered in the miner's fun as long as no one got hurt and it caused no damage to his property. Jack even hired John Little Man's wagon to haul those who celebrated a little too much back to the mines before they met up with the wrath of Tink Larribee.

I got to the saloon early. I didn't expect Jack to toss the preacher out as long as the preacher kept his mouth shut. What I went to see was if that preacher had the ability to do so. I opted for a seat at Sandbar Jack's table to get close to the action.

"You're here early CJ?" Jack said after the usual pleasantries.

"I'm feeling extra thirsty tonight," I hedged.

Jack turned to stare at me. He eyes said it was time for me to 'fess up and don't try lying.

"Rio Rosa; it's getting where a man can't do anything new without raising suspicions."

"Okay," I said aloud. "Look that is the truth. It's just not the whole truth and I promised to keep my mouth shut."

We passed some time drinking in silence. Jack finished his drink and glanced at his watch.

"What time is the preacher coming?" he asked.

"Just after sundown," I said it without thinking; realized what I had done and knew I'd been had. "Dang it Jack, how do you do that?"

"Relax; you haven't given away any secrets. I heard about his calling on you and figured it out. Guess he's counting on Larribee to keep him safe."

"He did seem a bit concerned about his safety."

"If God's given the man the good sense to keep from preaching in here, there's no place safer he could be … Ah, there's our guest now."

Jack rose and walked across the bar to meet Rev. Fellowes at the door. The preacher looked as nervous as a cat in a room full of rockers. Jack shook Fellowes' hand then bowed gracefully to his escort, Clara Ann.

"Welcome to the Trails End," Jack said.

"Hello, Jack," Clara said.

Jack ignored Clara and kept his eyes on Rev. Fellowes.

"Good evening, Mr..?" Fellowes began.

"Jack will do fine preacher. Come join CJ and me if you like," Jack offered.

"No thanks," Clara answered. "We'll just sit over there by the window."

"Make yourself at home," Jack said and swept the room with outstretched arm.

Jack stopped at the bar to whisper to Clyde Bristow. Clyde disappeared and returned with a tall pitcher of lemonade that he presented to the preacher with Jack's compliments. The preacher seemed glad to have something to occupy his hands.

There were no fireworks. Members of the preacher's flock slipped out the back as soon as he arrived. The miners didn't seem to care one way or the other, but the atmosphere in the Trails End just wasn't the same somehow. That was anathema in Rio Rosa and the festivities ended early.

Chapter 11

The next morning Sandbar Jack knocked on my door as we had arranged. He looked like a regular churchgoer. His black hair was slicked back on his head, his moustache waxed and a genuine twinkle in his eye. He wore a knee length flocked coat and string tie over a starched white shirt. A belt buckle of sparkling silver bought in Tombstone's topped black linen pantaloons and highly polished boots. Jack wore a red rose (where he got it God only knows) in his lapel and the widest grin I've ever seen.

"You're enjoying this already, aren't you?" I felt like smiling myself.

"Darn right, I am, but the best is yet to come."

"Lead on Mc Duff," I said.

We walked right down the middle of Main Street. Saint and sinner alike leaned from the windows or fell into our wake. By the time we reached the church, you'd have thought it was the Independence Day parade. The Reverend Fellowes was presented with the largest congregation ever to gather in Rio Rosa. Sandbar Jack marched boldly down the aisle and settled in on the front pew. Fellowes was going to be eye to eye with him all morning. Initially, Fellowes had a hard time of it. However he soon found his voice and launched into a vigorous sermon delighted to have the object of his reproach seated before him. Jack joined the congregation providing the preacher with a generous supply of Amens and Hallelujahs...

When the service ended, Jack made the rounds to shake hands with each and every member of the Temperance Society. His extreme pleasure was directly proportional to their obvious discomfort. Of course, he saved the best for last. Ginny Honeywell stood beside Rev. Fellowes as the congregation filed out.

"Mrs. Honeywell, lovely meeting don't you agree?" Jack asked.

Ginny's face went bright red. She looked like she stuck her hand into a bucket of worms when she took his hand. Jack reveled in her discomfort.

"I hope you felt the fire of Hell that God has in store for you," she said through her best smile. "How dare you enter this House of God?"

"Madame," Jack said, "I dare the same as all the whiskey sipping deacons who come here every Sunday. That includes your husband, though God knows he has cause to imbibe. Good day to you, Mrs. Honeywell."

"And a good day to you too, Reverend," he added.

Chapter 12

Sandbar Jack checked his watch--again.

"How many times you going to check that watch?" Clyde asked.

"As many times as it takes," Jack snapped.

"Just asking." Clyde returned to polishing glasses that didn't need polishing.

John Little Man was three hours late with the week's shipment from Bisbee. Jack drummed his fingers on the bar and watched the street. He decided the view was better from the door; found the street empty and returned to his drumming.

"Clyde, go send a wire to Matt Spooner. See if John picked up the shipment and what time he started out," Jack ordered. "Tell Matt I'll pay for the answer …wait for it, okay?"

"Sure thing," Clyde said.

He was back a half hour later. John Little Man had loaded his wagon and left Bisbee at his usual time. Spooner watched him drive out of town. Nothing out of the ordinary in Bisbee.

"I'm going to ride out and see if I can find him," Jack announced.

Jack kept his horse at a walk until Rio Rosa was out of sight then spurred him to a gallop. Jack found John Little Man face down in the road five miles north of town.

Little Man had taken one hell of a beating. He was still alive … barely. His jaw and at least one of his legs were broken. The bloody ax handle used to beat him lay beside the overturned wagon. Beer barrels were strewn across the road and broken bottles were everywhere their contents vanishing into the thirsty soil. John's team was gone.

Jack got a rope around the wagon and managed to set it upright. He hitched his own horse to the traces and loaded John Little Man into the back as gently as he could. On the trip back to Rio Rosa John slipped in and out of consciousness. His wakeful moments were punctuated by groans. The ride was almost as bad as the beating.

John spent the next week at the Trails End. Doc Brown came around every day and tried to shoo away the hovering Sandbar Jack. The sheriff dropped in the second day. There was not much information to be gleaned. John quite literally never knew what hit him.

Chapter 13

Sandbar Jack glanced over his shoulder. Billy was still there. Jack let it be known he was headed out of town. Billy got the

158

dusty duty of shadowing Jack on the trail. Jack didn't mind. He liked Billy. Jack crossed Five Mile Gulch and decided to end the game. When Billy dropped into the gulch, Jack slipped his bay behind an outcropping of rock.

Billy climbed out of the gulch to an empty trail. "Oh no," he groaned.

The Sheriff was going to be steamed. Billy swung down from his roan and tried to pick up Jack's trail. He wasn't much of a tracker, but with some intense concentration, he found Jack's track. "Want some company, kid?" Jack shouted.

Billy jumped, twisted awkwardly and landed on his butt. His heart hammered in his chest with the sudden shot of adrenalin while Sandbar Jack roared with laughter. He had to hold the huge rock to keep from joining Billy on the ground.

"Good Lord, Jack," Billy gasped.

Sandbar Jack continued to rock with laughter. Billy got to his feet and dusted himself off.

"Sorry, kid." Jack said. "I couldn't help it. The offer still goes; want to ride together and make things easy on both of us?"

"Suits me," Billy answered.

A mile down the road, Sandbar Jack turned his bay on to a barely visible trail and Billy followed suit.

"Mind my asking where we're going?"

"Not at all," Jack said. "We are headed just over that rise. I have a call to make."

"A call? We're in the middle of nowhere."

John Little Man's home was a squat, flat topped, adobe set back into a small hillside overlooking a small valley planted in corn. Beside the house grazed a matched pair of bays and three painted ponies. A young woman in a bright camp dress emerged from the adobe followed by two black haired children. Her raven hair fell in long tresses around her dark face. The children sheltering in the folds of her dress reflected her dark good looks. The woman waved to Jack and he returned the gesture.

"Hello Mary," Jack said. He stepped down from his horse. Mary raced into his arms. She buried her face against his shoulder and shook with silent sobs. Jack held her until the tears subsided. Billy noticed Jack covertly wipe away a tear from his cheek.

"Mary," Jack said. "This is Billy. He's a deputy in Rio Rosa."

"He's looking for the men who nearly killed my Johnny?"

"Yes he is," Jack lied. "We're riding the trail to Bisbee hoping to pick up some clues."

"Come in the house. Johnny will be glad to see you."

John Little Man called a welcome from the bedroom. His leg was mending, but he was still unable to walk. Billy realized he had never been inside the home of an Indian before. Mary was an attentive hostess. She plied them with fry bread and beans. Billy was soon entirely at ease.

Christopher and Sarah played at Sandbar Jack's feet and climbed into his lap. However, they kept a wary eye and a safe distance from the white stranger. Billy watched a bankroll pass between Jack and Mary.

Jack spoke to Mary in Pima. She snickered; answered in kind and a moment later excused herself. When she returned she spoke to Jack in Pima again. Jack finished his beans and announced it was time to go. Mary kissed Jack's cheek and led them to the door. Billy followed and looked up into the angry faces of six mounted warriors.

Chapter 14

Sandbar Jack left Billy in the custody of John Little Man's family with instructions to make Billy a welcome, but captive guest until morning. Jack skirted Bisbee to avoid being recognized and headed for Tombstone. After a quite night under the full moon, he arrived in Tombstone about the same time that Billy was explaining to Tinker how Jack gave him the slip.

Jack didn't know Billy wasn't his only shadow. Familiar eyes watched him bound up the steps into the office of the U.S. Marshal. Jack's shadow didn't wait around to find out Jack's business with the marshal. He knew. Jack was hedging his bet. If the marshal got involved now, everything could go very bad, very fast.

Sandbar Jack rode into Rio Rosa a day after his shadow. He tied his horse in front of the Sheriff's office and went inside. By then, Larribee knew where Jack had gone. The sheriff was feeling ahead in the game. He leaned back with his feet propped up on the desk and didn't bother to move when Jack came in.

"Hello Sheriff, CJ," Jack said.

"Hello Jack," I replied.

Larribee just kind of nodded.

"I came in to see about Billy. Is he all right? Indians jumped us on the road. I was wondering if Billy got away okay."

"Billy's fine," the Sheriff said. "He tells it a little different than you do, but what's new about that?"

Without missing a beat, Jack answered. "Yup, things don't change much in Rio Rosa. Will I see you tonight, CJ?"

"Of course," I answered. "Like you said, things don't change much in Rio Rosa."

Jack wheeled and went out the door. The Sheriff and I watched him ride out of sight towards the Trails End.

"He's got nerve, I'll give him that," Larribee said.

"You got to admit he covers his tracks pretty well," I added.

"Not well enough this time though, eh?"

"No, I reckon not. So, what's your next move Sheriff?"

"I'm still thinking on that. One thing is sure; no marshal's going to interfere in my town. Maybe it's time I got behind this ridiculous ordinance and put an end to all this."

Chapter 15

Sandbar Jack's church attendance caused an unpleasant ripple effect to run through Rio Rosa. The ladies of the Temperance Society, by various female wiles, put an end to their husbands' visits to the Trails End. Their number included the most powerful men in town.
These men did not intend to be the only ones to give up drinking. Employees were warned to stay away. Notes were called in and businesses threatened. One by one Jack's customers disappeared. The odd bottle was still delivered or sold out the back door, but the turn out at the Trails End definitely fell off. I was subjected to a little pressure myself. However, holding a monopoly and lacking a wife, I was able to continue spending time with the "regulars".
Freighters, knowing what happened to John Little Man, flatly refused to haul for Jack. John Little Man wouldn't be back in business for weeks. Jack was faced with the choice of selling only the tequila that came up from Naco and what he ran off himself or closing up one day a week and hauling whiskey from Bisbee on his own. It really wasn't much of a choice. Tequila and home brew would do for the Indians but to keep the miners coming to Rio Rosa, Jack had to have the whiskey and beer that was hauled in every week.
Jack closed the Trails End the next Sunday while he and Clyde made the trip to Bisbee. The heretofore weaponless Sandbar Jack rode with his new shotgun across his lap to prevent any further unpleasantness along the trail.
With this departure from the routine, the rhythm of life in Rio Rosa spun out of control. Perhaps, given time, things would return to normal. Rio Rosa was out of time. The fires of change were already burning and fuel was about to be thrown on the fire.

Chapter 16

The third Sunday that Jack and Clyde Bristow set out on their run to Bisbee, things seemed to be settling into a routine. When they pulled away from the Trails End at first light, most of the town was awake. Only the two men on the buckboard knew a storm was coming.

With Sandbar Jack out of town and the Trails End closed, the Temperance Society decided to hold a celebration of sorts. They had been successful in closing the saloon on the Sabbath and felt the need to crow about it. In their wisdom, and Christian humility the Society decided to hold the celebration in front of the Trails End itself. Their plans called for a grand procession down Main Street. Once a crowd gathered, Clara Ann and Rev Fellowes would speak on the evils of drink and of one saloon in particular.

Anyone with a lick of sense had to know this kind of secret, guarded by a flock of cackling hens, was already public knowledge. I got up early to see if Jack would really leave town and let them have their fun. I was surprised to see wagon roll out of town. Had the hour been later, I might have wondered why Jack gave in so easily. As it was I climbed back in bed until the sun got up a good deal higher.

Like clockwork, church let out at the stroke of noon. The congregation broke into rousing hymns and marched to the saloon accompanied by the beat of an old bass drum. Rev. Fellowes led the flock, marching arm in arm with Ginny Honeywell and Clara Ann. The Society's newest member stayed near the back and kept an eye on the growing crowd.

I had only one customer at the time. Hiram Jenks wasn't interested in the proceedings.

"What the heck," I told Hiram. "I might as well go take a look."

I followed the crowd and took up a perch on the hitching post directly across from the saloon. Rev. Fellowes quieted the crowd

163

and launched into an excruciatingly lengthy prayer of thanksgiving to which everyone said a glad "Amen".

"Brothers and Sisters of Rio Rosa," he announced. "I want you to see what a great victory God has given His servants of the Temperance Society. By diligent, fervent prayer and trusting in the power of Almighty God, this saloon stands closed on the Sabbath. God has moved to silence this evil on His holy day. It is our hope and prayer to see it silenced forever!"

"I can only tell you of the evil and degradation of the saloon secondhand. However, there is one among us who has been, saved from this very pit of iniquity. Whiskey held her bound but God has set her free. Listen well, Brethren."

Clara Ann climbed the steps to stand beside Fellowes. The preacher nodded to her and swept a long outstretched arm over the crowd. Clara Ann stood ramrod straight, a large white Bible clutched to her chest with gloved hands. She wore yellow gingham mirrored blond tresses that cascaded over her shoulders. Her face was almost angelic. Clara's voice cracked at first; grew in strength and there spilled from her saintly lips the biggest pack of lies that ever touched my ears in one helping.

She told of young girls lured from decent homes. Forced into prostitution, the soiled doves turned to whiskey to soothe the pain. She cried over years spent in drunken stupor and of the torture of being denied whiskey. Sandbar Jack had done all this and more.

Clara told how she wanted to go to the law but had no proof except her word. Who was going to believe her word against that of a rich man she asked. She said God had set her free and He was keeping her safe from Sandbar Jack's retribution. She called on every one to close the saloon and help to rescue the other women held there. Clara closed with a cascade of crocodile tears.

Movement from the corner of my eye. An arm swung towards the crowd. The street exploded. Screams mingled with the staccato sound of gunfire. Honeywell threw his wife, Ginny, to the ground.

Other members found their way there all on their own. A second round of gunfire burst in the street. I turned towards the shooter and looked into the smiling face of Sandbar Jack.

Jack lit another string of firecrackers and tossed them into the street. Jack pointed towards the saloon. Aggie Winslow and Lois Rigsby, a bottle of whiskey in each hand, climbed from an upstairs window. The women turned up the bottles showering the cowering Rev. Fellowes with whiskey. The storm of explosions stopped; replaced by stunned silence. Townsfolk laid in the street too scared to run. A few men with guns drawn looked for a target that wasn't there.

"Drop your weapons," bellowed Larribee.

The men holding guns immediately complied. The crowd regained its feet. Muddy rivulets ran down Ginny Honeywell's face and her best Sunday-go-to-meeting dress was covered with a generous layer of street dust and fresh horse manure. Whiskey dripped from Rev. Fellowes face and clothes. Light began to dawn on the shell shocked faces of the crowd. The anger that arose over having been the butt of Sandbar Jack's joke was given no outlet.

"Everyone and I mean *ever-ry-one,* go home and do it now!" Larribee ordered. "Move!"

Congregation and onlookers alike cleared the street.

I remember thinking, *"What's with Tink?" Is he in on this?* That's when I saw the shotgun Clyde had in the middle of the Sheriff's back. The Sheriff towards the Trails End and Jack motioned for me to follow.

I don't know how Larribee managed to control his temper and keep from getting shot. Maybe it's not as difficult as it looks with two barrels of double ought buck trained on you. The sheriff's face had gone dark, throbbing red. I swear you could count every muscle and vein in his neck and jaws. His hands were clinched into white knuckled fists. Larribee could explode any minute. Sandbar Jack had a tiger by the tail. I hoped he would be able to turn loose without any one getting hurt.

"Please sit down Sheriff," Jack said once inside the saloon. Clyde handed Larribee's .45 to Jack. Jack sat at the table nearest the bar; put Tink's gun on the table and waited. Clyde retreated behind the bar and put the shotgun out of sight.

"C'mon, Sheriff, sit down," Jack repeated.

Larribee sat. Jack read murder in the blazing stare aimed at him. Still, Jack managed to smile.

"I don't want any trouble. We were just having a little fun with the teetotalers on their big day. No one got hurt, except for some wounded pride. Let it go Sheriff."

Billy Rubin and Johnny Sheffield entered from each side of the bar, guns drawn.

"Oh, put those guns away boys," Jack ordered.

Billy holstered his gun. Johnny waited for the order from his boss. The Sheriff nodded and Johnny holstered his gun. Larribee continued to sit stone faced.

"Beer all around Clyde,' Jack ordered.

I was glad for the beer. My mouth felt like it was stuffed with cotton. The rest must have felt the same for the tension eased a bit.

"Let me put it to you this way," Jack said. "Near as I can tell, we didn't break any laws. We made a little noise and poured out some whiskey. Just a little ironic, don't you think? Nothing compared with what happened to John Little Man."

Tinker Larribee was unmoved.

"I know, I know," Jack said. "I got no proof they were behind destroying my goods and beating John within an inch of his life. Thing is, Sheriff, I don't need any. Even if you just chalk it up to God answering their prayers like they say, they're still behind it. I run a legitimate business. Meanwhile, these fine Christians people shout about how they intend to destroy it and celebrate a man nearly getting killed for doing his job. I'm not the bad guy here."

Jack pushed Larribee's .45 across the table to the sheriff. Larribee seemed to soften just a bit. He holstered the weapon and took a sip on the beer before him.

"None of them stuck a shotgun in my back," he said.

"No, they didn't, but they're willing to put a political gun to your head."

"That shotgun was there only to make sure no one got shot," Clyde volunteered."

Larribee said nothing.

Sandbar Jack broke the silence. "That's our story. You've got your gun back. Do your duty."

Larribee drained his beer and asked, "Johnny, does Clyde still have his hands under the bar?"

"Sure does," Johnny answered.

"Then you and Billy cover us. We're getting out of here."

Larribee kept his eyes on Sandbar Jack and backed out of the Trails End with his deputies in tow. The sheriff stopped in the doorway.

"Okay, you haven't broken any laws. I could make a case against your barkeep for holding a shotgun on me, but it's not Clyde I want. This will keep. Believe me it ain't over. It ain't never going to be over."

Chapter 17

The Trails End went dark. Sandbar Jack stepped through the batwings onto the boardwalk. The flare of a match lit his face. His silhouette was visible even on the moonless night. He smoked and studied the lights that burned along Main Street. There weren't many. One at the Sheriff's Office, where Billy was guarding a drunken miner caught his attention, as did the other above the Undertaker's Parlor. Things didn't change much in Rio Rosa.

The sound of breaking glass from the Trails End shattered the peace. Jack charged through the saloon doors. More shattering glass; followed by a scream and orange flames blossomed in the Trails End. Jack grabbed his shotgun on his way towards the sound. He jumped through the spreading flames in the storeroom and kicked open the back door in time to see a single rider gallop away. Jack cut loose with both barrels. The rider jerked at the shotgun's roar, lurched in the saddle but held on and cut sharply behind the Livery.

Jack debated only for a moment then plunged back into the saloon. More shrieks sounded from over head. Clyde Bristow was beating down the flames in the storeroom with a blanket. The outcome was still uncertain but Clyde seemed to be gaining the upper hand.

"I'm okay. Go!" Clyde yelled.

Jack took the stairs at a run. The hall was packed with women who continued to scream in terror. Jack pushed them aside. Donna Evers was beating out the last of the flames on the smoldering bed. Aggie Winslow knelt in the middle of the room cradling Lois Rigsby in her lap. What remained of Lois' hair was singed stubble over a blacked, blistered face. Lois gasped for breath like a fish out of water. Aggie held a wet cloth to what was left of Lois' face and cooed to her through free flowing tears. The fire was started by lighted whiskey bottles thrown from the street. The one that struck the casement of the upstairs window exploded and rained fire down on Lois. Her screams drew the flames into her lungs. Her throat was now rapidly swelling closed.

"Fire's out down…." Clyde stopped; hammered by the sight of Lois Rigsby's last breath.

"Clyde, get the Sheriff," Jack ordered.

Clyde met Billy Rubin on the stairs and turned the deputy around.

"You don't want to go up there, boy," Clyde said.

"What's going on?" Billy asked.

Clyde didn't answer and Billy didn't press. Main Street was alive with the citizens of Rio Rosa. Their natural curiosity into their neighbors' affairs drove them towards the Trails End. Clyde noticed Rev. Fellowes moving against the tide.

"Billy, you go on and get the Sheriff. I'll catch up to you." Clyde set out after the preacher. Fellowes was indeed headed for the church. The church lights were on.

"If Fellowes isn't there, why are the lights on?"

Rev. Fellowes disappeared inside the church. Clyde followed his movements though the windows that ran the length of the building until Fellowes entered his office. There were no windows along the rear of the church so Clyde returned to the side of the building and waited for the preacher to reappear.

His patience was rewarded. Rev. Fellowes left his office only minutes later. Half way down the aisle, the preacher stopped; pulled a handkerchief from his pocket; and wiped something from the floor. He glanced at the handkerchief before stuffing it back in his pocket. Fellowes reversed himself and returned to the office. Clyde headed for the back door. The bartender rounded the corner and light from inside the church fell on a familiar face.

"What the...." Clyde began.

The door swung closed. Clyde was plunged into darkness. A muzzle flash blinded the bartender and the darkness became eternal.

Chapter 18

I was still a young man back in 1888. I'd never seen anything like the burned body of Lois Rigsby. In her final moments, her face had swollen into an unrecognizable, blackened, blistered mass. Her ears had melted to the sides of her head. As bad as the sight of her was, it couldn't compare to the smell. Jack, Clyde, Billy and I laid the body on a blanket and carried her to the undertaker.

The Sheriff questioned everyone in the saloon. Everyone but Clyde and Jack had been asleep. Clyde had been in his windowless room and Jack out front. In short, there were no witnesses. Tinker found two whisky bottles filled with kerosene and stuffed with rags behind the saloon, no blood to indicate Jack's shotgun had found its mark.

"We're coming up empty," Larribee told Jack. "You got any ideas?"

"None you'd buy into Sheriff," Jack answered.

"You can't seriously expect me to believe Rev. Fellowes did this?"

"Like I said, No ideas you'd buy," Jack repeated.

"Look," Larribee prodded Jack's chest with a meaty finger. "You got something to say, say it."

Jack met Larribee's eyes and he moved the finger from his chest.

"I'm saying the Trails End has never been a problem to anybody until that Bible thumper came to Rio Rosa. There ain't no one got an ax to grind like Fellowes and you're too blind to see the truth."

"I'm going to overlook your mouth this time Jack, But only because one of your girls was killed."

"She had a name. Her name was Lois."

"Lois, then," Larribee said. "But don't you dare push me again. You'll lose. I promise you."

"Don't make promises you can't keep Sheriff. This ain't an election," Jack snarled.

Larribee swore and launched a roundhouse right at Jack's head. Jack blocked the blow saving himself a concussion. The force of the big man's fist sent Jack stumbling sideways. Jack planted his foot and threw all his weight behind a right hand of his own. The punch caught Larribee square on the chin. Larribee went down but only for a second. He sprang to his feet with his Colt drawn.

I stepped between Larribee and Jack. It was a stupid thing to do. I could have been shot. That thought along with a horrendous case of the shakes hit me an hour or so later.

"Whoa, hold it." I shouted. "Let's talk this over."

"Get out of the way Winters," Larribee snapped. "This puke's going to jail."

"No he's not," I said. How I got the guts to say "no" to Tinker Larribee, I'll never know. My stupid blunders were piling up.

"Everyone's skittish and on edge," I continued. "A woman's been killed, for God's sake. Let's all just cool down."

Hatred seethed in both men's eyes but Larribee lowered his gun and Jack unclenched his fists. Somehow I'd backed the bulldog off the meat wagon. Larribee holstered his Colt.

"Let's all just go home. Things will be better in the morning," I offered.

"You've been warned Jack," Larribee said without as much as a glance my way. "Next time, I won't bother about taking you in. I'll kill you. Oh, and one last thing; if anything, and I mean *anything* happens to the Church or Rev. Fellowes; I'm coming for you. You clear on that, Jack?"

"I'll be counting on it Sheriff," Jack answered.

Gunshots ripped the night and the tension building in my office. Jack and Larribee moved apart following the crowd headed towards the church.

The back door of the church stood open. Light spilled onto the small knot of people gathered there. Clyde lay on the ground; blood soaked the front of his shirt and pooled beneath him. Rev. Fellowes knelt beside him, but it was too late for prayer. Clyde Bristow was dead.

Sandbar Jack was frozen. He had a sense about things that always seemed to keep him a step ahead of everyone else. That sense had failed him. He was having trouble comprehending what he saw.

Clyde was going for the sheriff. How could he be dead behind the church? Life and color drained from Jack's face; silent tears rolled down his cheeks.

"Billy, take Jack home and stay with him," Larribee commanded.

Billy obeyed and, strangely enough, so did Jack. He walked back to the saloon and never once looked back. Tinker continued to bark orders.

"Johnny, you take the Reverend to my office and wait for me. A couple of you boys help me and CJ carry the body over to the undertaker's. For God's sake, everybody else, go home and stay put."

We laid Clyde's body beside what was left of Lois Rigsby. The room reeked of burned flesh and embalming fluid I wondered if the stink would ever go away and hoped this would be the last delivery I'd make that night.

I followed Tinker back to his office. When we came through the door, Johnny Sheffield yielded the desk to Larribee and sat next to Fellowes. The preacher was ashen and visibly trembling. A crust of Clyde Bristow's dried blood covered his hands.

"Johnny, get the Reverend a bowl and some water so he can wash up," Larribee directed.

"How about I make some coffee? Or you need something a little stronger?" I asked.

"Coffee's fine. Thanks CJ," Tink said.

I fumbled around putting on coffee while Johnny tended to the Preacher. I hadn't noticed until then how shaky my own hands were. For several minutes we all sat wrapped silently in our own thoughts. Johnny served up the hot brew all around and after a few sips, Larribee was ready.

"Reverend, I want you to take your time. Just tell me everything that happened behind that church. Let's start with what you were doing there in the first place."

"Well, I was in my room reading when I heard a gunshot. I got dressed and went down to see like everyone else. When I got down to the street, I noticed lights on at the church. I was sure I had put them out. It took me a while to get through the crowd. When I finally made it to the church, I knew something was wrong. Not only were the lights on; the door was unlocked. I went back and looked in my office. Everything looked fine. I blew out the lamp and started out. Then I saw this on the floor. Well, just the blood really, the handkerchief is mine."

Fellowes passed the stained handkerchief to Larribee. The sheriff looked it over and laid it open on his desk.

"Any idea whose blood this is?" Larribee asked.

"No, Sheriff," Fellowes continued. "About the time I wiped that up; I heard a noise from my office. I went back to see and the door was locked. The door locks only from the inside. The lights were back on too."

"So, someone was in your office?"

"There had to be, Sheriff. I could have left the light on or not got it out good, but someone had to work that lock from inside."

"Did you have the key with you?"

"That's just it. There's not a key. There's just a bolt on the inside."

"So what happened next?"

"I started around back thinking I could get in that door with my key. That's when I heard the shots. The back door was wide open and that poor man was just lying there. There was blood all over him and it was bubbling from his mouth when he tried to breathe. Merciful God it was awful,"

"Did you see anyone else nearby?"

"I couldn't take my eyes off that man. I tried to comfort him. He didn't seem to see me at all. He coughed and more blood flew everywhere." Fellowes was seeing it all again. I started to pray. The next thing I knew people were standing all around."

"Who got there first?" I asked. "Oh, pardon, Sheriff."

"It's okay. Go ahead Preacher," Tink said.

"I don't know…I just can't. Oh, God," Fellowes said and began to weep.

"Okay, that's enough for tonight. Johnny take the Reverend home. Then you'd better check on Billy. Tell him to sit on Sandbar Jack tonight and to by-God-pay-attention. The last thing we need tonight is more trouble from him. We'll try sorting this out in the morning. CJ looks like you've got work to do."

"Yes it does. I'll be in the office; let me know if I can help with anything Sheriff," I said.

"I'll be by tomorrow."

"Okay, don't make it too early. I need my beauty sleep."

Chapter 19

We buried Clyde Bristow and Lois Rigsby side by side. Jack saw to it they had the very best. Reverend Fellowes insisted on conducting the funeral. He said it was the least he could do for a man who died in his arms. Either Fellowes didn't share Tink Larribee's suspicions that Clyde Bristow was the mysterious intruder, or he was a forgiving man after all.

As to who did the actual shooting, the only one's Tink ruled out were Jack and I. That was only because we were with him at the time. Everyone else was suspect. In his heart, Tinker believed one of Jack's people did the deed by mistake and was too afraid to own up to it.

Jack believed Clyde surprised the arsonist and got killed for his trouble. Neither man allowed much room for other theories. By the end of the week, Larribee gave up hope of solving the arson and murders.

The Temperance Society and Sandbar Jack held an unofficial armistice. Both sides blamed the other for stirring things up in Rio Rosa and neither side was ready to concede defeat.

Fellowes still quietly pursued his ban and lining up the council votes. Jack was busy checking out church members for minor shotgun wounds and small caliber handguns. The rest of Rio Rosa held its collective breath and waited to see what would happen next.

Chapter 20

Clara knew about the new night time patrols and kept to the shadows to avoid being seen. The church was dark. She hoped she was not too early. The church gave her the creeps and she didn't want to have to wait there alone.

"Why did it have to be the Church?"

Clara crossed the moon washed street a hundred yards south of the church. The church door was hidden in shadows; once across, she was safe. Clara drew a deep breath when she finally reached the shelter of the church. She tried the door. The knob turned freely. Clara stepped inside.

"Rev. Fellowes? Anybody here? It's Clara, Preacher."

Silence. Clara allowed her eyes to adjust before she moved through the small entry. Uneasiness crawled up her spine. Moonlight through the open door allowed Clara to find the lamp. She held the lamp to the light, lit the wick and trimmed the lamp.

"Rev. Fellowes?"

A loose floorboard groaned behind her. Clara whirled around in time to see a large fist. Brilliant light exploded in Clara's head. She heard the thud of her head hitting the floor. Then blackness swallowed her whole.

Dawn on the desert never failed to be spectacular. The sky blazed with reds and oranges atop indigo mountains. Rio Rosa woke early. Later the sun would soon drive folks into the shade but while the day was new they were out and about their business.

Billy Rubin began his day earlier than most. He dressed and got to the office to make coffee before the sheriff arrived. Tinker was always easier to get along with if he could enjoy a quiet cup of coffee when he got to work. Billy rode passed the church every morning on his way to work. This morning the church doors stood open.

"Not good, not good, not good," the inner Billy whispered. The unusual never boded well in Rio Rosa. Billy rode up to the church. He swung down and drew his gun. His hands shook despite his command to be still.

"Oh, Lord. Here we go," the voice said again.

Billy willed his feet to move up the steps to the church door.

"Still in one piece," but Billy wasn't quite sure if he meant himself or the door.

Rev. Fellowes always locked the church. Billy could see the lock had not been forced. If there was an intruder, he had a key.

"Intruder? At Church? Who says it was an intruder? The part that doesn't want to find a dead Preacher in here, that's who."

Billy peeked inside. Though the sun wasn't quite up; the interior of the church was filled with dark shadow.

"Preacher?" he said. "Preacher, are you in here?"

His rising hackles were the only answer. Billy started down the aisle. The sun was up. Light hit the stained glass. A woman lay on the altar; a naked woman. The kaleidoscope of color streaming through the glass washed her body, but Billy could tell she was covered with blood.

"Oh, God," Billy whimpered. "Oh, my God."

The figure on the altar moaned.

Billy took Clara Ann to Doc Brown's. She was unconscious, but alive. The doctor told Tinker he wasn't sure when, or even if, Clara would ever wake up. A bedside vigil was begun. Being a night owl, I volunteered to man the midnight to six watch. For the first three days Clara slept. Her breathing was ragged. At times it stopped altogether, caught with a loud gasp and ground on. The swelling on the outside was beginning to go away. Clara grew paler everyday and most of the bruises turned a sick yellow. Fever burned inside her where Doc said the real injury was.

The town went about its business trying hard to find comfort in its day-to-day routine. However, the atmosphere remained charged and folks walked softly each one afraid of disturbing the uneasy calm. There was a monster among them. Clara had not just been beaten. She had been raped. Holes had been punched in her hands and the blood sprinkled on the pews. The words "The Mother of Harlots" was written in Clara's blood on the wall behind the pulpit.

For Rio Rosa there was only one person who would dare such things. Only one person also had a score to settle with both Clara and the Church. That person was Sandbar Jack. That was the name everyone expected to hear from the battered lips of Clara Ann Tyler. The Trails End was deserted. Even the miners choosing to come to Rio Rosa was dwindling.

On the seventh night of my vigil, Clara began to stir. I sent for Doc Brown. The doctor listened, poked, tapped and scratched his head.

"I think she's going to make it," he pronounced at last.

"She's going to wake up soon, then?" I asked.

"Well, I can't say when, but, I'd say, yes she'll come around with time and care. Keep up the good work. I'm going back to bed. See you in the morning."

A couple of hours before dawn, Clara began to speak. It didn't make any sense, rambling mostly. Finally, she opened her eyes.

"Am I dead?" she asked.

"Not yet, my dear, but soon."

I don't know where that whore found the strength to scream. I guess it doesn't matter. It wasn't loud; little more than a whisper after I held the pillow over her face. Amazing how long it took for her to quit struggling. I went back downstairs to tell the doctor the bad news. Clara had awakened, mumbled a name, and died.

The name? Sandbar Jack, of course.

Chapter 21

It's easy to lie to a man who doesn't care if you are telling him the truth. Tink Larribee wanted to hear Sandbar Jack named as Clara's killer. Once the name was spoken everything else was irrelevant. He was only too willing to accept the story without question. When I told Larribee I'd testify that Clara, with her dying breath, named Sandbar Jack that was all he needed to hear. He called in Billy Rubin and Johnny Sheffield; deputized George Honeywell and Frank Tilden and went to arrest Jack.

The Sheriff was determined to prevent Jack from being warned. He offered Doc and me the choice of tagging along or being in "protective custody" until Jack was locked up. We opted to tag along. It was potentially the biggest arrest in Rio Rosa's history; we had to be there. Larribee's plan called for Billy and Johnny to come in through the back while Larribee took Jack head on through the front door. Honeywell and Tilden would provide outside back up. They were ordered to shoot without hesitation if Jack made it to the street. The deputies left first and took different tracks to the back of the Trails End. Honeywell and Tilden followed. Honeywell was posted on Main Street while Tilden backed up the deputies. Larribee, Doc and I then headed for the saloon.

Sandbar Jack was not an easy man to surprise. Knowing everyone in town suspected he was the killer, Jack made a few preparations. The back door and the board platform to the Trails

End were intentionally a poor fit. The platform squeaked and the door stuck as unobtrusive alarms. A coil of rope was also tied to Jack's bed frame as an emergency egress from the second floor. Jack had always condemned Booth as an idiot for jumping from a balcony while trying to escape. Jack's shotgun stayed close at hand. This time though, events and precautions conspired against Sandbar Jack. Everyone was in place quickly and without drawing any attention. However, not everything went perfectly for Tink Larribee either.

Johnny Sheffield's boots sounded a squeaky alarm. Sandbar Jack had his shotgun in Johnny's face by the time the deputy got the door open. Jack had the deputies cold. Only with Clyde gone, there was no longer anyone to watch Jack's back.

"Drop it!" Larribee growled.

Jack slowly straightened. Billy and Johnny had their guns drawn but Jack still turned his head towards the Sheriff.

"That's right, just try it," Larribee said. "You're a dead man either way. C'mon, let's end this right here."

"I don't think so Sheriff," Jack replied and raised the shotgun over his head.

"Get that shotgun CJ," the sheriff ordered.

I jumped at the sound of my name. Then, I cut a timid path across the room and reached for the shotgun.

"Sorry, he made me come," I whispered to Jack. I took the shotgun and beat a hasty retreat back behind the Sheriff.

"Cuff him, Johnny," Larribee ordered. "What's the matter Jack? You ain't got anything smart to say?"

"You can't talk to a man who don't want to hear, Sheriff."

"I heard Clara well enough. She woke up long enough to name her killer. Now, I'm going to see you hang."

Jack looked at the men surrounding him. It was Billy he spoke to: "Billy this is not what it looks like. Ride to Tombstone and get the Marshal. Let him look into this and you'll see."

"I…I can't Jack. I can't," Billy stammered.

Johnny had the cuffs on and pushed Jack towards the door. "Move it. Let's go," he ordered.

"Billy I'm telling the truth. I didn't do it. If you don't go for the marshal, you'll be hanging an innocent man."

Larribee saw belief in Billy's eyes.

"Shut up," he snarled and brought his gun down on Jack's head.

Jack staggered but stayed on his feet. The blow had split his scalp and blood began to flow down Jack's face. He raised a hand to wipe the blood from his eyes. When he did, Larribee punched him in the ribs. Air rushed from Jack's lungs and he hit the floor gasping for air.

"Get him up," Larribee commanded. "Johnny, you go up and tell his whores to start packing because if they're still around after he hangs, I'll throw them out of town myself."

Johnny set off up the stairs while the rest of us led Jack to his cell. By the time we reached the Sheriff's Office, a crowd had gathered outside.

Chapter 22

Sandbar Jack had three visitors during his incarceration. I was the first and the only one who came at Jack's invitation. Larribee made Billy stand guard day and night. That wasn't unusual. There was a cot for the guard to nap on when he needed to. However, that wasn't the reason Billy got the duty. Jack just might have the power to persuade Billy to go to Tombstone. But, Tinker *knew* Billy would never leave his post to do it.
Jack was determined to give it a try anyway. Jack made enough headway that on Friday to get Billy to let me in to see him. I pulled a chair up to the bars so we could talk loud enough for Billy to hear and close enough to be private if we needed to.

"Sorry I can't offer you the usual hospitality CJ," Jack said.

"Maybe next time," I smiled.

Jack shot a glance towards Billy. "Not going to be a next time. These folks mean to hang me sure. If I can't get that U.S. Marshal to step in, they'll do it."

"I'll go to Tombstone and get him," I offered.

"Thanks, CJ. But, no good. You're a friend. You're expected to cry 'unfair'. It's got to be someone from the Sheriff's own office or the council. The Marshal's not going to interfere in Larribee's jurisdiction unless he's got good reason to believe Tink's up to something illegal."

Jack gave Billy a glance. The kid looked miserable but he wasn't going to buck Tink Larribee.

"Anyway that's not why I wanted to see you," Jack added.

"You want a lawyer?" I asked.

"Hell no," Jack chuckled. "I'd just as soon hang. I want you to go see Aggie. She's got some papers for you to see."

"Papers?"

"Just some business matters; final arrangements and such. Will you take care of it for me?"

"Sure, you know I will."

"Thanks," Jack said. "One last thing you can do for me."

Jack motioned me closer. "Find out who Clara talked to. Larribee's keeping his cards close to the vest. I guess he's afraid I might buy off his witness. Which is not a bad idea."

"Forget the bribe, it was Fellowes."

"You're sure?"

"Absolutely. I was there."

Like I said, it's easy to lie to a man when you're telling him what he wants to hear…even a man like Sandbar Jack.

"Thanks for coming CJ. You're a friend," Jack said.

"You bet," I said. "Things might work out yet though."

I offered Jack my hand. He shook it a deftly palmed the key he found there. A big smile spread across his face.

"Well, you never can tell, can you?" Jack said.

"No you just never know. Oh, by the way," I added. "There's a council meeting tonight at the church. It's about the whiskey law. Looks like some opposition is growing. Reckon there's some who wouldn't mind filling your shoes. I suspect Honeywell smells a buck and Ginny-be-damned. Larribee *wants* the church's support next election, but he's *got* to have Honeywell's. There just may be a bigger fight over who is going to be the new saloon owner than over outlawing the stuff."

"Do tell," Jack said.

Jack's second visitor passed me as I left the Sheriff's office. I gave him quick thumbs up and a quick smile. Emmett Kirkland was Rio Rosa's only lawyer. Most of the folks in these parts claimed his shingle hung from Josh Honeywell's pocket. Kirkland was sharp. In court he was as deadly as a rattlesnake with the morals and ethics to match. He was just the kind of lawyer a condemned man needed.

Kirkland got himself appointed as attorney for Sandbar Jack. Billy escorted Kirkland into the small cell area and broke the news to Jack.

"Don't be so darn apologetic," Jack told Billy. "You're just doing your job."

"If you would be so kind to give us some privacy; I need to speak with my client," Kirkland said.

Billy backed out and resumed his perch at the desk.

"Jack, I'm going to get right to it. Forgive my directness, but it doesn't look good for you." Kirkland held up a preemptive hand. "Not hopeless by any means but…shall we say, bleak. There's no witness for me to attack. The case is going to hinge on Clara's deathbed identification. There will be a lot of sympathy for her."

"You haven't even asked me if I did it or not," Jack interrupted.

"Doesn't matter to me...all that matters is what that judge and jury are going to think," Kirkland explained.

"That's what I love about you lawyers, your constant pursuit of truth."

"Yes, well, be that as it may. Let's be practical here. Have you given any thought to what you will do if you are found guilty?"

"I'm going to hang you fool! Have I been thinking about it? Just what do you think I've been doing?"

"I'm talking about your assets, your estate," Kirkland retreated.

"No. To tell the truth, I kind of figured since I'll be dead...why worry."

"What if you don't die? Suppose there's a way to make a deal for a prison term instead of a rope."

"I don't see Tink Larribee going for any deal," Jack reasoned.

"Larribee can be handled...by the right people."

"Okay, you have my attention," Jack said.

"I have another client who can guarantee you don't hang."

"Honeywell?"

"I'm not at liberty to say. But this client is prepared to offer you your life and $50,000 in exchange for the Trails End," Kirkland explained.

"My, my, your client is serious about this. If he has $50,000 why doesn't he just buy a saloon and cut out all the scheming?"

"Because the Trails End has a reputation that money can't buy. It has an established a hedge against competition," Kirkland said.

"I have a condition," Jack said.

"I'm all ears."

"It's got to be cash. A friend will pick up the money at your office tonight; right before the council meeting. Once the cash is in hand, I'll sign the deed over to your client."

"Agreed. Who is the friend?"

"He'll be the one asking for $50,000 cash."

Jasper Ruffin considered himself an artist. He loved his work and he loved giving his audience a good show. Jasper also loved the notoriety that went along with being the best damned hangman west of the Missouri. Jasper was never hard to spot. Always the showman, he dressed all in black, from his broad rim hat to his polished boots. Around his neck hung a red string tie with each end fashioned into a noose. Jasper walked with a slight limp. It was a souvenir from a rebel Minnie ball Jasper took in the right thigh at Cold Harbor. He could walk just fine but used the 1x4 lever from his first gallows as a cane. The cane was studded with inlaid stones to mark each subsequent customer. It was all a part of the Jasper Ruffin show.

Jasper arrived in Rio Rosa on Friday to supervise preparations for Tuesday's hanging of Sandbar Jack. Construction of the gallows and stands were already well under way even though the trial didn't start until Monday. When I spotted Jasper headed for Larribee's office, my curiosity was naturally piqued. Everyone knew the Sheriff was at the council meeting. Something was up.

"Well, well. You're a might early ain't you Jasper?" Jack asked.

"A mite, I suppose," Jasper answered. "Then again, I ain't had a case I so looked forward to in quite a spell. The crowd is really getting excited to see me work."

"And here I thought it was me they were coming to see," Jack said.

"How egotistical the criminal mind. No one wants to see the petty criminal. It's justice they come to see; justice that exacts a harsh revenge on the guilty. It gives everyone a sense of security. They want to know that the law, when it can't protect him, it will get even. I am the instrument of revenge. It will always be the hangman they come to see."

"Then shouldn't you be out with the adoring public?" Jack asked.

"Plenty of time for that," Jasper said with a brush of his hand. "A hanging is a very complex operation. There's much to do."

"Sorry to be such a bother Jasper."

"Oh no bother, it's all part of the show. You see no one, no one except you, knows this shall be my final performance."

"You'll be joining me on the short drop? Why, Jasper, how kind of you."

"I'm glad to see you're so upbeat about this," Jasper started. "It makes what I have to tell you all the sweeter. You see this gold nugget?"

Jasper held the pea sized yellow ore up into the evening sunlight. "This shall be Sandbar Jack. It will be the final addition to my cane. It will mark my finest performance."
Jack started to answer but Jasper cut him off.
"My career has been a long and glorious one. It needs a spectacular finish; something truly memorable. You were the answer to my prayers. Rape and murder in the church house…such a bad, bad boy. Now the greatest hangman of all times comes to town to send the guilty straight to hell. But, wait! God takes a hand; something is not quite right, the noose does not snap the killer's neck. He is left to dance at the rope's end; his eyes bulging; his face blue and bloated; his bowel and bladder let go as he slowly strangles to death. It shall be a show they will never forget. Jasper Ruffin's first mistake is his greatest hanging."

Jack hung his head on the bars of the cell door. Was he weeping? Billy and I leaned forward to see. So did Jasper. Jack slammed the unlocked cell door into Jasper's face. The hangman went spinning across the small space in a spray of blood. Jack followed close behind. He punched the stumbling Jasper breaking his nose a second time. When the hangman hit the floor, Jack was on top of him before Billy could move. Jack came up with Jasper's Navy Colt.

"Billy, how many times has the Sheriff told you about disarming visitors?" Jack asked. "Now put your gun on the desk and step over here."

Jasper Ruffin was finding his feet. Jack kicked him in the gut.

"Get in that cell Billy. CJ, I'm afraid I must ask you to join him. I'm going to insist you gentlemen remain quiet. You heard Mr. Ruffin; I have nothing to lose by shooting you now."

Jack closed the cell door behind us then returned to Ruffin's side. Jack fished the gold nugget from Jasper's pocket and tossed it to Billy.

"A little gift from Sandbar Jack," he said and was out the door.

It took a great deal of coaxing to get Jasper to crawl to the desk for the key. His face was a bloody mess. Jasper had two tiny slits for eyes, but he found Billy's keys and unlocked the cell.

Chapter 23

"That saloon is the devil's playground. It is rotten to the core polluting everything around it. It is a pit that harbors all manner of sin and infects this town with the vermin that crawl through its doors. We have seen the depravity of its owner demonstrated in this very church. We must stand as one for the saloon's destruction or be destroyed by..."

The church door imploded. The preacher froze open mouthed. Heads swiveled in unison and the congregation drew a collective breath. Sandbar Jack started down the aisle. His steps echoed in the silence. Cradled in the crook of his arm was his new shotgun.

"How dare you presume to defile the house of God," Rev. Fellowes shrieked.

Jack rolled the shotgun to his hip and pulled the trigger on both barrels. Double ought buck caught the preacher just above the waist and nearly ripped him in half. His body slammed against the pulpit with a wet slap. Fellowes' blood and guts splattered the altar. Josh Honeywell leaped from his pew in an attempt to separate Jack and his shotgun. Jack drew a .45 from his belt and blew Josh's brains all over his wife. Ginny Honeywell promptly fainted dead away, which probably saved her life.

Jack pivoted and his next shot caught Harvey Green in the chest. Harvey went down in a lifeless heap. At the same time most of the women found enough breath to begin screaming. The congregation sought refuge in the pews and frantic prayer. Jack leaned over the pew to make sure Harvey Green's frothy pink respirations had stopped. They had.

Sandbar Jack holstered his .45, broke the shotgun and reloaded. In response to the gunfire and mindless shrieking, Johnny Sheffield charged through the open church doorway, gun drawn. The explosion of Jack's shotgun met him. The blast lifted him off his feet and carried Johnny back through the door to bleed to death in the street. Jack reloaded.

"Stand up Butch," Jack commanded. "C'mon, Butch. I know you're there. Be a man and show your face. Here's your chance to put an end to Sandbar Jack."

"I'm not armed," Butch Davies answered rising to his feet.

"You're a liar, as well as a coward," Jack said. "Either way I'm going to draw on you. You do as you like."

Butch Davies drew the Colt from under his coat. Jack's .45 appeared from nowhere; thunder reverberated; the gun bucked in Jack's hand. A trail of red followed Butch's body down the wall and pooled in the floor.

"Where's Larribee?" Jack demanded. "I know the lying bastard's here. Now, where is he?"

187

No one present could manage more than a whimper. Jack dropped the shotgun into the nearest pew.

"I'll kill every last one of you if you don't tell me where the sheriff is," Jack said.

Jack reached into the pew and pulled Mary Vernon to her feet. Jack drew his revolver and pointed it toward Jane Tilden.

"Where's Larribee?" He snarled in Mary Vernon's ear.

Mary managed a weak shake of her head. Jack shot Jane Tilden in the right arm. The Colt turned on Molly Goodpasture.

"Where's Larribee?" Jack asked again.

"Right behind you," Larribee growled.

Jack turned and fired. He was fast, but Larribee was faster. Tinker's speed was the doom of Mary Vernon. Her body still shielded Jack. Larribee's round exploded Mary's heart and exited from her back. Jack felt the bullet burn a path across his ribs. Jack got his shot away. However, the force of the bullet and the pain in Jack's left side threw his shot wide of Larribee's head. But it was close enough though to jerk Larribee's second round into the ceiling. Tinker dove behind the gore splattered pulpit.

"Let her go, Jack,"

"Sure, Sheriff, why not. You killed her."

Jack let Mary fall and reclaimed the shotgun. The thud of Mary Vernon's body on the floor brought Larribee to his feet with his gun blazing. Sandbar Jack was waiting. Jack again let both barrels of the shotgun roar. The shot was short and caught the top of the pulpit. Larribee went down with a howl of pain. The splintered pulpit riddled his face and chest. Larribee fired blind until the hammer fell on empty chambers.

Billy ran through the church door. The smell of gunpowder and blood was stifling but it was the sight of the eviscerated Rev. Fellowes sitting at the base of his blasted pulpit that brought the deputy to a sudden stop. Jack drew a bead on Billy but couldn't pull the trigger. Not Billy; Jack couldn't kill the kid. He couldn't be sure Billy would feel the same. Jack dropped his Colt and raised the empty shotgun over his head.

"Easy now Billy," Jack cautioned.

"Shoot him!" Larribee screamed.

It took Billy a long moment to move. It was long enough for Jack to escape. Jack dove through the window. Larribee reloaded through the blood that flowed down his face into his eyes. He staggered to the broken window, but even Larribee's clouded vision was good enough to know Sandbar Jack was gone.

I left the jail knowing where Jack was going. Let Billy be the hero; I headed the other direction. I had an appointment with a lawyer. The exchange went well until the thunder of Jack's shotgun began. Emmett must have guessed what was happening. Panic made it difficult to handle the money so I lent a hand. We left Emmett's office as Sandbar Jack flew through the church window. He rolled once; was on his feet and headed for the Trails End. He saw me, bag in hand and tipped his hat. Kirkland stepped around me to see what was going on. Jack shot him right between the eyes.

Jack crossed the street. Jasper Ruffin, almost blind, was emerging from the Sheriff's Office. Jack got up pretty close. About the time it dawned on Jasper who he was looking at; the blast from both barrels turned out Jasper's lights forever.

At the Trails End, Jack found his horse saddled and waiting.

That was the easiest $50,000 I ever made.

Jack climbed aboard and started south; doubled back and head for Bisbee. Billy was leading Tink Larribee from the church. Larribee had a blood stained towel over his face but was busy shouting orders...

"Somebody get my horse. Billy, telegraph Naco. Tell Sheriff Shaw to close the border."

189

Doc Brown pulled a few of the larger splinters from Tink Larribee's face and sewed up the lacerations over his eyes. The bleeding stopped; Larribee was ready to lead the posse. I considered it my civic duty to tell the Sheriff that Sandbar Jack was not making for the border.

He's headed for the Pima Reservation, "Tinker relayed my news to the posse. "Let's ride!"

There was a ton of work to be done in town. I decided to attend to it…tomorrow. So, I saddled up and joined the posse. A dozen others did the same. Adam Goodpasture rode up as we got started.

"We've picked up Jack's trail," Adam said. "He's not headed for the Rez."

"He's headed for John Little Man's place," Billy volunteered. "Follow me."

The posse spurred towards the San Pedro with Billy leading the way. At Little Man's we found Jack's lathered bay tied out front. There was no friendly reception for the lawmen this time. Larribee kicked open the door and a half dozen of the boys followed him in with guns drawn. The search only turned up a terrified Mary and two children cowering behind the bed.

"Where is he?" Larribee screamed.

Mary hesitated. Larribee yanked her to her feet.

"Where…is…he?"

"I don't …." was all Mary got out.

Larribee backhanded her across the mouth. Mary flew back onto the bed, but sprang back like a cat; claws bared. Larribee's fist caught her before she even got close. Her nose and jaw broken; Mary fell to the floor. That was going to hurt when she woke up.

Billy came in through the back. "I found tracks Sheriff." A look of stunned horror clouded Billy's face when he saw the unconscious Mary. "Outback," he mumbled.

Two sets of tracks led west from the adobe. After about ten miles, one set turned south while the other continued west.

190

"They've split up. Which way, Sheriff?'" Billy asked.

"South," Ed Burke said. "The rider going south is leaving a deeper track. He's carrying extra food and water. The other's headed for the Rez."

"You're right," Larribee pronounced. "Elmer you ride back to Rio Rosa and get a telegraph off to Ft Huachuca. Get them to seal the border. Matt, Luke, Henry, you boys follow the track west.... Just in case. When you find John Little Man arrest him.

The main body of the posse turned south. We tracked Jack for two days. He was using every ridge and arroyo in the Sonoran desert. On the third day, exhaustion, heat and hunger had worn the posse down. Then, Jack's trail turned due south. No deception; it was a race for the border. Larribee drove the posse onward. Jack was following Weber Creek. He would cross into Mexico just west of Naco right between Sheriff Shaw and the Army. Jack just might make it.

Three miles from the border, we found Jack's horse hobbling along the creek on a broken foreleg. Jack knew we were close. He left us the job of putting it down and giving away our position. It was all or nothing now, but Jack was afoot. Larribee shot the horse and we dashed ahead. We need not have hurried.

A half mile further on we found Sandbar Jack propped against a cottonwood. His shotgun was across his lap; his head on his chest. His breathing looked ragged and irregular, even from a distance. Jack didn't move as we approached. Remembering the jail, we all moved very slowly. I was the only one to get close. I made it to Jack's side and he still refused to move. Jack looked at me. His face was ashen; deep dark circles appeared under his sunken eyes. Jack dropped his head without a word. He was done for and he knew it.

"He's burning up with fever," I told the others.

I opened Jack's shirt. The path Larribee's bullet had taken across Jack's ribs was a raised, angry red. Sick yellow pus oozed from the wound with each ragged breath Jack took. It gave off a

191

God-awful stink. I turned to find Larribee looking over my shoulder.

"I'll be switched if that murdering bastard's going to die in bed. "Get a rope," Larribee ordered.

No one moved.

"By God, I said hang him and I mean hang him...*Right Now*!

"But, Sheriff....." was as far as Billy got with his protest. Larribee's gun was out.

"I'll kill the next man that doesn't jump when I give an order. Any takers?" Larribee asked. "Josh, Billy, get him up on a horse."

Instant compliance followed. Jack swayed in the saddle, but stayed upright. Larribee slipped the noose over Jack's head and cinched it down next to his ear.

"Sandbar Jack, you're guilty of murder. According to the laws of this territory you're sentenced to hang. Got any last words?" Larribee asked.

Jack's voice was hoarse and barely audible over his breathing.

"Yes, I do," Jack said. "Always search your prisoners and tie his hands before you hang him."

Jack's hand trembled, but his aim was true. The shot hit Larribee just below his collarbone and carried the sheriff from his horse. Jack's horse bolted and dropped him to the end of the rope. Jack's neck snapped leaving his body swinging from the branch in a declining arc. Sandbar Jack was dead.

Chapter 24

Larribee ordered us to leave Jack hanging there, but he was in no shape to enforce it. I cut Jack's body down and laid him across my horse. Josh and Billy fashioned a travois from some cottonwood branches and got Larribee onto it. I took the sheriff's horse and the posse headed for nearby Naco where hot meals and beds waited. Doc Brown rode in from Rio Rosa to tend to Larribee.

The posse stayed on in Naco for a couple of days until Tink was strong enough to sit a horse. He wasn't about to go home in the back of a wagon. I decide not to wait and took Jack's body back to Rio Rosa the next morning.

The Sheriff and posse made their triumphal entry to Rio Rosa a week after riding out. Everyone in town turned out to see the heroes. Tink Larribee made a speech that was sure to win him reelection. He congratulated the people of Rio Rosa for cleaning up the streets. The town needed a celebration and they got it. There were fireworks, dancing and a huge dinner on Main Street.

I missed a good deal of the party catching up on the work that had been piling up. I did manage a little time away. However, there would be one more customer to call on me.

Tink Larribee sat through the celebration in pain. He was unwilling to concede anything to Sandbar Jack, especially the opportunity to bask in the town's adoration. When the party ended Larribee walked home and headed for bed. Sara Larribee helped him out of his shirt. The bandages on Tink's chest were soaked with blood. Sara's tears could not move him to call for the doctor. He told her he would go see the doctor in the morning and that was final. It was an appointment he never kept. During the night the clot sealing his lung broke loose and Tink Larribee drowned in his own blood...the last victim of Sandbar Jack.

Chapter 25

Well, folks that's the story in a nutshell. There are a few gaps I want to fill in. I'm getting close to the end of the trail myself and I'm told confession is good for the soul. We'll see about that. Anyway, it couldn't hurt.

Sandbar Jack was a scoundrel. Tink Larribee was power hungry. That made them easy to play against each other. I never did go and see Aggie about those papers. I didn't need to; I'd already seen them. Aggie shared them with me while we shared her bed. Sandbar Jack left me everything and Aggie wanted to be on good terms with the new owner.

We offered Clara a share to help us usher Jack into early retirement. The unwitting Rev. Fellowes made it easy. Clara performed splendidly until she botched the fire at the Trails End and got spotted by Clyde. It was a good thing Aggie was right behind her coming out of the church.

Clara saw Aggie shoot Clyde and that meant she had to go. It was a shame. Even that didn't go quite as planned; Billy happened along before Clara died. I had to smother her before she could talk, but it worked out well. Jack was arrested and worked up enough to take out Fellowes and all the whiskey opposition. The Trails End went on in tribute to its notorious owner and business boomed again.

It was nice of Jack to work out that $50,000 bonus for me and shoot the witnesses to boot. Tink Larribee's death was a wonderful parting gift. It served him right for being sloppy.

Aggie was an excellent partner. She managed to get the most valuable information. Unfortunately, for Aggie, the only kind of partner to have in this business is a silent one--forever silent. There was no Billy to come along for Aggie.

I do regret what happened to John Little Man. He was the true innocent in Rio Rosa. He finally mended and I hired him to continue his Bisbee run.

All the killing revived my regular business. Thanks to Sandbar Jack and Tinker Larribee I embalmed and buried more bodies in a month than I did most years. Yep, 1888 was a *very* good year.

I hope there's enough CW Winters passed along in the family so my kids don't go getting all righteous on me. A man makes his own way in this world and God help those who get in the way. No one got hurt in Rio Rosa who didn't deserve everything he got. I like to think that includes old grandpa CJ. In one year I made a fortune and won the entire town of Rio Rosa.

The other reason I'm telling all this is because, from time to time, I've experienced a few weird goings on at the hotel. When Prohibition hit, I converted the Trails End into a hotel. It seems old Sandbar Jack is still hanging around. Don't worry, he won't hurt you. He thinks he can scare a Winters into letting the story out. If he does; he does. CJ Winters is only a sideshow. Sandbar Jack deserved to hang and hang he did.

Epilogue

Jay closed the book and slid it across the table to Seth Winters.

"Hell of a story. Is any of it true?" Jay asked.

"Far as I can tell…every word of it," Seth answered.

"But aren't you….well….uh…." Charli started.

"Ashamed of my family tree?" Seth supplied the words. "No, what's done is done. Nothing I can do about it now. CJ Winters inherited fair and square, even if he wasn't the man folks thought he was."

"But he murdered two women," Charli said.

"Yes he did, Missy. It only proves he wasn't the only one in those days willing to kill to get what he wanted."

"Your grandfather wanted the story kept in the family. Why let it out?" Jay asked.

"Because, Sandbar Jack still brings in the customers. I used to let anybody read the story. I had a kind of library here. Not many folks cared one way or the other so now I keep it for those Jack singles out. If I let him get the story out to whoever he wants, maybe he'll find peace. It hasn't happened yet; but who knows-- maybe someday.

"Wisdom is better than weapons of war: but one sinner destroyeth much good." Ecclesiastes 9: 18

Tokens of Perdition

A storm was brewing; coming up a cloud, as folks around the territory put it. The black mass building on the southwest horizon was a late confirmation of the message Will's knee had been sending him all day. Will shifted in the saddle. It eased the pain, if only temporarily. His back would protest if he sat twisted in the saddle too long. It was disheartening how much consideration he gave to his body these days. The thought brought a heavy sigh.

There wasn't a gray hair among the black ones under Will's hat--not yet. It would turn up sooner rather than later. He stopped looking in mirrors hoping to postpone the inevitable. The Chickasaws believed a man lived longer if he didn't remember how old he was. It sounded good in theory. Unfortunately, Will's joints were unbelievers whose chief delight was to remind him that his boyhood was gone long ago.

God, he hated getting old. He hated it for slipping up on him disguised as life; hated it for stealing from him bit by precious bit. But, most of all, Will hated getting old because he couldn't remember when it happened. He still thought young man thoughts and dreamed a young man's dreams. The charms of next hill; the next town; the next night under the stars still seduced him. How could he be old?

He didn't know how--or when. He did know that riding over the next hill or on to the next town was getting harder and harder to do. Everyday another part of him began complaining about the trip.

Will pulled makings from his vest and rolled a smoke. His hands worked the tobacco and paper with practiced ease. Without thought or effort, like magic, the cigarette appeared between his lips. Will cupped the match in his hands that somehow, somewhere, had grown old too. They had become his father's hands.

"But they still work," he said. A smile touched the corners of his mouth and lit his dark brown eyes.

There was more to his smile than the joy of dexterity. Will was fourteen days in the saddle. His mouth was as dry as last year's bird nest and relief was only about two miles away. Below him where the rock strewn hills gave onto a wide flat expanse was a town. It wasn't much to look at. The marvel was that it existed at all. No matter how you looked, it was an illegal settlement. The Red River was a good twenty miles further south. This was Indian land; Kiowa or Comanche, he wasn't sure which. Not that it mattered. He had been following the North Fork for a couple of days and found plenty of signs that both tribes were nearby.

Will wasn't overly worried about Indians. He was close to the trail that brought Texas beef north to Dodge. The Indians were apt to ignore a lone rider in the area as long as he kept moving. But, a town didn't make sense.

He could understand the Army turning a blind eye. The town had a pair of large stock tanks and a stable. Fresh water, beef and horses two days ride from Ft. Sill would be a welcome sight to tired troopers. What he couldn't understand is why the Indians tolerated the town's existence.

There was something else odd about this town. It wasn't built along the trail. It was laid out in a pair of concentric circles. He counted ten buildings in all; five per circle. The inner circle looked like shops. The building backed by a corral was definitely a livery. Will licked his parched lips. Lord willing one of the others was a saloon.

Except for the one at the south end of town, the outer circle was houses. His eyes couldn't get a good hold on far building. His eyes must be going too.

Will crushed out his smoke. He wanted a drink. Darn it all, he *needed* a drink. His knee was throbbing like a Comanche war drum. Still, he couldn't quite bring himself to top the hill and ride down. The southwest sky rumbled. He would have to decide soon.

"There's bound to be a saloon," he told himself. "Maybe there's a bed."

He'd settle for a saloon. The worst he could do was soft hay at the livery. Why was he just sitting here? Will rolled another cigarette. His hands were shaking.

"Ride around old man," the voice in his head warned. He'd grow old trusting that inner voice; not this time.

"Like hell I will," he said and nudged the dun over the crest of the hill.

The dusty corner of Indian Territory into which he rode was a land of extremes. Summer heat baked the red clay hard as brick. Come winter, the same ground was frozen under layers of ice and snow. Woven through the seasons were the storms. The wind was perennial as the grass.

The cattle, hindquarters to the storm, stood in the shelter of the island oaks that dotted the sea of short, coarse grass. The storm was going to be a big one. The scent of rain blew up the hill to meet him. Will drank it in letting it carry away the stagnant unease swirling inside him. Thunder rolled in the west. It was closer now-- much closer. The light was going. Behind him the sun hung between the growing wall of clouds and the jumbled piles of granite that passed for mountains in this country.

At the edge of town, the grass gave way to dust. Little red clouds danced around the mare's hooves and lingered in her wake. The advancing wall of rain was a miles away. Will reined in beside a battered shingle nailed to a solitary fence post. The name of the town was scratched in the weathered wood.

Perdition.

Will rolled the word around in his head. After a moment, the meaning came to him. Will shrugged and smiled. His Ma had been right all along. He *was* on the road to perdition.

There were no streets in Perdition only paths worn in the packed clay. The trail led straight to a canvas topped collection of old lumber. Large red letters painted with an unsteady hand advertised the structure as the Hell Hole Saloon. Will smiled and shook his head. He wondered if the people were as friendly and inviting as the names they chose. He decided he didn't care.

A combination blacksmith and livery flanked the saloon to the east. A trading post occupied the same spot on the west. Neither held any special interest. He wanted a drink. Staying dry had a certain allure too. The temptation to slip inside the saloon collided in Will's head with the practical reality. Walking to Texas because he left his tired, hungry horse in the street shoved beat a pair of immediate comforts. Will headed for the livery.

Five dollars to stable the mare overnight sounded like robbery, but Will decided against saying so. Sometimes it was best to go along or move along. Will paid up and slid off the saddle careful to keep his weight off his complaining knee. He brushed down the mare and forked hay into the stall rather than trust to the owner. A bucket of water finished up his duty. He lingered in the door to roll a smoke and watch the stable hand saunter to the saloon. The air was heavy with the smell of rain on thirsty grass. Sundown was a couple of hours away but the storm was spreading a blanket of early darkness over Perdition. Dust kicked up ahead of the storm turned the lightning a dull orange. In the flashes that lit the south end of town, Will could make out the building that eluded him from the hilltop. It was a seriously neglected church. The steeple was in shambles. The cross had fallen over and was hanging upside down. It looked like God must have pulled out of some time ago. Will shrugged off a chill and hobbled over to the saloon.

The Hell Hole's keeper had yet to light the lamps. The interior gloom matched the coming weather. Will rested a hand on the Colt tied to his hip while he waited for his eyes to adjust. The stench of unwashed humanity hit Will a second before the abrupt silence. Will, conscious of their eyes, touched the brim of his hat and walked up to the bar.

"Whiskey."

A tall, thin man in an apron streaked with several days work pulled a bottle from beneath the bar. He retrieved a glass and poured the whiskey. The man's dark weasel like eyes never left the stranger. Will tossed back his drink then let his eyes met those of the weasel. The man was measuring him like a tailor, but Will saw no emotion in the flat, black eyes. The bartender coughed; turned his head and spat on the floor.

"I'll take the bottle," Will dropped a dollar on the bar. Long boney fingers snatched up the treasure. "Is there someplace a man can find a bed around here?"

"Got a cot in back," the barkeep offered. A greedy glint flashed in his eye. "Cost you another dollar fer the night."

Will fished another dollar from his pocket. The coin brought a tobacco stained smile to his host's face.

"Where you headed stranger?" The barkeep asked.

"Lubbock." Will nodded at an empty table in the corner. "First, I need a nice quiet drink."

Will headed the table hoping the bartender and his friends got the message. A sandy haired man at the next table nodded a greeting as Will sat. The barkeep scurried from behind the bar suddenly aware the lamps need lighting. He made sure to light the stranger's lamp first.

"Mighty fer piece. Got family there?" the bartender asked.

"Nope, just a bunch of cow's needin' company on their way to Dodge."

The bartender opened his mouth to say more.

"Leave the man alone, Josh," the sandy haired man said.

"I was just…"

"I know what you was just," the man said and shooed away the pesky barkeep. "Now, finish lighting the lamps."

Will offered the man a wave of silent thanks.

"Josh ain't the sharpest tool in the shed." The man returned to his drink.

Will did the same. The whiskey was vintage army rotgut; but it would serve. A second shot transformed the throbbing in his knee into to a dull ache. A warm glow spread through his middle. Will let himself relax.

Outside, the sky outside came unraveled. A sizzling crack stood Will's hair on end. It was followed by a deafening roar. A few heavy patters played a warning on the canvas roof just before the sky opened up. Wind whipped sheets of rain slapped the bar and snapped the wet canvas like a bullwhip. None of the bar's regular patrons seemed to share Will's concern that the roof might come loose from its moorings. They went on drinking and playing cards. Will tried to do the same. He poured another drink. This one, he sipped. It wouldn't do to be too far gone in a strange place.

Will understood the sidelong looks in his direction and the averted glances. That was natural enough; they were sizing up the stranger. Small town folks were a suspicious lot on a good day. From the looks of Perdition good days were few and far between. It was the nervous glances the men gave one another and their constant checking the door that troubled Will.

Except for the sandy haired man at the next table, the men in the Hell Hole shared a hollow-eyed look and cowering manners of a pack of hungry coyotes. Like varmints, alone they were probably harmless enough. But together, well, that was a different story; even coyotes could get vicious. Whatever the case might be, Will felt there was more going on than just looking the stranger over. Uncertainty dug a ragged barb into Will's nerves. Without thinking, he adopted their habit of checking the door.

Will Bannister wasn't one to run from trouble. He also wasn't in the habit of seeking it out. Perdition smelled like trouble. No one had done more than glance at him, but the air was heavy with tension. Something was building. It was not too late to ride out. His knee had quit shouting and wet was better than dead.

"Whoa." Will dug in his heels and hauled back on the reins of his runaway imagination. *"They aren't even armed."*

The thought was small comfort. Armed or not, they still out numbered him nine to one. He had six shots to improve the odds, but was it enough? Maybe was the best he could do.

The conversation he picked up was the usual talk; breeding stock and next year's calves. However, it lacked the good natured joking and heated opinions of cattlemen's banter. He'd heard livelier conversations in a St. Louis funeral parlor.

Suddenly, Will's mind registered something his eyes had been trying to tell him since he sat down.

"How could you be so stupid?" Will kicked himself.

The card players on the other side of the room were only going through the motions. There was no money on the table.

His hackles were up. Perhaps his worries about growing old were a bit premature. Will raised the glass to his lips and pretended to drink. He didn't know what he had ridden into, but he was certain of one thing; it was already too late to ride out. If he tried to leave in this downpour, he'd spook them. Once the storm eased up, he could make up an excuse and ride out. Meanwhile, he'd sit tight; nurse his drink and wait for them to make the first move.

He didn't have long to wait. The sandy haired man got to his feet and headed in Will's direction. Will's hand slid off the table. He eased the Colt free. The man appeared unarmed, but that didn't seem to matter anymore.

"Mind if I join you?" The man's lips trembled trying to hold his smile in place.

"He's scared," Will thought. He nodded for the man to sit.

One of the card players, a round man in a tall beaver hat, started to say something to Will's guest. The other players shook their heads and beaver hat returned to the phony game.

"Your friends don't approve." Will pointed at the card players.

"No, probably not. We're an unhappy lot here in Perdition."

"That kind of makes sense." Will chuckled at his own joke.

"What? Oh yes, unhappy in perdition, I get it." There was no humor in his voice. The sandy haired man held out his hand. "Drake, Drake Mather."

"Will Bannister. So, what makes folks in Perdition unhappy?"

"They can't get out."

Will started to laugh; saw the lost expression on Mather's face; and caught himself. The notion of being trapped on the open prairie stuck Will as nonsense. There was no doubt, Mather was serious. The stormed seemed to agree with the sandy haired man. The sky streamed tears down the canvas roof while wind moaned around the walls in sympathy.

"Why not?" Will whispered.

"Doesn't matter; not to us." Mather moved closer; his voice barely audible over the wind and rain. "You can still get away."

The hair on Will's neck stood on end. A chill ran down his back. When would he learn to trust his gut?

"I didn't want to risk leaving in this storm," Will confessed.

"Believe me, the storm outside is nothing compared to what goes on in here."

"I don't understand," Will said. "Just what is going on in here?"

"You don't have to understand; just get out." Drake's eyes snapped to the card game and back. "Go now."

It was more prayer than demand. Will was grateful for the warning, but he wouldn't turn tail and run now. They'd all know he had been scared off. What was worse, he'd know it too. He didn't think he could live with that. Mather seemed to read his mind.

"You're a prideful man, Will Bannister." Sorrow filled Drake's eyes. "Pride goeth before destruction, and an haughty spirit before a fall."

Drake's fear was palpable. A small gold cross slipped from his trembling fingers. Will leaned closer.

"Are you some kind of preacher?"

"It doesn't matter." Drake gathered the cross back into his hands. "This place is evil."

"I've heard that before."

"I'm sure you have. For once in your life believe it." Drake laid a hand on Will's. "I can help."

Mather's weakness turned Will's stomach and stiffened his neck.

"How? You can't even help yourself."

The words hit Mather like a fist in the gut. The spark went out of him and a single tear leaked from the corner of his eye.

"You'll be one of them by sun up," Mather whispered and went back to his table.

The storm was over as quickly as it began. All that remained was an occasional flurry of raindrops on the roof. The calm that followed stayed outside. Inside the bar Drake Mather sat at his table his face buried in trembling hands. Josh, the bartender was pacing in a clumsy attempt to appear busy. The card players abandoned all pretense of their game and sat staring at the door. Perdition held its breath.

The whiskey soured in Will's gut sour. But, his mind was made up. He would not be run out. One at a time or all together this bunch couldn't stampede him. He eased the Colt to his lap. The image of a St. Louis funeral home was back brighter than ever. So be it. Pine boxes for everyone.

"It'll be soon." The thought had scarcely formed when Josh gave up pacing. He stood in the doorway and pretended to watch the sky.

"Storm's over," Josh announced. "Guess you'll be wanting that cot now, eh mister?"

Will Bannister was the least curious of all God's creatures. He wasn't a builder or a pioneer; he was a drifter. When things weren't to his liking, Will shrugged his shoulders and rode on. The old cat killer usually left him alone. This time he had to know what the rats were hiding.

"I want to know what's going on," Will demanded.

"Whaddya mean?" Josh asked.

"Y'all are skittish as a bunch of yearlings. What's coming through that door you keep watching?"

The round man in the beaver hat left the card game and joined Will at his table.

"Name's Mort McCall." He gave Will a conspiratorial wink. "What's coming through that door is a couple hundred pounds of mean named Eli Warner. Eli's used up a lot of good men. It might be better if you weren't here."

"Mister, Eli and his mama run this town," Josh added. "You might say they own it."

"They can have it," Will said.

"That much is certain stranger." A hungry grin grew on Mort's face. "We was just giving you fair warning. Eli's trouble-- more trouble than you know. He's evil; quick with a gun; and he don't like strangers in his town. Especially strangers who might buck when he says jump."

"Looks to me like he's already got plenty of frogs." Will glanced around the room.

"Don't matter to Eli. He's gonna try you. One way or the other you'll jump. When you do--you'll lose."

Drake was back at the table. "Ride out while you can. It's easier all around."

A hulk of a man with blacksmith's arms and a leather faced codger in a faded slouch hat joined the table. There was more of pleading than pressure in their eyes.

"How about it, mister?" the blacksmith asked.

"I came in for a drink," Will assured them. "I don't aim to cause trouble."

"Then, we're all agreed," leather face announced. "Tell you what, stranger, you get outta sight before Eli gets here and the bunk and the bottle are on me."

The old codger slid two dollars towards Will. His hand trembled as he did.   "Keep it." Will pushed the money away. "I pay my own way. I make my own way too. I'll ride out, but I ain't hiding and I ain't running. Your friend Eli has as much to say about what happens here as me."

"Eli ain't our friend," the big man whispered.

"Then what is he?" Will looked around the table.

"He's the devil," Mort said. "And if he finds you here and we'll catch hell. Help us out. Help yourself too."

"What's the matter with you men? How long do you plan to let Eli push you?" Will returned the Colt into his holster.

"That kind of talk will get you killed," Drake warned.

"You let us worry about Eli," Mort said.

"Start worrying boys," a voice from the door warned.

There was an audible intake of breath. In the silence that followed, Will could hear the old codger's shallow wheezing. Sweat trickled from the blacksmith's temples and ran down his cheek. A glass slipped from Josh's hand clattered on the floor and rolled to a stop against a spittoon. Twelve open-jawed men stared at the door. A pimpled faced kid, guns slung low on both hips, stared back.

Eli Warner might be a kid, but he was six feet and two hundred pounds of kid. His eyes had the flint of age. Oily strands of black hair escaped his hat lay plastered against the dark skin.

There was something in the boy's face; could be Comanche; not that it mattered.

"What's yer hurry stranger?" Eli asked.

"No hurry." Will settled back into his chair.

"Good." Eli smiled at Will. "Stay and have another drink with us. The evening's just gettin' started."

"Evening Eli," came the chorus from the barroom.

Will's companions abandoned him. There was a small stampede as they hurried back to their usual places. Eli's smile reminded Will of a dog baring its teeth. He was clearly pleased by their fear. Eli studied each face; making sure each man's gaze crumbled to the floor. Even the burly blacksmith trembled under the kid's stare.

"What are they so afraid of?" Will wondered. *"He's nothing but a big kid."*

"Drake, it's time for confession." Eli pulled a pair of chairs into the center of the room. "Sit down preacher, and hear everyone's confession. I want the stranger here to know who he's dealing with."

"Honest Eli, we ain't..." Mort started.

Eli delivered a stinging backhand that sent blood flying from the round man's lips.

"You shut up." Eli waved a gun at Mather. "C'mon Drake, take a seat and shame your daddy."

Drake Mather rose slowly from his seat. His knees buckled threatening to drop him back in his seat. Blanched knuckles wrapped around the gold crucifix, the preacher walked toward his appointed place. The man was trembling so hard he could barely walk.

"Move it," Eli shouted.

He punctuated the demand by shooting Mather in the foot. Drake screamed in pain and went down. Nobody moved. Drake struggled to regain his feet. The sight of blood dripping from his boot mollified Eli for the moment. Eli gave Will his best say-something-I-dare-you look as Drake hobbled to his chair.

The challenge was lost on Will. These men said they would take care of Eli--well, let them. He had nothing to say. There was nothing was going on here that hadn't happened before. It would go on happening after he rode on. It wasn't his fight. Will leaned back to take in the show. Drake's whispered warning played inside his head.

"You'll be one of them before sun up."

Eli took center stage. His eyes danced with anticipation. The pleasure he took from his power over these men couldn't compare to the thrill he got from putting it on display.

"Who'll be first?" Eli looked at the heads hung in silence. "Mort, you had something to say. Step right up here."

Mort's hands and feet shook as badly as Drake's had. His eyes searched in vain for help that wasn't coming. He didn't repeat Drake's mistake. He hurried to his seat and sat, head bowed, beside the preacher.

"Forgive me for I have sinned," Mort began the litany. He looked up at Eli tears flowing down chubby cheeks. "Please Eli, tell me what to say."

"Why, Mort," Eli voice was sugar coated cyanide. "You know how this works. Confession's good for the soul. You tell your old friend, Eli, what you told the stranger."

"I...I..." Mort stammered.

Eli rested the barrel of his pistol against Mort's ear. He thumbed the hammer back. The loud click brought a whimper from the reluctant repentant. Drake shielded his face to ward off the coming splatter.

"He's gonna do it," Will thought.

"He didn't say nothing." The words were out before Will could stop them.

Mort and Drake's eyes grew wide at the interruption. Eli turned on the newcomer, eyes narrowed to slits, his lips drawn back like a dog bereft of his favorite bone. Eli holstered his gun and slammed both fists on Will's table.

"*What* did you say?" Eli hissed.

Will eased his chair back to the floor and leaned forward. Noses not more than a foot apart, the two men measured one another. The certainty of the young was in Eli's eyes. Eli didn't fear death--he didn't even consider it a possibility.

Will knew better. He didn't want to kill the kid, but he had anted up and now he was in the game. It wasn't his business if these men were willing to let Eli push them. It sure wasn't his fight, but the price of riding out Perdition peacefully just went up. Will had to call or fold.

"We were passin' the time of day; that's all." Will let his eyes drop.

Eli was enjoying himself. He turned to be sure his town saw the stranger blink first. When he looked back at Will, Eli's savage smile said it was not going to be that easy.

"Not in my town you don't. I say what passes for the time of day around here. They all know it. You're about to learn it too, mister."

"I won't be staying that long," Will said.

"You ain't going no where till I say so." Eli was back in Will's face. "You've been meddling. I think it's time you 'fess up. Maybe, then I'll let you go."

So there it was. Join the rest of the sniveling pack at Eli's feet or fight. Drake's warning echoed through Will's head a third time. His didn't believe he'd get to wait for sun up to decide. A stone like cold rose up in Will's face and steeled his hands. It was his pot now. He wasn't folding.

"Like I said, we was just passin' the time of day," Will answered.

"Is that so?" While you was passin' the time of day..." Eli pointed at the men in the impromptu confessional. "Did they tell you what happened to the last gun they hired?"

"Musta slipped their minds," Will sipped his whiskey. "Why don't you tell it."

The men in the room jumped like they'd been slapped. They melted into neutral corners. Eli let them go. He cocked his head and smiled at Will.

Eli squared his shoulders; hooked his right thumb in his belt and let his fingers lay loose on the grip of his pistol.

"He crawled outta here trailing his guts between his legs. The buzzards ate most of them before he died."

A hint of smile touched Will's lips. He took a slow sip of whiskey. He'd seen the kid draw. Eli was fast all right. He was also hot-headed enough to be his own undoing. He just needed a push.

"You think that's funny, Mister?" Eli snapped.

Will ignored him; choosing to concentrate on another sip.

"I asked you a question," Eli screamed.

"You got it all wrong, boy." Will pushed the bottle aside. "I'm just passin' through."

"Don't call me boy." Eli eyes narrowed into black slits.

Will shifted in his seat. "Who's backing your play in this little town?"

"I don't need no one to back me." Eli's voice jumped up the scale.

Will poured a drink; tipped his glass to Eli and tossed it back. "If you say so."

"You're a liar, mister," Eli snarled.

It was marginally true, but Will didn't like it. He bit his bottom lip and tasted salty copper. He let go of the insult and poured another drink.

Eli drew himself up a little taller. It was time to remind Perdition not to buck Eli Warner. The warped floor squeaked under Eli's boots as he took a half step back from the table.

Will sighed. He couldn't say he wasn't warned.

"I said, you're a liar." Eli's hands clenched into tight fists; relaxed; clenched again.

Will's fingertips brushed the grip of his Colt. The boy's pent up rage pushed his breathing faster.

"So you say." Will tried once more to give Eli an out.

"Dang right I do. Your a liar *and* a coward."

Will stood. Men scrambled to get out of the line of fire and cowered with their companions. No one fled the bar.

"They want to see somebody killed." Flashed across Will's mind.

"You've got a lot to learn, boy," Will cautioned. "Like how to tell a bull from a steer."

"You aim to teach me?"

"Not tonight. I'm going to bed." Will stepped towards the bar.

Eli got his first clear view of the Colt tied on Will's leg. The kid blinked; a tiny tremor touched his hands and was gone. Eli took a step back, but held Will's gaze.

"Goodnight folks," Will told the bystanders. "Which way is that cot barkeep?"

Josh looked at Eli, then back at Will. Neither seemed to notice the trembling bartender.

"Right out back." Josh raised a boney finger to point the way.

Will nodded; picked up his bottle and side-stepped from the table.

"Hold it right there," Eli growled.

Will stopped. He blew out a deep breath. He'd given it a good try.

"I didn't say you could go," Eli told him.

"Boy, you ain't got the sense God give a goose." Will's voice was flat--dead.

Eli didn't notice. His hands hovered above his weapons.

"These folks dance to your tune because they're scared," Will said. "I don't know why, but I'd bet good money it ain't you that's got 'em scared."

"You're about to find out mister."

"I ain't much of a dancer," Will warned. "Let it go while you still can. I give you a wide trail, but you've reached the end of it."

Will stepped towards the bar. Eli's hands dove for his guns. Thunder rolled through the bar. Fire and blue smoke filled the air. Before Eli could touch the grips, the back of his head jumped across the room chased by a sea of blood and gore. Life drained from Eli's face. His shocked expression collapsed in on itself. Eli fell to the floor.

The wide-eyed citizens of Perdition crawled from cover to huddle over the dead man. No one spoke. They were transfixed by the blood pooling under Eli's head. When the red trail staining the rough plank floor oozed towards the stunned blacksmith, the big man jumped away as if it were deadly poison. Will smelled the terror rolling off them.

Outside, the wind changed direction. A cold draft filled with the musty odor of old bones rode in to mingle with the scent of gun powder, and blood. The smell seemed to take on a life of its own that hovered over the dead man. The preacher fell to his knees and pounded the floor.

"No, no, no, not again," he pleaded.

"What did you expect?" Mort said.

Some of the men began to cry. Silent tears ran down Josh's cheeks.

"What's the matter with you?" Will shouted.

"What's the matter with *us*?" Mort said. "With us? We ain't gunned down a man in cold blood."

"Cold blood?" Will was incredulous. "He drew on me."

"So?" Mort replied.

"What do you mean...so?"

212

"You're a professional gun. You wanted him to go for his gun. You forced him to draw."

"You're all crazy," Will protested.

"Why'd you do it, mister?" The blacksmith, unable to take his eyes off the blood, shook his head. "Poor Eli, he never had a chance."

"What'll we tell his mama?" Josh asked.

"Oh God," Drake moaned.

"It's murder, that's what it is." Mort pointed at Will. The others murmured assent.

"Are you blind as well as stupid?" Will backed away from the pack.

Josh slid slowly towards the bar. Mort stepped away from the body to block the door. The blacksmith shuffled to Will's right. The circle was closing. Josh reached for the shot gun he kept under the bar. Will let the whiskey fly. The bottle connected in an explosion of blood and glass. Josh howled in pain. Mort reached for the peppermill in his coat pocket. Then let the little pistol rattle to the floor. Will's Colt was an inch from Mort's nose.

"Everybody stay put or old Mort here is gonna die," Will said. "You want to die tonight, Mort?"

Mort shook his head.

"Good." Will stepped around Mort putting the round man between him and the others. "Now, tell your friend to come out from behind that bar--without the gun."

"You heard him Josh."

The barkeep crept from his hiding place. Blood streamed through Josh's fingers and fell from his elbow. Big drops of dark blood hit the floor with a plop and a small puff of dust. Will motioned for all the others to join Josh at the bar.

"Everyone on the floor." Will nodded at the blacksmith. "You, get my horse."

The big man rushed to do as he was told. The others sunk to the floor. Will pushed Mort to the doorway the muzzle of his Colt pressed just below Mort's left ear.

"Tell me something," Will said. "The preacher said, 'not again.' Do y'all make a habit of blindsiding strangers?"

Silence; not an eye looked up. Will pressed the Colt into Mort's neck.

"Yeah." Mort nodded.

"Why?"

"You'll find out soon enough."

The blacksmith returned with Will's horse. Will had the big man put his weight in the stirrups to show it was cinched before he backed Mort out of the saloon. The men in the bar followed as far as the door. Will pushed Mort in their direction and swung up into the saddle.

"Wait," Mort said.

Will's hand stayed on the Colt. But there was no fight left in these men. Mort looked at Will; a sadness consumed the round man's face. The man's play for Will had been as phony as his card playing.

"You want to know why?" Mort asked.

"I want to know why you're still so afraid of that kid?"

"Cause this ain't over," Mort told him. "Didn't you wonder what this town's doing out here? Didn't you wonder about the Indians?"

"The thought crossed my mind," Will admitted.

"We were waiting for you," the blacksmith said.

"What?"

"Not you exactly; just someone like you," Josh explained.

"Someone with a quick gun and too much pride to move on," Mort added.

"You're all crazy," Will said.

"We'll see who's crazy come sun up."

"Drake what are they talking about?" Will asked.

214

"I tried to warn you," Drake said. "You killed her son. She'll come after you."

"She? She--who?"

"The witch," Josh said. "You're hers now."

"This is nonsense," Will protested.

"You don't understand," Drake said. "She'll..."

"Shut up Preacher," Mort ordered.

"She'll come after you." Drake warned. "Maybe there's still time. Hurry..."

Mort silenced the preacher with a solid right hook.

"You'll find that out soon enough," Mort told Will.

Will had heard enough. He swung into the saddle and spurred the mare south. The little knot of men stood in front of the saloon watching him ride away. Will didn't believe anyone would follow, but he was done taking chances. He cut west across the open grassland until he struck the North Fork near Otter Creek. He forded the river a few miles downstream and pulled up behind the bank to watch his back trail. Satisfied no one followed him, he let the horse pick its way along the river for another couple of miles.

Will decided to make camp in a stand of cottonwoods where the river cut a slow series of "S" turns through a sandy bottom. The banks here were high enough to hold the rain swell. Will's knee was shouting again. He shouldn't have thrown the bottle at that worthless bartender. He wished he'd ridden around Perdition altogether.

"If wishes was gold we'd all be rich," he recited.

His father was to thank for that precious nugget. The old man had an endless supply; each one meant to illuminate the boy's shortcomings. Will's father, ten years in the grave, was still able to put a spur in his son's flanks. Now, Will was the old man, but there was no son to receive the Bannister wisdom. Will pushed the thought aside. He was too tired to think about that now.

Will found a few branches dry enough to build a fire. He was dog tired and could have done without a fire, but he didn't think sleep would come anytime soon. He spread his bedroll and busied himself staring into the flames and watching the stars. The late rising moon escaped the tattered clouds turning the grass into a sea of silver. Rings of moonlight danced on the water where hungry mosquitoes and the fish that found the insects so delectable touched the surface. Will was not the only one unable to sleep. A nearby bullfrog called to his neighbor. Crickets and cicadas serenaded winsome maidens with their songs. The sharp cry of coyotes running off the opposite bank floated back to him on the breeze.

The river was on the rise. Come daylight it would be dangerous, but for now, the water flowing through the darkness was soothing. Will tried to focus on the familiar sounds of the night and the parade of stars. He wanted his world back. The world free from haunted by visions of Perdition and tales of witches.

He'd tried, blast it all. He tried to walk away. He tried a darn sight harder than he was accustomed to doing; that's for sure. It was the kid's fault. The kid forced him into a fight.

"Did he?" His conscious asked. *"Did he really?"*

It was true, he goaded the kid. He got the kid all worked up. He could have walked away. He should have walked away. Was his pride so precious? Drake Mather was right; he was prideful. They were all right; Eli was just a kid.

"A kid with a gun," he said aloud.

In the end that's all that mattered. Eli had a gun. He shot Drake and he would have shot Will too. Just how many unsuspecting strangers had Eli killed?

"Would you feel better if you were dead?" Will asked himself.

That question was answered the moment Eli reached for his guns. It was that simple. Will could live with simple. His eyelids drew down. Will slept.

The men of Perdition watched Will ride away. There was no need to pursue him. Bannister would be back tomorrow. He would be one of them. In Perdition patience wasn't a virtue, it was fact of life.

"One last round?" Josh asked.

"Why not?" Mort turned to Drake. "Care to join us preacher?"

"No. I think not."

"Suit yourself." Mort shrugged and led the others back into the Hell Hole.

A trace of gunpowder still lingered in the air. Mac, the oldest man in Perdition, leaned over Eli's body as if seeing it for the first time.

"Hoo-wee," he hooted, "that Bannister was fast as lightning. Got him square between the eyes too."

"You want we should take him over to the church?" The blacksmith joined Mac's inspection of the body.

"You two are going to wait for the rest of us," Mort said. "Now, get over here."

The steeple with its fallen cross cast a long shadow over the preacher. Drake once dared dream of escaping Perdition. He had grown up since then. Dreams were only a disguise worn by despair, in his case, an endless, torment of despair. These days he no longer dreamed at all.

"Vanity of vanities, saith the Preacher, vanity of vanities; all is vanity." Drake jumped at the sound of his own voice.

Drake shivered. Quoting the Bible made him sound too much like his father. He didn't need that; not now. Color rose in his in his face; Drake wound up and threw the stone he was holding. It felt good to let it fly. The stone hooked sharply right. Ten yards away the stone stopped in mid air and fell to the ground. Drake's heart fell with it.

"None of them is lost, but the son of perdition," he quoted; sighed and climbed the steps into the church.

Drake lit a candle. The flame pushed the darkness back a few feet. It was enough. Drake knew every broken, overturned pew and every loose board in the decaying floor. He knew exactly how many steps from the door to the altar. Most important of all, no matter what his eyes told him, Drake knew he was not alone.

"Mandrake Mather, son of Cotton," a seductive stirring of the air breathed the words into his ear.

He knew the voice; knew it was coming. He started anyway. Feminine laughter floated from everywhere and nowhere at the same moment. A breath sent dust swirling above the altar. The whirlwind glowed with emerald phosphorescence. She was as beautiful as the first day he saw her. She smiled at the want kindled in his eyes.

"You've been hiding from me," she teased. Long, smooth fingers caressed his cheek.

"You lie when the truth is so easy," he said.

"And you love to have it so." Her kiss brushed his lips.

Drake pulled away. "It's not love that binds us together."

"No, it's something more elemental." She molded her body to his. "Isn't it?"

Her embrace was heaven and hell. God help him, he wanted her.

"I want you to let him go," Drake said.

This time it was she who pushed away. "You know that's impossible."

"We could begin again," he pleaded.

"Are you..." she cocked her head letting candle light play in her hair..."jealous?"

"Yes."

"*I* maybe a liar, my dear, but at least *"I'm"* good at it."

"I won't let you go." Drake moved to block the door.

She threw back her head letting laughter, black and cold as the Styx, wash over her. Drake recoiled from the sound. His revulsion pleased her all the more.

"As if *you* could stop me." Long nails raked fire into his eyes.

On the dark banks of the river, Will Bannister dreamed.

The river was no more. Will rode a black horse through a burned wasteland; the charred ground littered with glowing embers. Tendrils of acrid smoke burned his eyes and hot air scorched his lungs with every breath. Will's parched tongue touched his cracked lips. He tasted of smoke. The canteen hung from the saddle made a hollow clink.

His mother once told him of a rich man in hell asking for a drop of water from the finger of Lazarus. Was this hell? He didn't think so, but he wanted that drop of water more than life. Will closed his eyes against the sting of smoke and let the horse have its head. Pain ripped his right shoulder. Something thick and hot ran down his arm. Will forced his eyes open. Barren, twisted trees had closed in along the trail. Their sharp branches raked his arms. Smoking skeletons of briars rose up to bite at his legs. Trapped on the narrow trail, Will clung to the saddle. His life was seeping from his wounded arms and legs. Will's eyes grew heavy. When they closed, he would fall into the smoking dust and never get up--so be it.

Will gathered handfuls of the horse's mane; bent low on the animal's neck and dug in his spurs. The horse bolted. Whether he hung on for minutes or hours Will would go out fighting. Then, he *was* falling.

Will felt the ground at his back. It was hard, but cool. He tried his eyes. They were assaulted by a burst of bright light. He could hear the river; feel the grass. He blinked and there was the Oklahoma sun. He was alive. He smelled...

Coffee.

He wasn't alone. The outline of a woman eclipsed the morning sun. He could not make out her features or see any weapons, but the scent of coffee suggested he was in no immediate danger.

"You don't look like a hired gun," the woman said.

"You don't look like a witch. Guess you can't believe everything you hear in Perdition." Will propped himself up an elbow.

She was a far cry from what he expected. She was young; far too young to be Eli's mother. Her seamless face was the color of the hills. A sea of raven hair washed over her bare shoulders and the blanket she held closed at her breast. Her wide mouth framed by soft pink lips opened into an easy smile. Her eyes were pale as river ice. Her beauty had somehow become twisted in the son.

"Are you telling me you didn't kill my Eli?" she asked.

"I'm telling you he drew first. He gave me no choice."

She held her right hand toward him. While Will wondered if it was a peace offering, her hand snapped into a white knuckled fist. Iron bands clamped on Will's throat. He gasped and fought the unseen strangle hold trying to suck in enough air to stay alive. He was losing badly. His face turned blue; his vision red; then, everything went black.

When Will came to, she was smiling at him. Her hands were folded together in her lap, but otherwise she had not moved.

"I wanted to kill you," she admitted. "It would have been easy. Do you believe me?"

Will nodded. He didn't trust his voice. Her eyes on his, she rose to her feet and stepped towards him. Will's world began to swim. He rubbed his eyes to clear his vision. She came to him through a swirling fog and dropped to her knees. Her face was inches from his. Her eyes were the same icy blue. The change that had spread over the rest of her sent shivers down Will's spine. Her hair, streaked with lightning bolts of silver, floated around her head on a wind that wasn't blowing. Her flesh was withered like an apple left in the summer sun. Will recoiled. His head hit the ground sending a shower of light through his eyes. The rotten tide that ebbed and flowed between her blackened teeth made his empty stomach lurch. He rolled; tried to find his feet, but they were hopelessly tangled. She followed him, her face pressed to his cheek.

"You took my Eli, but I took him back." Her scaly hand caressed his cheek.

"What...?" Will gagged.

She pulled away. Able to breathe again, Will drew in a deep breath that caught in his throat. Over a tattered black dress she wore an apron yellowed with age. The apron was tied below her breast and stretched over her impossibly pregnant belly. She patted her swollen middle.

"He gets stronger every time." Her mouth twisted into a mocking smile. The christening is on Sunday. I think we'll name him Eli."

The words hit Will like a hammer. It wasn't real. He was still dreaming. He had to be dreaming. Will jumped to his feet. His breeches twisted tight around his ankles; he stumbled and nearly went down. Cackling laughter accompanied his frenzied attempts to get his pants up.

"What did you do?"

"Why, nothing you ain't done before."

Her laughter was back; fueled by Will's red-faced embarrassment. She caught the drift of his eyes despite her levity. Her laughter faded. Her smile vanished.

"You want the gun, do you?" She held out a welcoming hand. "Go ahead."

Will snatched up the gun belt. The Colt was dead center on her chest in an instant. She nodded at him and her smile reappeared. Will's arm shook; his muscles strained and cramped, but neither his finger nor the trigger moved. He let the gun fall. His heart sank along with it.

"Come," she ordered and started for his horse.

Will stood his ground. He wasn't one of her townie lap dogs. He didn't take orders from anybody. She didn't seem to notice. She reached the horse and turned to find herself alone. Cold fire blazed in her eyes. Will could see it even at a distance. Her hand reached for him and slowly began to tighten. As it did, the breath was squeezed from him. His vision narrowed; consciousness was fleeing. Will pushed his right foot forward. The grip on his throat tightened. His left foot slid to join his right. The crushing stopped. Another step and he could breathe again.

"You'll be one of us by sun up," Mort's voice filled his thoughts.

"Ain't gonna happen," Will promised.

He wasn't sure how he'd keep that promise, but saying it seemed to help.

"I don't repeat orders." She threw a bony leg over the saddle. "Dead or alive, you'll do what I say. You can walk back to Perdition. It'll give you some time to think it over."

"It's kind of hard to make a dead man obey," Will told her.

"Not as hard as you might think." She smiled at his innocence.

Will sat in the shade of a tall cottonwood and watched her ride away. He drew a bead on the witch's back. A moment later, he lowered the gun. In the distance she raised an arm and waved.

"How did she know?" he whispered.

He plucked the Colt from his holster and blew the limb off a nearby tree. Everything worked. Why couldn't he pull the trigger on her? He had never shot a woman, but in his mind, she hardly qualified. What kind of hold did she have him?

It was twenty miles along the fork to the Red River. He could shave a few miles going cross country. How many miles after that to find a horse? God only knew. On the other hand, it was shy of ten miles back to Perdition. But distance had nothing to do with his decision. No one, man, woman, or witch took his horse from him. He was too old to change that now.

"Too old and too proud," his conscious told him.

"That too," he said.

Will set out to reclaim his horse and a measure of dignity. He didn't have a clue how to get the job done, but he knew where to start and, as she said, he had all day to think about it. The first thing he had to do was get across the river. It wasn't called the Red for no reason. It's muddy waters carried the clay of Indian territory south during the rains. Once it got settled down in Texas, the wind blew it all back again. The river was never more true to its name than after a storm--or more dangerous. It wasn't bank full, but it was a darn sight deeper than it had been the night before.

The river was wider here than in most spots; shallower too. The witch had crossed easily enough, but he wondered how much he could trust that. Not much, he decided and found a stout branch to feel for the bottom. There was a sandbar where he crossed last night; he set out to find it. He followed his tracks back to the spot and started across. driving the branch into the sandy bottom helped to steady his steps. The current wasn't as swift here as in a lot of places, but it was dangerous enough to make him cautious.

Will leaned on his branch using it as a lever to pry his feet from the muddy jaws of the river bottom. As soon as a foot came free, the waist deep water threatened to sweep him downstream with the rest of the debris. The temperature had climbed into nineties and taken the humidity along with it. A fine sheen of sweat covered Will's chest and ran from his hair to sting his eyes. The chilly run off made laboring with the current almost bearable.

The current took advantage of the deeper water near the east bank to push him farther downstream with each step. Will drove the branch into the mud and hung on trying to catch his breath. He was almost across; only another ten steps to safety. He yanked the branch free; swung it to the right and dove it into the bottom. He pulled his feet free and sidled sideways. A loud crack sent his pulse thundering. A few yards upstream a monster cottonwood left its moorings and headed straight for him.

The race was on.

Will stepped and poled with all his might. The runaway tree took aim and tumbled after him. Will was losing and he knew it. His eyes swept the bank for help. An exposed root six feet behind him offered a slim chance. If he could catch it, if it held his weight, if...if...if, Will worked through one more step and dove for the bank.

His hands found purchase; the root held. He was half way out of the water when the tree hit him in the chest. Pain screamed down his left side. Will's head went under. His weight slammed against his grip. The current did the rest. His left hand broke free and Will tumbled in pursuit of the fallen tree. Muddy water washed his nostrils with fire. He gagged and sucked water. Will's head broke the surface on the next tumble. He stole a breath of air in time to catch a glimpse of the tree trunk wedging itself between the bank and a large rock. Unable to stop himself, Will crashed into the stalled tree trunk. Water and air exploded from his lungs. He hooked an arm around the tree trying desperately to stay above water, but the current was taking him under again. Will's feet hit bottom. He took advantage of the contact to push upward with all his strength. His body flew out of the water far draping him over the tree. Will clung to his precarious perch gasping for air.

When a measure of breath and strength returned, Will inched along the tree toward solid ground. He prayed the tree would hold long enough for him to reach the bank where his pack rested in a crooked mesquite limb. Maybe, this once, God was listening. Will collapsed on the grass; every breath hurt. A blue-black patch under his left arm told him two, maybe three, ribs were broken.

The sun passed noon before he could coax his body to move. The three hour walk back to Perdition took six. In that the witch, or whatever she was, was right about him having time to think. The trouble was that thinking had never been Will Bannister's strong suit. He was a good hand with a gun, a fact he kept quiet. He knew cattle. He'd survived two years riding with General Forrest. Through it all, his thoughts were as concrete as his stubborn streak. He was always better charging straight ahead, but none of those things had worked very well so far.

"The boy learns slow, but he learns good," his Pa always said.

The less than flattering assessment was close enough to true. Who knew the apple's resting place better than the tree? James Bannister was no dullard, but coaxing a living out of the piney woods of east Texas left a man little time for abstract thought. James firmly believed hunting and hard work were more important skills than anything they were teaching at the schoolhouse. Will learned to ride, to shoot and to face trouble head-on with both fists. He might have fared better in Perdition had his father believed in witches and magic spells.

"Go ask your mother," was Pa's answer to all questions spiritual.

"Do I believe in witches?" Will asked himself. *"Do I believe in God for that matter?"*

No answer came readily to mind. Growing up Will assumed his Ma did enough praying for three people and called it square. He remembered how she'd pull her big, black Bible off the mantle at night and read aloud to her men. Will, like his father, politely tuned her out. He was not completely successful. To this day, bits and pieces laced with thee's and thou's intruded on his thoughts.

However, not all Ma's stories came from the Good Book; there were interesting ones too. Stories from her childhood back East about Jack o' lanterns, lights that bounced through the woods at night, and spells cast in secret glens. She knew Indian stories about little people who took special joy in bedeviling wayward children. And witches--there were stories about witches; women who changed themselves into dogs and chickens or peered into stump water to spy on their neighbors.

If only he had paid more attention. There was an answer somewhere in that head of his. He was sure of it. But where? Thoughts swirled through his head like the breeze in the grass, but no answer came.

He made four miles before his knee gave out the first time. Will dragged himself into the shade of an old oak to massage the away pain. The throbbing eventually gave way to frustration. He knocked his head against the tree not sure if he was punishing himself or just trying to shake something loose. Whatever the case, he came away with a headache and a knee that demanded two more stops before he reached Perdition.

The west-bound sun painted the rocky hills surrounding the town a deep rose. Somewhere in the long shadows that covered Perdition Will's fate was waiting. The rumbling in his stomach joined the throbbing in his knee and the pounding of his side in symphonic assault. There wasn't much to be done for the latter pair. A faint glow from the saloon said there was still a chance for something to eat and a drink. Will found his horse tied in front of the Hell Hole. There may not be a hot meal in Perdition, but he wouldn't go hungry. There was jerky and hardtack in his saddle bag. The temptation to just ride out returned; strong, but fleeting.

Will reached for his saddle bag. A bolt of white pain stole his breath; the sky went black and stars danced before his eyes.

"Jesus," he panted. It was more complaint than prayer, but the pain eased--a little.

Holding his elbow tight against his side, Will waited for the pain to pass before walking his right hand up the mare's hindquarters to work the saddle bags loose. He was careful to slide the bags down by the same path and not let the weight free fall.

"Old man," a voice in his head chided.

Will ignored the thought and pushed his way through the batwings with his good shoulder. Drake Mather was waiting. Drake's left eye was a narrow slit in a bulging sea of purple and black. His right eye was blood red. Three jagged lines ran from temple to temple. Here and there beads of dark red proclaimed the seal of the wounds was tenuous at best. A bottle and unused glass sat before an empty chair. Drake motioned for Will to sit.

"You look as bad as I feel." Will poured a drink; tossed it back and poured another.

Drake offered a wan smile in reply.

"Where is everybody?" Will asked. "I figured Mort would want to be around to gloat.

"Mort's beyond caring," Drake said. "They all are."

"What's that supposed to mean?"

The preacher shook his head and waved away the question.

"I want to know what's going on around here," Will demanded and winched in pain.

Drake nodded at the bottle. "Have another drink. Whisky makes it easier to believe. It'll help with that side too."

Will downed another drink. He doubted he would find faith in a bottle, but Drake was right, it would help ease the pain. After the drink, Will rolled a smoke while he waited for the preacher to explain. His host seemed lost for a place to start.

"The beginning's always a good place," Will suggested.

"First, let me review your day."

"Okay, have at it." Will nodded for the preacher to begin.

"You had company his morning. She was a young Indian woman with eyes like blue ice. That changed, that is she changed and so, I expect, did her cheery mood. She let you know she was capable of inflicting a great deal of pain or even death. The particulars vary, but by the time she left you to find your way back, she was very pregnant and you were very confused. How'd I do?" Drake searched Will's eyes.

"Like you was there," Will admitted.

"One more thing." Drake looked Will over. "You're missing something; something personal."

"What?" Will joined the visual search.

"I don't know," Drake said, "But your life depends on finding out."

A spark of memory touched off the mental kindling Will had been gathering on his walk to Perdition.

"That's how she gets a hold on you, isn't it?"

"That's as good a way to put it as any," Drake said.

"You seem to know everything." Color rose in Will's face. "So, tell me preacher, what do I do now?"

"Don't call me that!" Drake snapped. His face softened slowly. He returned to his seat. "Drake will do."

"Okay Drake, what do I do?"

"Do you trust me?"

"No."

"That was mighty quick." Drake gave Will a real smile for the first time. "But it's the right answer. Trust nothing and no one in Perdition."

"Done. Then what?"

"You let me take a look at that side of yours. After that, you get a couple hours sleep. We'll talk more later. Right now, drink up. This is going to hurt."

Will abandoned his glass in favor of some long pulls from the bottle. Working his arms out of his shirt occasioned a few more. Drake disappeared into a back room. He returned moments later with a sheet which he tore into long strips. He looped a strip around Will's chest and motioned for the cowboy to have another drink. When the whisky hit bottom, Drake cinched the cloth tight.

Will's eyes rolled up. His jaws locked down turning an obscenity into a grunt of pain. Will swayed unsteadily until the next turn of the cloth shot him upright again.

"That ought to do it." Drake knotted the last strip just above Will's waist. "Stay here."

Will nodded agreement through a fog of pain and whisky. Following Drake's order saved him the embarrassment of trying to stand and failing. The sun of clear thought burnt through the fog just as Drake returned with large bucket.

"Relax," Drake assured him.

"Easy for you to say," Will said. "What's that?"

"Reinforcement." Drake sat beside him and began to apply handfuls of red mud to Will's side. "I don't figure on being able to talk you out of going after her. This may feel heavy, but it will dry hard and protect those ribs."

"And what do we do in the meanwhile?"

"You sleep. I'll stand watch. She won't come looking for you tonight, but I'll watch anyway."

Will pushed himself to his feet. He was relieved when they held his weight. The bandages restricted his breathing, but kept the pain at bay. Measured steps carried Will across the bar toward the waiting cot. He was too focused on maintaining his balance to notice the sticky red puddle on the floor that stuck to his boots and marked his trail to the back room.

Will lay in the windowless room listening to the ragged sound of his own breathing. How long had he been asleep? He swung his legs over the edge of the cot and pushed himself up. Fresh pain flared in his side. It was not as hot or as bright as it once had been. Will let the pain pass before getting to his feet. A faint line of charcoal gray oozing beneath the door showed the way back to the bar. A loose board groaned under his weight. Will froze-- waiting; all remained quiet.

Will pushed open the door. The night sky filtering through the batwings blanketed Drake as he lay draped over a table snoring softly. Will glided passed the sleeping preacher into the dark shadows of Perdition. At the far end of town a faint yellow glow from the church told him not everyone was asleep. His hand touched the gun at his side.

"That's *your* strength," the preacher told him while splinting his side. "It won't work."

The words echoed in his head. It was true. He trusted in his gun. Perhaps he had relied on it once too often. Whatever this woman was, she would expect him to shoot first. Another rusty wheel turned somewhere inside Will's head.

It had been thirty years since Will Bannister darkened a church house door. His heart told him it was time to return. His head reminded him duty is equal parts blessing and cursing. Will raised the stakes when he shot Eli. Now, all bets were down. It was time to see who held the winning hand. Will withdrew his hand from the Colt. It felt good--right somehow. A thin smile touched his lips.

Keeping to the shadows Will worked his way across Perdition. In the blacksmith's shop he found neither forge nor anvil. The non-existent shelves in the general store held no goods. The town was a hollow shell. Perdition was a lie.

"So where is everybody?" Will asked the wind.

A south wind moaned around the eaves of the lifeless town.

"Figures." Will checked the Colt's load. "Just in case."

In Will's experience towns predated churches. It was not so in Perdition. The faded whitewash and patches of mold clinging to the structure tucked against the rocky hills south of town spoke to him of another place and time. Will was convinced the abandoned church was the only truly occupied building in Perdition. The thought of who, or what, occupied the church sent a shudder speeding down his spine. His last encounter with...

...was he really going to admit to witches?

"It's as good a name as any," he told himself.

But was it? What was it Ma used to say? Something about the smell of a rose...but more. Will sat on a deserted porch and stared at the church. How was a man suppose to think when it hurt to breathe? And if this woman was a witch, what then?

"Thou shalt not suffer a witch to live."

Will turned towards the voice. Pain screamed along his side. His hand trembled but held the gun on the intruder. Drake raised his hands in surrender.

"Sorry, I thought you heard me coming," the preacher said.

"I should have," Will admitted. "How'd you know?"

"What you were thinking? I didn't. It was a lucky guess. I saw the way you were taking the measure of the church."

"I take it killin' a witch is easier said than done." Will lifted a questioning eyebrow.

"Infinitely easier," Drake said.

The late rising moon sat on the hilltop and stared back at the two men. Their conversation melted into brooding silence. There was only so much words could do. The unspoken challenge that glowed from the church would have to be answered.

"I can't help you." Drake hung his head.

"Can't or won't?" Will asked.

"It amounts to the same thing." Drake continued to study the ground at his feet. His voice fell to a whisper. "I love her."

Will shook his head. There it was; no more needed saying. He stood and straightened his gun belt. Will let out a long breath and stepped off the porch.

"Don't make me kill you," he told the preacher and walked away.

He didn't like turning his back on Drake. The preacher had warned against such trust, but Will decided sooner or later faith was going to sit in on this gamble.

"*Might as well deal it in now,*" he told himself.

Halfway to the church, Will chanced a look back. Drake was gone.

Alongside the church was planted small plot of stone markers and wooden crosses. Will didn't want to read the names, but his feet did. Confirmation that the graves belonged to men who were drinking and playing cards last night made Will's heart sink. He'd always known that there was more to life than ranching and driving cattle. The revelation of how much more was like being kicked by a mule. Dead men walking; a gun slinging son of a witch; magic spells, what else might the church hold?

The mixed grass prairie is a thirsty land. Evidence of last night's storm was gone, yet amid a sea of sagebrush, tumbleweeds and red dust, every crack and crevice of the church was black with damp decay. The rocky hills that wrapped the church in perpetual shadow left the air dark and heavy. Even the yellow light from within refused to venture beyond the glass.

"Everything in; nothing out." Will jumped at the sound of his voice.

He hadn't meant to speak aloud. The sudden revelation which seemed to come from outside him could not be contained. He drew a deep breath and moved closer. One look at the ancient stairs told him surprise was out of the question. He'd be lucky if they didn't collapse altogether. The first stair sagged and groaned but remained solid. Will shrugged.

"Likely I'm expected," he said.

As if to confirm his notion, the church door swung open on rusted hinges. Will let the door run its course before stepping into the threshold. Along both long walls candles guttered from brass sconces gone green with age. The soft light fell short of the center aisle weaving a shadowy path between the broken pews to a tall pulpit. Blackness shrouded the altar and the preacher's seat.

"Come in," a voice beaconed from beyond the altar. "Oh Will, where are your manners? Put that gun away."

Will didn't remember drawing the Colt, but there it was in his hand. He holstered the weapon and took a step inside. A quick glance over his shoulder sent a strange mix of relief and disappointment washing over him.

A small feminine voice tittered laughter. "Thinking of running?"

Will tried without success to pinpoint the voice's origin. He inched his way towards the altar.

"Keep her talking," he told himself.

"I didn't get your name." Will scanned the darkness.

"I have many names."

"But what do I call you?" He moved closer.

"*You* don't. When it amuses me, *I* call you. I say 'Come' and you run to do my will just like all the others."

"How about I call you Witch?" Will searched for movement still trying to get a fix on her.

"Will, that's so rude. Besides you know there's no such thing."

"*Got you.*" Will thought. He stepped alongside the tall pulpit.

Will burst upon empty darkness. Laughter turned his blood to ice. Will turned to find her sitting like obscene royalty in a high backed altar chair. Her dress was open over an ancient tapestry of dark veins and sallow skin folds. She made no move to cover her nakedness A leg flung over the arm of the chair swayed lazily to and fro. Will could not take his eyes from her swollen belly.

"Tomorrow." She lifted her pendulous breast. "Milk's already coming."

Will ripped his face away glad for the dark. Fresh laughter filled the church.

"Oh Will, you're such fun," she said in a voice grown rich and smooth.

She floated from her throne, her raven hair trailing from a seamless face. She opened her arms inviting him to flawless skin the color of the earth.

"You haven't always been so coy," she cooed.

"Don't mistake shame for shyness." Will forced his eyes away.

The honey left her voice and beauty fled. Fire the color of ice flared in her eyes.

"*I* don't make mistakes." Her voice struck like an angry rattler. "You will soon learn yours."

A fetid breath of wind rose from the floor. Churning air engulfed her calling the dust to dance. Debris of worship long forsaken filled the air.

"*Dust devil,*" Will made the connection.

A swirling current awash with evil made Will's stomach lurch. He fended off the remains of a hymnal and backed away from the storm. A leg from the crumbling communion table caught him under his left arm shattering the makeshift cast and thundering pain across his chest. Will stumbled against a pew. The rotten wood crumbled spilling him to the floor. A choir of corpses rose from the baptistery as the infernal whirlwind moved to hover above the altar.

The tempest ended in a rain of battered hymnals and broken furniture. Untold years of dust followed in the storm's final breath. Withered, hunched and barely human, she stepped from the altar to stand over him. Malevolent hunger writhed beneath her skin. Fear seized Will's guts and pulled. His hammering heart skipped a beat--then, another.

"God help me," he meant to scream, but only and unintelligible squeak came from his lips.

Her black lips parted as she moved closer drinking in his fear, sucking the life from him. His boots skittered over the floor as he tried to crawl away. Will saw his life end groveling amid the God-forsaken ruins of a dead church. He'd thought about dying before. But not like this; never like this.

"Confess sinner!" the voice rumbled over the pews and shook the walls.

Will knew that voice. It was not the voice of God he hoped for. It was the voice of the preacher. Words, strange and unpracticed, poured from Will's lips. His heart vomited its blackest secrets.

His speaking ended in a thunder clap of silence. Wide eyed with disbelief, the witch recoiled as if struck. Will tried to stand. His knee buckled spilling him onto the floor. He was not as strong as he felt. Weak or strong, his fear was gone. Strong hands lifted him to his feet.

"Drake?"

"Steady," the preacher whispered. "You're not safe yet."

"So, you've decided to play preacher?" The witch tapped her teeth with a long, yellow nail. Her eyes bored into Drake's. "You'll pay dearly, my love."

"Let him go," Drake demanded.

His voice had lost it's thunder. Will could see Drake's courage melting. The preacher seemed to be shrinking.

"Or you'll do what?" She bored down on the retreating preacher.

With the witch distracted, Will struck. He ripped the medicine pouch from her neck and bolted away. She snatched at him, but found only air.

"Or you die." Will snapped the Colt from his holster.

She matched his draw with a backhand flip of the wrist. Will was lifted into the air. His shot ripped a hole in the ceiling as he went crashing into the wall. Will hit the floor with a thud. Through a haze of pain he saw her turn on Drake. The preacher was trembling. Will had seen her transformation before, but not with such detached interest. Deformity to beauty; darkness into light; her spell wrapped Drake tighter. Will had to do something. But what? He was sure stealing her medicine pouch had been enough the key. He couldn't afford to be wrong again--not now. Ignoring the pain Will scrambled to his feet. The witch wheeled on him.

"Interfere and I'll kill you," she said.

Will froze in place.

"Don't believe her," Drake shouted.

It was hard not to believe. She had just tossed him like a rag doll. He knew her capable of worse.

"But you won't," he said. "Not yet."

"You're pretty sure of yourself," she said.

"You need me for something or I wouldn't be here." Will moved between the pews.

"We'll get to that soon enough. To every thing there is a season. Isn't that right Preacher?"

"Even heaven and earth pass away," Drake warned. "Please, let him go."

Fury galvanized her hands into claws. She lifted Drake over her head and hurled him against the back wall. Will heard bones crack. Looking for help, Will worked open the top of the medicine bag. It was empty.

Will knew better. He tipped the bag and let the contents tumble into his hand. A horseshoe nail, a diamond stick pin and a small gold nugget rolled across his palm onto the floor. Will's hand closed on the next object. He slipped the .45 caliber round into his belt and tossed the pouch aside.

"What's a little petty theft between lovers? She flashed him a salacious smile.

Will inched his way closer to the center aisle. The balance of power was shifting. He could feel it. She backed towards the altar. Will pursued slowly trailing his hand atop the pew in front of him; keeping it close to the Colt on his hip. Will reached the aisle.

"In a moment, in the twinkling of an eye," he whispered under his breath.

The Colt jumped into his hand. His finger closed on the trigger. He heard the click of the hammer falling back; saw her mouth and eyes widen.

Will's world went black.

Drake let the table leg slip from his hands. His breath was coming in short, sharp gasps.

"Come, it's time," she said.

The only thing worse than the ringing and pounding in Will's head was the smell. The air around his head was alive with the odor of rotting meat. He tried to move away, but strong hands held him.

"Take it easy," Mort said. "It's almost over."

Will forced his eyes open and the room began to spin. He waited for his head to clear and tried again. First his right eye; figures in a crimson fog. He closed it and tried the left; figures swan slowly into focus.

"The man wants to see," Mort said. "Lift him up, boys."

Unseen hands pushed him upright. This time closing his eyes couldn't stop the waves of nausea looping through his gut. Will retched, but there was nothing to come up and no relief. His head was the anvil of a cruel smithy. Hammer blows of pain forged the image before him into memory.

Will sat on the floor between the altars. The pulpit was gone. In its place Drake held the witch's head as she travailed in birth. Between quaking contractions, she spat curses dripping venom.

"She won't kill you," Josh's voice came through the pain.

"But you'll pray to die," the blacksmith assured him.

"We'll save you a seat back at the saloon." Mort added.

Then the hands were gone. Will's head hit the floor. White light flashed behind his eyes. Will rolled unto his side and pushed himself up. He hurt too much to be dreaming.

The congregation of the dead blocked the door. Will might be able to shoot his way through them, but that wasn't the same thing as escaping Perdition. A high pitched shriek from behind the altar told him time was running out.

"He's coming. Eli's coming." A deep grunting push choked off her announcement.

The men who once shared Will's fate turned away as a small dark head slipped from between the witch's legs. The head was followed by two withered arms. What came next was not human. A mucoid gray mass slithered from her and raised itself on tiny, gnarled arms. A long, serpentine tongue tasted the air.

Eli smiled.

It was not the innocent smile of the new born, but a greedy, hungry smile of the beast that's found its prey. Eli's slug-like body slid towards Will on a slime trail of afterbirth and its own secretions. It was fast--very fast.

Will tried to dodge the mouthful of needles that closed on his boot top. The Eli thing spit leather and came again. Will kicked, and missed. The thing snapped at his thigh as Will rolled right. Will spun on the floor hoping to get to his feet before it struck again. He'd nearly made it when the thing launched itself at his throat. Will ducked under the flying monstrosity and rolled under a pew. He came up between the pews in time to see the witch rise from the platform. Flush with triumph, her face shifted as she closed the distance between them. Beauty and monster shimmered in her blazing eyes.

The Colt was in his hand. Will's fingers tightened.

Click. Misfire.

A fist like gloved steel caught Will above the cheek. He went over the pew; into the floor. Will groaned. There was no strength left. The gun fell from his fingers.

"Get him Eli," she screeched.

Will raised a boot to ward off the attack. The heel and sole, dark and sticky from the saloon floor, met Eli in the air. The collision of bloody leather and spongy flesh sounded like a blast of locomotive brakes. The rotten egg smell of sulfur filled the church.

"Eli!" screamed the witch.

The melting mass of flesh that was her son could no longer reply. Will crabbed away. The dead slug thing clinging to his boot came loose with a wet sucking sound that brought a wail from its bereaved mother. Will paid no mind. He had to find a weapon before her sorrow turned to rage. His hand closed on the toe of a boot. He was surrounded by dead men. Cold hands lifted Will from the floor; he was done for and, at last, he knew it.

"Her name is Lilith," Mort whispered in his ear.

Will's gun was pressed into his hand. His strength nearly gone, Will struggled to lift the weapon. A hand closed over his; the Colt rose.

"Kill her," Josh prodded.

"No." Drake stepped between them. "Don't do it Will."

Will hesitated. Drake seized Lilith and dragged her towards the altar. Opportunity was slipping away. Lilith's hair began to rise on a nonexistent breeze. Fire rose in her eyes and hot steel in her bones. Drake still had her moving toward the altar, but that couldn't last much longer.

"Lilith," Will called after them. "Now you die."

Bared fangs and a spitting hiss answered him. Lilith's thin shroud of humanity fell from her face and shoulders. Will squeezed the trigger. Mort gasped. The Colt bucked and the church exploded. The sledge hammer of sound blew the church apart. Drake and Lilith were drawn into a whirling vortex of fleeing light and shadow. Debris chasing the collapsing church pummeled Will as Perdition folded itself into the wake of the retreating witch. The world was vanishing.

But another was on the rise. A large oak appeared in the fading sanctuary. Will threw his arms around the sturdy trunk and held on against the vacuum drawing the town and its citizens to God-knows-where.

Consciousness returned slowly. The storm had blown itself out. A bright world swam reluctantly into focus. Blinking back the sun, Will looked out on an open expanse of prairie. His horse cropped grass in the shade of a nearby hackberry tree. Somewhere high in the branches cicadas sang a trilling melody to the sweet, clean grass.

Perdition was gone. The saloon, the trail, the church, all of it--gone. Will wandered over the ground searching for some trace it ever existed.

"Not a splinter." Will shook his head running a hand through his hair to soothe the puzzlement beneath it. "Was any of it real?"

Sunlight on something shiny caught his eye. Will returned to the spot where Perdition's church once stood. He found a bare patch of red dirt. It slightly smaller and finer, but the shape was unmistakable. It was a hand. On the bare earth lay a length of thin rawhide with a single black bead clinging to one frayed end. Next to the thread rested a small gold cross. Will scooped them up; tested the weight of them in his hand.

"There are more things in heaven and earth than you know Will Bannister," his mother's voice reminded him.

Will pulled a knife from his pocket. He cut the rawhide down the middle; threaded one strip through the cross and knotted it behind his head. It was real--all of it. But who would believe it? Will climbed into the saddle; pointed the mare south and gave her a nudge.

As he rode away, Will fingered the cross hanging from his neck. "Tokens of Perdition."

He looked back only once.